I love you more than all the stars in the sky...

Copyright © 2024 by Nikki Ash

All rights reserved.

Visit my website at www.authornikkiash.com

Cover Designer: Jersey Girl Design

Photograph: Wander Aguiar Photography

Editor: Jovana Shirley, Unforeseen Editing

No part of this book may be reproduced or transmitted in any form or by any means, electronic or mechanical, including photocopying, recording, or by any information storage and retrieval system without the written permission of the author, except for the use of brief quotations in a book review.

This book is a work of fiction. Names, characters, places, and incidents either are products of the author's imagination or are used fictitiously. Any resemblance to actual persons, living or dead, events, or locales is entirely coincidental.

Hooked on You Playlist

Treat You Better – *Shawn Mendes*
What Ifs – *Kane Brown*
Little Do You Know – *Alex & Sierra*
Fight Song – *Rachel Platten*
Roar – *Katy Perry*
I Wanna Dance with Somebody – *Whitney Houston*
The Comeback – *Danny Gokey*
Rain On Me – *Lady Gaga & Ariana Grande*
Stand By You – *Rachel Platten*
She's So High – *Tal Bachman*
This Love (Taylor's Version) – *Taylor Swift*

Author's Note

This story contains subjects that
may be sensitive for some readers.

Content warnings (which contain major spoilers)
can be found on Nikki's website.

To all the parents who are so focused on their children they forget to think about themselves.

It's okay to find love and happiness for yourself. And don't you ever feel guilty about it.

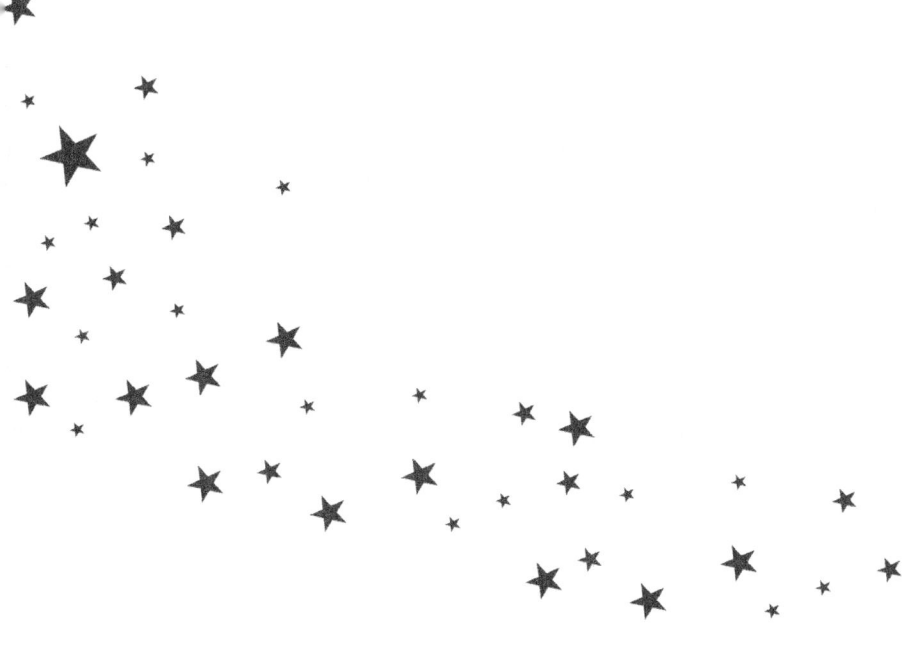

Prologue

RYDER

"Ryder, your wife is on line one. She said it's an emergency."

"Thank you, Julie," I say to my assistant.

I quickly press the line and bring the phone to my ear. "Nora, is everything okay?"

"No," my wife shouts through the phone over the sound of a screaming baby. "Everything is not okay. I need you to come home now."

I'm already standing, worst-case scenarios flitting through my head. Did our daughter fall and hit her head? Did she choke on something? Was there some kind of accident? Addie is only four months old, but anything is possible.

"Let me call you on my cell."

I hang up and grab my phone, seeing a dozen missed

calls and texts from Nora. *Shit.* I had it on silent because I was in a meeting earlier and forgot to turn the ringer back on.

"Hello," she breathes, the screaming in the background still going strong.

"What's wrong?" I ask, snagging my keys and running out the door.

"I don't know! The nanny isn't here, thanks to you giving her the time off, and I have no idea what the hell is wrong with her."

I step into the elevator and press the button for the parking garage.

"Did something happen?" I ask in confusion.

"How the hell am I supposed to know? I tried to feed her, but she threw up all over me. I was supposed to be meeting my mother for brunch, but I can't go now because I'm going to have to shower, and the formula stained my dress, and I have no one to watch Adeline."

"Forget your fucking brunch for a second," I bark. "Why is our daughter screaming like she's in pain?"

"Because the nanny and you have turned her into a spoiled brat, and neither of you are here, so I'm left to deal with it."

"She's four months old," I remind her as I get into my car. "She has needs, and the only reason she'd be crying, unless there was something wrong with her, is if they weren't being met."

"Well, I don't know how to meet her needs. Maybe

we need to hire another nanny. She literally gave us zero notice."

"Her mother passed away," I say dryly, wondering how this has become my life. "You can't exactly give notice when you don't know your mother is going to have a heart attack and die."

She called Friday night and told me her mom was in the hospital and she wasn't sure what was going to happen. Nora was on a girls' trip with her mother and friends, so I spent the weekend with Addie.

Last night, the nanny called and said her mom didn't make it, and of course, I told her to take off as much time as she needed. Because I had to go to work today, Nora was left to take care of Addie. It's only been about two hours since I left.

"Can you please just get home?" Nora huffs over the line. "I don't know how to fix this."

"I'll be there soon."

I click End, and the car immediately goes silent, giving me a few minutes to calm myself so I don't lose it on my wife. For a woman who wanted a baby as badly as she did, it's insane, the way she wants nothing to do with caring for our daughter.

The nanny mentioned that Nora has gotten worse, relying on her to do everything, but I didn't fully grasp the severity of the situation until now, as I walk inside and hear my daughter screaming at the top of her lungs.

"Jesus fucking Christ! What do you want from

me?" Nora yells, sending chills up my spine.

It brings me back to when I was little and my parents would fight. And then my dad would leave, and my mom would take it out on me. Nothing I did was right. I was too messy, too noisy, too much work. I tried to be cleaner, to keep my mouth shut, to make it to where she wouldn't be upset. All I wanted was for her to love me ... and instead, she left.

I follow the cries, and they lead me to the nursery, where I find Nora standing over our daughter in her crib. Addie's face is bright red and blotchy from crying, and when her hazel eyes—identical to my own—meet mine, my heart shatters into a million pieces.

I shouldn't have left Nora with Addie. This morning, when I told her the nanny wouldn't be coming in, she threw a fit over having to care for our daughter herself. I called her a selfish bitch and told her she could handle one damn day of taking care of Addie. But I should've listened because based on Addie's face, she's been crying for a while.

"Come here, Chunky Monkey," I whisper, pulling Addie into my arms.

Within seconds of me holding her, her cries soften from an ear-piercing scream to a sob as her head flops onto my shoulder and she clings to me like the sweetest little monkey.

When she was born, she came out screaming like a pissed-off cat. She was only four and a half pounds with her skin hanging off her bones. But my little girl loves to eat, and all too soon, she was gaining weight and filling out. She also loves to be held, hence the nickname—because she's clingy and chunky. Nora hates it, says it sounds juvenile, which only has me loving the name that much more.

"What's the matter with my sweet girl?" I coo.

"She wouldn't stop screaming," Nora huffs, as if our crying daughter is such an inconvenience.

"Did you try holding her?" I ask, glancing at my wife, who shoots daggers back at me.

"I told you not to go to work today. I can't do this without Freida."

"I had an important meeting, and you're her mom," I hiss. "The nanny is here to help because you demanded it, but she's not meant to replace you. She needs her mom, not some stranger."

"I'm not good at this!" Nora throws her arms in the air, sounding like a petulant child.

"It takes time." I pace the room, patting Addie's butt lightly. Her sobs have stopped, but her breathing is still heavy from her earlier exertion. "Maybe if you help Freida more ..."

"This isn't what I signed up for."

"What are you talking about?"

"This." Nora flails her arms about. "Her." She nods toward Addie. "This isn't how I thought my life would be."

"This isn't how you thought your life would be?" I retort with a humorless chuckle. "How the fuck did you think your life would be when you tricked me—not once, but twice—into getting you pregnant?"

She opens her mouth to argue, but before she can get a word out, I continue, "And before you try to say both pregnancies were an accident, don't bullshit me. I overheard your conversation with your mother. I know you lied about being on birth control and that you tampered with my damn condoms."

I hit her with a hard glare that has her taking a tiny step back.

"If you didn't want a baby, you should've listened to me about waiting after we lost the first baby. But you didn't. Instead, you kept track of when you were ovulating …"

Her eyes widen in shock, and I shake my head.

"Yeah, I saw the app that was downloaded from the App store. You're on my account."

I didn't say anything because what's the point? Addie is here, and what's done is done. I might despise my wife and the fact that she trapped me into this bullshit of a marriage, but I love my daughter something fierce. Adeline Elizabeth Du Ponte is my entire world, and I'll never regret her being born. In the four short months she's been alive, she's managed to wrap me around her tiny little finger, and I wouldn't have it any other way.

"Okay, fine," Nora says, raising her chin in the way

she does when she goes on the defense. "So, I might've done things to increase my chances of getting pregnant."

I roll my eyes at the way she's spinning shit. It's so typical of her. God forbid she takes responsibility for her actions.

"But this wasn't how I envisioned my life," she adds. "I wasn't meant to be a mom, and *this* isn't worth it."

"What's not worth it?" I hiss. "You live in a multimillion-dollar home, drive an expensive car, have access to my black card, spend the majority of your time shopping or at the salon when you're not doing *girl days* with your equally spoiled friends, and you have a fucking nanny who helps take care of our daughter ninety-nine percent of the time."

I was originally against the nanny because I had been raised by one. After my mom left, my dad was given full custody, and he immediately hired a nanny. Don't get me wrong. Greta was as sweet as they came, but she wasn't my mom or dad—although in my case, she was better because she actually cared about me. But when I was old enough to no longer need to a babysitter, she moved on to take care of another family, and I was left alone. I never wanted that for my daughter. I want her to know that her parents love her and put her first.

But when Nora threw a fit and it was clear she wasn't in the right state of mind to take care of Addie, I gave in. After two months, when she still wanted nothing to do with our daughter, I did some research and thought maybe she was going through postpartum depression. But when I asked her to let me get her help, she refused.

Now, it's been four months, and she still has no desire to be a mom. I've known this, but I kept hoping, for our daughter's sake, she would come around. Feeling unloved and unwanted isn't something I would wish on anyone, especially my own daughter.

"None of that matters when I'm trapped in this hellhole with you and her." She looks at me with fire in her eyes. "I want out. Fifty million, and I'll sign over my rights."

I lay Addie down in her crib, pulling her blanket over her bottom half, and then walk out of her room with Nora on my heels as I try to wrap my head around what my wife just said.

Like Addie, I was an accident. My brother, Erik, is ten years my senior. My mom wanted out—out of her marriage, out of being a mom, out of the life of being a Du Ponte—but then she found out she was pregnant.

When I was three, she took off to start a new life, leaving me to be raised by Henry Du Ponte, who only cares about himself. He hired Greta, and I only saw him when it was convenient for him. I wanted more for my daughter, but it looks like no matter what I do, what I give Nora, it'll never be enough.

Really, I should be thrilled she wants out. Paying her off would mean getting out of this farce of a marriage and not having to deal with her every day. But a part of me feels like a failure. I wasn't worth either of my parents sticking around for, and now, Nora wants to get away from me. And what about my daughter? What will I tell her one day when she asks where her mom is and why she didn't want to be a part of her life?

"We both know you don't want to remain married to me," Nora says once we're in my office, snapping me out of my thoughts. "Fifty million, and the baby is all yours." When I don't say anything, she adds, "Isn't she worth that much?"

"She's worth *everything*," I hiss. "But what I don't get is how she's not worth it to you. You carried her for nine months. She's your blood, Nora. You're her *mother*."

I close the gap between us and palm her cheek. "Let me get you help, please. I know you don't think you have it, but I've read about PPD and—"

"I don't have PPD!" she barks, taking a step back. "Stop trying to see the good in everyone. Stop trying to fix me! I only wanted you for the money and the lifestyle. But I was dumb because you're the cheapest rich person I know. You're the only person I know who is worth millions and acts like he's poor. I thought once we were married, things would change. And then I had your baby! But nothing's changed. You want this ...*family*, and I want to have fun. I want to travel and enjoy my life. And I don't want to be shackled down by you or that damn baby."

She crosses her arms over her chest. "Fifty million, and she's all yours."

"You'd really do that?" I ask despite knowing she would.

She reminds me of my mom, only the polar opposite. My mom hated being rich—Nora loves it. My mom hated my dad traveling and the social obligations she was forced to attend—Nora thrives on them. The problem is, I'm not my dad, and I prefer to be home with my family over traveling and attending social functions, and it drives Nora nuts. She wants the picture-perfect family without having to be part of a family. And I just want the family.

I kept hoping whatever she was going through was a phase and she'd come around and want to be part of this family. But it's clear that she's never going to.

"I don't want her," she says, finality in her tone. "She was only a means to an end. If I could go back, I never would've gotten pregnant. I'm still young, and I have time to live the life I deserve. It's bad enough she ruined my body. But now, she's ruining my life."

"You know how bad it's going to look that you're giving your daughter up? Any respectable, rich man isn't going to want that type of woman."

"Well, after you pay me, I won't need a man, and I'll be damned if I ever get pregnant again."

"And what does your family think about this?"

Reputation means everything to people like Nora, so I'm shocked she'd risk her reputation like this—which has me believing something is wrong with her. I know she doesn't agree she has PPD, and I'm not a woman or in her body, but it's just crazy to me that she tried so hard to get pregnant, only to turn around and say she no longer wants to be a mom.

"I'll deal with them," Nora says. "My mother warned me not to latch on to you, and I should've listened."

"Fine." I sigh in defeat. "But I'm not giving you fifty million dollars. One, you signed a prenup, so you're not eligible to receive a dime without being married for at least five years unless I've been unfaithful, which I haven't. And two, I've been recording this entire conversation."

I lift my phone out of my pocket and shake it. "I can easily take you to court and get custody—and I will because, as you pointed out, I have a shit ton of money—but since neither of us wants to go through all that, I'll give you five million as a parting gift, and you'll walk away because *my* daughter deserves better than *you* anyway. But understand that walking away means you will have no contact with Addie. Not you or your family."

It has to be a clean slate. Otherwise, she'll be confused. One day, this will affect her, and the last thing I want is Nora's family demanding to see her when her own mother doesn't want anything to do with her.

Nora glares at me, probably debating whether she should argue and try to get more money, but after several seconds, she nods. "Okay. Five million, and I'm gone, and I'll make sure my family stays away."

"Okay, but you need to leave now. Go stay somewhere else while I have my attorney draw up the paperwork. I don't want you anywhere near my home or my daughter. As far as I'm concerned, you're dead to us."

One

RYDER
EIGHT MONTHS LATER

"Dada, up!" Addie lifts her arms, releasing the side bar of her crib, and drops onto the mattress in a fit of giggles.

How my daughter wakes up in such a happy mood every morning is beyond me, but since it's better than her waking up cranky, I can't complain—even if waking up takes place at six in the morning.

"Good morning, Chunk," I say, reaching into the crib and pulling her out.

She squeals in delight as I lay her onto the changing table so I can change her diaper and get her dressed for the day.

Once she's ready, I make her a bowl of oatmeal with fruit and a sippy cup filled with milk. She inhales it like a champ, laughing and babbling the entire time. My little girl loves to eat.

After I clean her up from breakfast, I set her on her play rug that's filled with toys while I make my own breakfast. Since she's now learned to walk, she takes a quick look around and then pops up onto her feet, chasing after me.

"Dada, up!" she squeals, latching on to my leg like the most adorable spider monkey.

And because I can't say no to her—I know, I know, every parenting book says that's bad—I lift her onto my hip and go about making my coffee and breakfast one-handed.

As I drink my coffee and eat my breakfast, I watch the morning news while Addie plays with her blocks. It's a routine we've fallen into since I returned to work and put her in our recently opened corporate childcare.

After two months of being home with her—while I loved the time we spent together—it was time for both of us to leave the house. I love my job, and Addie loves going to the childcare three days a week and playing with the other kids.

"Dada, look," Addie says—the word *look* sounding like *ook* since she hasn't mastered the L sound yet. She points to the block tower she created, hits me with a toothy grin, and then slices her fist into it, sending the blocks flying everywhere.

She falls into a fit of giggles, and I can't help but join

her. Everything about her is infectious—her smile, her laugh, the way she looks at me like I'm her entire world.

The first few weeks after Nora left were rough—mostly because I let the nanny go. I was determined to do this on my own. So, I took time off from work and dove into the deep end of single parenthood. But between the books I read, having my best friends—Julian and Ana—there to help, and many days and nights filled with trial and error while praying I wasn't fucking up my daughter too badly, I'm proud to say that Addie and I didn't drown. She recently turned one and is thriving.

Nora took her five million, signed her rights over, and disappeared—despite her family begging her not to and agreeing that she's going through something. While I hate that my daughter will grow up without her mother in her life, I realize now that it's for the best. I can't help someone who doesn't want to be helped, and I need to put my daughter first—something neither of my parents ever did for me.

When the alarm goes off, indicating it's time to leave for work, I double-check the diaper bag to make sure we have everything we need, get Addie buckled into her car seat, and then take off to the office.

Since we live in Rosemary—a small town in Texas—the ride is quick, and all too soon, I'm handing Addie and her diaper bag off to Cynthia, her childcare teacher she's grown rather fond of.

"Good morning, Addie," Cynthia coos, taking my daughter and bag from me. "Are you ready to have a good day?"

"Yay!" Addie exclaims.

The second Addie spots Ana and Julian's son, Kingston, already playing, she wiggles her way out of Cynthia's arms and toddles over to Kingston, plopping down next to him to play.

"I have a meeting at noon, so I should be by to get her around two."

"Sounds good," Cynthia says with a smile.

Because the corporate world has evolved over the past few years, many of us no longer work in the office full-time. I generally come in three days a week and then work from home two. I've considered hiring a nanny to help me at home with Addie since she can be a handful now that she's mobile, but I haven't bitten the bullet yet.

"Morning," I say, popping my head into Julian's office since the door is open.

He's not only one of my best friends, but he's also the co-CEO of Kingston Limited—the liquor company I work for—along with his wife, Ana. Having two CEOs in a company isn't the norm, but it works for them.

"Hey, man," he says, nodding for me to join him. "We still on for the game tonight?"

It takes me a second to remember what he's talking about, but then it hits me. Today is Thursday, and we always get together for a guys' night on Thursdays. I bring Addie over, and Ana spoils her, along with their son, while we eat shit food, have a few beers, and watch whatever game is on.

"Hell yeah," I tell him. "We'll be there."

The rest of the day flies by. I check on Addie between meetings. At three o'clock, since my meeting ran over, I pick her up, and we head out, stopping at the park to play.

I've learned when she burns energy, it means she'll fall asleep easier at bedtime.

At dinnertime, we head over to Julian and Ana's, and the second we pull up, she gets excited, recognizing their home.

"Hey there, sweet girl!" Ana says, taking my daughter from me. She's seven months pregnant, and they just found out they're having a little girl, so she's excited.

"Hi, hi!" Addie babbles.

Kingston comes barreling around the corner, and Addie worms her way down to play with him while I have a seat on the couch and grab some chips and salsa from the table.

"Beer?" Julian offers. "The guys should be here soon."

"Thanks."

"Hey, Ryder," Ana says, leaning against Julian. "Did you have a chance to check out the link I sent you?"

I roll my eyes and shake my head. "I've been a little busy," I drawl. "You know, raising a baby on my own."

"I know," she says, "but even single parents deserve to have a life. You should check out Plenty of Fish. It's an online dating site and not sleazy, like some of them. It's how Paige met her boyfriend."

Paige is Ana's best friend, who she met when she was living and working in London. Last year, Paige's boyfriend got a promotion and moved to Houston, so Paige moved as well. Now, she's the chief marketing officer at Kingston. I think it's great she found someone from an online dating site but …

"It's too soon," I tell her. "Nora's only been gone—"

"Nora and you might've been married, but you guys weren't really together," Julian says, stating the obvious. "When's the last time you even got laid?"

"Julian," Ana hisses. "He doesn't need to get laid. He needs to meet a nice woman."

I tune them out while they bicker over me getting laid versus dating, trying to remember the last time I had sex. Nora and I didn't even attempt it after Addie was born. I brought it up a couple of times while she was pregnant, hoping to connect with my wife, but she shot me down every time with the excuse of being pregnant and not feeling up to it—including on our wedding night.

Jesus, that means the last time I had sex was when Addie was conceived—holy shit—almost two years ago.

"Well, regardless," Ana says, bringing me out of my depressive thoughts, "whether you're looking to get laid"—she glares at Julian—"or to date, you need to get back out there. You deserve to have some adult time."

I open my mouth to argue that I get plenty of adult time, but before I can speak, she says, "And by adult time, I don't mean you working while Addie goes to childcare or your weekly guys' nights."

I shut my mouth since those were the two situations I was going to name and shrug. "I'll check out the site," I tell her to get her off my back even though I have no desire to date or get laid.

The other guys arrive, letting me off the hook, and we spend the next few hours hanging out and watching the game. I might be in a dating slump, but Ana's wrong—I don't need more than this. I have great friends, a job I love, and the most amazing daughter I could ask for. Why do I need to push for more?

When Addie starts to fuss, we say our goodbyes, so we can get home and start our nightly routine. After a bath, a bedtime story, and some cuddles, her eyes are drooping, and when I lay her in her crib, she's already halfway to dreamland.

I turn the lights off, and close the door, leaving it open a crack to shine a bit of light in. And then I start my own nightly routine. It's only nine o'clock, but I'm exhausted, so tonight, I skip working out and head straight for the shower and then bed, knowing if I don't get some sleep, I'll regret it in the morning when my little girl is up at the crack of dawn, ready to do this all over again.

While I'm scrolling through my emails to make sure there's nothing I need to respond to since we have business associates all over the world and in different time zones, Ana sends me the link for the dating site again.

I know she means well, but right now, I honestly can't imagine dating someone. When I was single, it was easy to casually date, but I learned all too quickly that casual dating could lead to serious consequences. Not that I would ever consider my daughter a consequence. But I can't negate the fact that my carelessness led to the outcome—my daughter being raised in a one-parent household. I watched my mom leave, my dad choose work over his children, and while my brother and I get along, we're not close.

When I decide to date again, I need to make sure that whoever I let into our lives wants to stay for the long haul. The last thing I want is for my daughter or me to watch another person we care about walk out the door.

KIRA
ONE MONTH LATER

"Unfortunately, with it being only a few months before summer, we're not hiring," June, the principal at Apple Academy, says. "But if you'd like to fill out the online application, we'll be reevaluating once we know who is returning in the fall."

"And you don't have anything available for the summer?" I ask just to make sure since I'll take anything I can get at this point.

"No, we close for the summer, but you can check with Rosemary Montessori. They host a summer camp program every year. They might be hiring."

"Thank you. I'll do that."

I take my daughter's hand in mine, and we walk out of the school and back down the street toward the building where I parked the SUV.

Rosemary is a quaint but beautiful town and the perfect place to settle down, but it also lacks job opportunities and isn't exactly cheap. I'd probably be better off somewhere like Houston, where there are hundreds of schools and more places to rent, but I'm afraid that's exactly where *he'll* look for me … and I know he'll be looking, if he's not already.

When I spot a bench in front of the building, I stop so we can sit while I make a note to apply to the school we just left and check out the Montessori school she mentioned when we go to the library later.

"Mommy, I'm thirsty. And you know what I love? Chocolate milk. Can we get some?"

I glance down at my daughter, who's peering up at me with her innocent blue eyes—the same color as mine—asking for something so simple without realizing just how much she's asking for. And I hate that I'm going to have to tell her no.

What's worse is, she doesn't understand that it's not because she doesn't deserve it, but because something that was once the norm is now out of my reach. Milk is expensive, and chocolate milk costs even more. And to waste money on something that isn't a necessity isn't an option.

"Violet," I say, taking her small hand in mine.

She looks at me with such hope that my heart sinks into my stomach. The past month has been hard, but my precious four-year-old daughter has been so good every step of the way. She rarely complains, and she doesn't ask for much because, despite her age, I think she knows we're having a rough go at it right now.

"We can't get chocolate milk today," I tell her, swallowing past the lump of emotion that's lodged in my throat. "But tomorrow, you can have milk in your cereal." *When we sneak into the hotel around the corner and pretend like we're guests so we can eat breakfast,* I think but don't voice out loud.

She's too young to understand what we're doing, and I try to shelter her the best I can. Stealing from anyone, even a company that probably won't notice or miss it, makes me feel sick, but desperate times call for desperate measures. And the fact is, I'm more than desperate.

"Okay," she says softly, her lips turning down into the saddest pout. "Can we go play at the park?"

"That we can do," I tell her with a smile that forces one out of her as well. "Let's go back to the car and eat lunch, and then we'll go to the park."

She nods in agreement, and we're about to stand when a woman walks over and sits on the bench next to us. Normally, I wouldn't eavesdrop, but what she says gets my attention.

"I understand there's a shortage in childcare providers. Yes, I know." She sighs. "Well, if you do happen to know of someone looking to work part-time.

Yes, thank you. Have a good day."

The woman removes the phone from her ear, and I catch her sparkling diamond ring on her left finger. It has a princess-cut stone in the center, like the one I had—and pawned—but hers is bigger and more expensive.

She's dressed in a beautiful blue-and-cream floral wrap dress, and when she recrosses her legs, her blue pumps with the red soles catch my attention, invoking a flashback from *before*.

"I've given you everything you could ever want, and this is how you repay me." He grabbed one of my navy-blue Louboutin heels from the floor and flung it across the room, barely missing my head.

"I didn't want to be rude," I explained calmly. "When he asked for my number to schedule a playdate, I offered to take his instead so he wouldn't have my number. I was going to delete it."

"You're lying!" he barked. "Admit you were planning to cheat on me."

A loud sigh brings me back into the present as the woman next to me looks up at the sky like it will somehow have all the answers.

I hate to tell you this, but it doesn't.

I know because I've spent the past several weeks staring up at the same sky, hoping it will give me some kind of guidance. And I'm still as lost as I was a month ago.

"I swear it gets hotter every day," the woman says, glancing over at me.

Her manicured hand goes to her belly, and it's then I realize she's pregnant.

"It does," I agree. "How far along are you?"

"Seven months," she says with a small smile. "Although, in this heat, I feel like I'm past due."

"My daughter was born in July. The last couple of months of my pregnancy were brutal. I think I took, like, four showers a day."

We both chuckle, and then she says, "Well, I'd better get back in there."

She nods toward the building behind us and then places her hands on the bench, as if needing to mentally and physically prepare to stand. "Need to pull a childcare provider out of a hat."

Her words remind me of the conversation she was having when she first sat down.

"I, um ... I have a degree in early childhood education, and I'm certified in childhood development."

She glances from me to my daughter, who's leaning against me, watching the conversation take place. We've been to enough places of business that she's learned to have patience while I talk since I have no choice but to bring her along to every interview.

"I'm Kira," I tell her. "And this is my daughter, Violet."

"Nice to meet you," the woman says. "I'm Ana."

"Mommy, can we go to the park?" Violet asks, looking up at me.

"Yes, sweets. Just give me one minute." I kiss her forehead and then look back at Ana. "I don't know the job you're trying to fill, but I have experience in early childhood education, and I'm currently looking for a job."

"One of the childcare providers had to quit unexpectedly," she explains. "Do you have time to interview now?"

A wave of hope surges through me. "I would love to. But I'd have to bring Violet with me."

"That's fine," she says, standing. "I'm assuming if you're hired, you would use our childcare facility for her."

"You allow that?" I ask in shock.

"Of course. That's the purpose of the corporate childcare. It's only for those who work for Kingston Limited, and it's discounted based on income. Do you live nearby?"

"Right around the corner."

She smiles. "Let's go inside where it's cool, and we can discuss this further."

Since I'm speechless, I simply nod and follow her with Violet by my side.

When we step inside the building, a blast of cold air hits us. The main lobby is beautiful and modern with a marble floor and gold trim. It screams wealth and sophistication, and while I can't imagine this place housing a childcare facility, I thank the clothing gods I'm dressed in a button-down cream blouse and black slacks with my black Gucci pumps. It's the only professional attire I own since it's what I was wearing the day—

"Welcome to Kingston Limited," Ana says, cutting off my thoughts. "This is Margaret Cole. She runs the front desk, and this is Mr. Vega." She smiles at the security guard standing next to the desk. "He handles all the visitor passes. This is Kira ..."

"Miller," I say.

"Kira Miller will be interviewing with me. Can you get her a visitor pass, please?"

"Yes, ma'am," he says. "May I have your ID?"

"Oh, um ... sure." I reach into my back pocket and pull out my ID and hand it to him. I knew if I got a job, I'd have to give my information, but I pushed it aside, telling myself that once I got hired, I'd deal with the rest later.

"Kira Williams," he says, handing me my visitor badge.

I flinch at the use of my legal last name and force a smile. "Thank you," I tell him, then turn to Ana, wanting to address my last name before it becomes an issue. "I'm in the middle of a divorce," I explain, and she nods in understanding.

"Childcare is on the second floor," Ana says as we

get onto the elevator. "We have an indoor and outdoor playground, a full-sized kitchen and lunchroom, a naptime room, three playrooms, and a theater room."

The bell chimes, and we get off the elevator and step into an empty hallway. Ana guides us toward a door that reads *Kingston Childcare* and swipes her badge, unlocking the door.

"Nobody can get in without a badge," she explains. "And only employees with the special badges can get off the elevator and onto this floor. The children's safety comes first."

Unlike the opulence in the lobby, the walls are painted various primary colors with hand-painted designs. Ana takes us on a tour of the childcare facility, and I'm in awe at how welcoming and cozy it is while housing the most state-of-the-art equipment.

I meet two other teachers, who are very pleasant, and one offers to let Violet play with the other kids while I interview.

Before I can insist that she stay with me, Violet runs off in excitement to play, and I can't tell her no since I know she's been missing the stimulation from playing with other kids.

"At Kingston Limited, we want to make the environment more family friendly," Ana explains. "By offering childcare to our employees, it allows them to work and know their children are taken care of. Many of them will come down during lunch to visit their babies."

"Makes sense. A happy employee is a dedicated employee."

"Exactly," she agrees, opening the door to an office that only has the bare minimum—a desk and two chairs.

"This isn't my office," she says, rounding the desk. "But I'm too tired to walk all the way there."

I laugh and have a seat across from her. "I get it. I loved being pregnant, but toward the end, I couldn't wait to evict her."

"I'm counting down the weeks," she admits. "Now, Kira, tell me about yourself."

We spend the next half hour chatting, and I find Ana easy to talk to. We go over my experience, and she asks me about various situations to gauge how I would handle them.

When it seems that she's satisfied with my answers, she hands me an iPad so I can fill out an application with my references. I pray she doesn't notice that I've been unemployed for the past year. Of course, she doesn't miss a beat.

"There's no mention of any workplace during the past year," she says. "Mind if I ask why?"

"I was fortunate to be able to be home with my daughter," I tell her, giving her a half truth. "But my financial situation has changed, and I need to go back to work."

"And before that, you worked at a bar. Why not in

the educational field?"

"Bartending pays better." I shrug. "I worked in childcare for six years—two during high school and the four years I was in college as well as the months leading up to me giving birth. But after Violet was born, it didn't make sense to work just to pay for her to be in day care. So, I worked nights while my mom watched her," I admit truthfully.

She nods in understanding. "The position is only part-time. We already have two full-time providers on staff, but we need a third to meet the state requirements. So, if you need more hours …"

"I'll take anything," I say. "I've interviewed at several places, and nobody is hiring. Part-time is better than nothing at all."

"Okay, good. It's nine to five, three days a week—Monday, Wednesday, and Friday. It pays twenty-five dollars an hour, and if you aren't needed that day, you'll still be paid. Since you'll only have two, sometimes three children with you, if you want your daughter to stay with you, she can, but there's also room with her age group."

"Thank you. As much as I'd love to keep her by my side, I'm sure she'd enjoy playing with kids her own age."

"They grow up too quickly," Ana says, rubbing her belly. "This is our second. My son, Kingston, will be with you a few days a week. He's about to turn one."

"Kingston?" I ask, recalling the name across the

top of the building. "As in …"

"Yes." She laughs. "Kingston Limited. My father built this company from the ground up. Last year, he stepped down and handed the reins over to my husband, Julian, and me. You'll meet him eventually. He'll be the grump complaining that I need to go home and take a nap."

She rolls her eyes, but I can tell she secretly loves that her husband cares.

"Anyway," she says, "the agency we use will have to run a background and reference check. They're usually the ones to do the interviewing as well, but as you heard, caregivers are hard to come by, so I wasn't about to let you out of my sight."

She winks teasingly, and my heart soars at how sweet she is. She doesn't know it, but she's throwing me a lifeline.

"Does that mean I got the job?" I ask, excitement buzzing through me.

"As long as everything checks out, yes. I'll call you once I'm given the green light."

Shit. She'll call me …

"I actually don't have a phone," I admit. "I just moved here, and money's been tight. I do have an email though."

She looks at me for several long seconds, and it feels as though she's looking into my soul. Like she knows everything I'm thinking without me saying it.

She knows there's more to this story, and she's going to call me out on it.

I wait for her to bombard me with questions or to change her mind, but instead, she says, "You'll need a cell phone in case we don't need you to come in, but the company can provide one. I'll make sure it's part of your contract."

I sigh in relief. "Thank you."

After we head out so I can grab Violet, who whines that she doesn't want to leave, Ana walks us down to the lobby.

"I'll be in touch," she says, and I pray that's the truth because if I don't get this job, I have no idea what I'm going to do, moving forward.

And going *back* isn't an option.

Three

RYDER

"Chunk, we've gotta go!"

"Yummy!" Addie calls back.

Of course she would pick today to sleep in. The one time I forget to set my alarm, and I have an early meeting to get to.

And is she fazed? Hell no. The only thing she cares about is that I'm letting her munch on fruit chips for breakfast since we're running late and I don't have time to make her anything.

I grab her diaper bag and my briefcase and then scoop my little girl into my arms so we can get out of here.

She munches on the chips all the way to the office, and I make a mental note to ask Cynthia to feed her a better breakfast. It's crazy how one change in a schedule can throw the entire morning off.

When we arrive, since employees park in an attached garage, the private elevator takes us straight to the second floor, and I haul ass toward the childcare center, already five minutes late for my meeting. Thankfully, my assistant is buying everyone breakfast to hold them over until I arrive.

But when I plow through the door, instead of Cynthia waiting to take Addie from me, a woman I don't recognize is standing there. Straight brown hair with honey highlights, sun-kissed skin. And when our gazes clash, I freeze in my spot, taken aback by eyes so strikingly blue that they remind me of my pool in the summertime—warm and refreshing.

"You must be Mr. Du Ponte," the woman says with a smile that shows off her straight white teeth and a single dimple in her right cheek. "And this little girl must be Adeline."

My checking her out stops abruptly the moment she speaks because, one, I've never seen this woman before so how the hell does she know who my daughter and I are? Two, why is she calling my daughter by *that* name? The only person who's ever called her by her full name was her egg donor. And three, despite being annoyed and running late, I can't remember the last time I noticed, let alone was instantly attracted to, the opposite sex. And that scares the shit out of me on many levels.

"Who are you?" I ask, holding my daughter a little tighter even though she's wiggling to get down.

When the woman flinches in response, I realize I spoke too harshly.

After taking a calming breath, I say, "I'm sorry. It's been a crazy morning. I'm Ryder, and this is *Addie*. Is Cynthia here?"

"Cynthia quit unexpectedly to move across the country with her fiancé," Ana says, sauntering through the door with Kingston on her hip. "This is Kira. She's been hired as her replacement."

I whip my head around to look at Ana. "Is she qualified?"

I don't give a shit how gorgeous she is. My daughter's safety comes first.

Ana glares. "Of course she's qualified. Jeez, what's your deal this morning?"

"Addie actually slept in, and I forgot to set my alarm, so I'm running late for my meeting."

I turn toward Kira, who's still standing there. Only now, she looks extremely uncomfortable.

"I'm sorry," I repeat. "I was taken by surprise."

"It's okay," she says, her smile reappearing, but not as bright and without the dimple. "I can take *Addie* for you so you can get to your meeting."

She extends her arms, and I know this is the part where I'm supposed to hand my daughter over to her, but something in me prevents me from doing so.

Since I started bringing Addie to childcare, it's always been Cynthia. It took a while to trust her with my daughter, and now, just like that, I'm supposed to hand her off to a stranger. This is the shit they don't talk about in all those damn baby books.

"Mommy! Look at the babies!" a little girl squeals, bouncing on the balls of her feet.

"Who's this?" I ask in confusion because, holy shit, a few days of working from home and everything has changed.

"This is my daughter, Violet," Kira says, placing a protective hand on her daughter's shoulder.

"I'm four!" The little girl, who looks like an adorable mini version of her mom, holds up five fingers, and Kira's smile reappears, that fucking dimple popping back out.

"Minus one," Kira says, gently pushing a single digit down.

"Minus one," Violet parrots.

"She's too cute," Ana says with a laugh as she heads down the hall with me following even though I'm more than late for my damn meeting and I should've handed Addie over to Kira already.

But seriously, would it have killed Ana to warn me about all these changes? She knows I thrive on routine. It's the only way to keep my sanity intact.

When we arrive at the playroom, Ana puts Kingston down, and he crawls over to the toys. Violet follows him and plops down, showing him a puzzle.

"I'll only be working a few hours today," Ana tells Kira. "If my husband comes by to grab Kingston before I'm done, he can take him."

"Sounds good," Kira says. "And he'll have his ID, correct?"

"Yes." Ana smiles warmly. "And if you need anything, you have my number. I've submitted to get you a cell phone, but until then, you can use the landline."

"Thank you. Helen and Joy did a great job of showing me around the past couple of days, so I think everything should run smoothly. Thank you again for this opportunity."

"Of course. I think you're going to fit in just fine here." Ana glances at me. "Don't you have a meeting to get to?"

Right on cue, my phone buzzes—no doubt, it's Julie, asking where I am—and Addie whines, wanting to be let down so she can play with her friend.

"I'm only going to be a couple of hours," I tell Kira, setting the diaper bag on the nearby counter. "Nobody can pick her up but me."

"Got it," Kira says,

"And if there are any issues …"

I pat my pockets, looking for a pen, but before I can find one, she says, "I have your cell and office number as well as your direct line." Her patient eyes meet mine, and she places a hand on my arm. "I'll treat her like she's my own, I promise."

She smiles warmly at me, and there's something in her look that instantly settles my nerves. I don't know this woman, and this is going to sound crazy, but I can feel it—she means what she says.

"Thank you," I murmur. "She didn't have breakfast …"

"I'll get something in her belly."

"Okay, thanks."

I walk over to Addie and give her a kiss on the top of her head while she bangs the puzzle pieces and ignores me. And then with one more look back, I head to my meeting, telling myself that today is the same as every day. Sure, the childcare has a new teacher—with mesmerizing blue eyes and a smile that could brighten even the darkest skies—but nothing has changed.

Yet, as I go through the motions of my Monday morning meeting, my brain can't stop thinking about Kira—those eyes and that dimple and her soft, warm goddamn smile—and I can't help but feel like, somehow, everything has changed.

"… BAKE ME A CAKE AS FAST AS YOU—"

"Dada!"

The moment I step into the playroom, my little

girl spots me and comes toddling over, everyone and everything else forgotten. There's no better feeling than seeing the look in your child's eyes when they're happy to see you.

My stomach knots in memory of Nora signing over her rights and walking out the door without so much as a backward glance. There's no amount of money in the world worth not being able to hear my daughter's laughter, see her smile, and smell her sweet baby scent every day. I'll never understand how Nora and my mom were able to walk away so easily or how my dad could go days, sometimes weeks, without seeing me, but I'll do everything in my power to make sure Addie never feels as unwanted as I did.

Kira glances up and smiles at me, her eyes twinkling with happiness, and all my negative thoughts are shoved back into the box I keep hidden deep within me. A part of me was hoping I was playing up the chemistry I felt toward Kira this morning, but as she walks over, I know I wasn't. She's just as beautiful as I remember. But unlike this morning, when I was taken by surprise, I've had time to mentally prepare myself. To put up a wall to keep her charm away from me.

Ana and Julian say I'm too young to be this cynical, but they haven't experienced what I have. I'd be a damn fool to let another woman into my and my daughter's lives so she can wreak havoc on our hearts. And I might be a lot of things, but I'm no damn fool.

"Hey!" Kira says as I scoop Addie up into my arms. "How did your meeting go?"

I blank for a moment, lost in my thoughts, but quickly remember I mentioned I was late for my meeting this morning.

"Okay," I tell her, trying to keep it short but polite.

"That's it? Okay?" She scrunches her nose up adorably. "Was it good? Bad? Productive? Did you figure out the answer to world domination?"

I choke out a laugh. "It was productive. But unfortunately, world domination was not tackled. Maybe at next week's meeting."

"I look forward to hearing about it," she says with a wink. "Addie here didn't dominate the world either, but you should've seen her jamming out during our dance party. Girl has rhythm."

Kira reaches out and runs her fingers through my daughter's short blonde hair, and Addie smiles at her, clearly already enamored by her new friend. Everyone says she looks like me, right down to the same hazel eyes, but she has Nora's blonde hair while mine is brown.

"Where's your daughter?" I ask, noticing she's without her mini.

"She's playing with the kids her own age in the other room. She loves babies, but she loves the big-kid playground more."

She playfully rolls her eyes and laughs, and I remind myself that I need to keep my distance from her. Her smile is too sweet, her laugh too melodic—a recipe for heartbreak.

"That's good," I choke out. "We need to get going, but, um ... we'll see you on Wednesday."

"Okay," she says with a nod. "Bye, Addie. Have a good night with your daddy."

Addie waves happily to Kira as I grab her diaper bag and run for my life, wondering what the hell has gotten into me.

It's just because I haven't gotten laid, I tell myself.

It's been a while, and my dick is feeling neglected.

But later that night, when the house is quiet, I pull up porn, hoping to relieve some tension. When I blow my load, it isn't the chick getting fucked on the screen that draws it out of me, but the gorgeous brown-haired, blue-eyed woman with the dimple in her cheek who has captured my attention.

Four

RYDER
ONE MONTH LATER

"I TOLD HER IF SHE DOESN'T LAY HER ASS DOWN AND rest, I'm going to tie her to the bed," Julian says, trying to sound like there's even a possibility he has a say in anything his wife does when everyone knows she runs the show.

"So, how's sleeping on the couch going for you?" I ask, taking a bite of my sub.

Julian glares. "I'm not sleeping on the couch, dickhead. The woman is only a month away from giving birth, but I swear, she thinks she's invincible. She did agree this will be her last week going into the office though."

"We both know she can easily run this entire company from her bed regardless," I point out, making

Julian grin like a lovesick puppy.

"Yeah, she can," he says with a nod.

My phone vibrates with an email from my dad, and I roll my eyes at his formality even though it doesn't surprise me.

Ryder,

I hope you are well. As you know, Du Ponte Enterprises will be hosting their annual Fourth of July picnic. Margorie hasn't received your RSVP. I don't need to remind you that you missed the last two years in a row due to your situation. Am I correct to assume you'll be attending this year? It looks bad that I've yet to meet my granddaughter.

—Henry Du Ponte

"Bad news?" Julian prompts when I groan out loud.

"Family obligations. My father has requested my presence."

Julian chuckles. "The Fourth of July picnic?"

"The fact that he calls renting out several floors of a hotel and a private beach a picnic shows how out of touch he is from reality."

I was excused last year because of the shit that went down with Nora—during which he never once showed up to offer his support—and the year before because of the wedding, which he didn't attend. But he's not going to take no for an answer this year. The idea of spending an entire weekend with my father and our stuck-up family at the beach has me wanting to drown myself in the ocean.

Although I'm sure my grandfather will be there, and unlike my dad, he actually cares about me. He might be related to my dad, but they're nothing alike.

"Rich people problems," Julian drawls, half joking.

Unlike Ana and me, Julian comes from a middle-class family. He loves his job, but even after all these years of working at Kingston, he's not entirely comfortable around people like my father, who flaunt their wealth and judge others by the number of zeros next to their name.

"He acts like it's my fault that he hasn't met Addie when he's the one who chooses to never visit. My grandfather and Eric both made the trip to meet her when she was born, and my grandfather has visited a few times since then."

"Don't let him get to you," Julian says. "He's just bitter that after all this time, you still haven't caved on working for him, and there's nothing he can do about it."

Thankfully, my grandfather believes in following your own dreams, and the trust I was given was only contingent on me furthering my education. The day I graduated from college with my degree, I was given access to more money than I'd ever spend. My dad was pissed because he wanted me to work for the family business and tried to convince my grandfather to require it, but he refused—thank God. The thought of spending my days working for a man who has treated me more like a stranger than blood is not appealing, to say the least.

"So, are you going to the picnic?"

"Yeah, I haven't seen my grandfather in a few months, and he'll be there. I want Addie to know him."

With him being in his eighties, I don't know how much longer we have with him, and I'll regret Addie not getting to know him because I hate being around the rest of my family.

While my grandfather was busy working when I was younger, he still made it a point to spend time with me. Both he and my grandmother—who passed away a few years back—were the only family I really felt somewhat close to, growing up. Neither of them agreed with the way my father chose to raise his children—or put work above his wife. Meanwhile, my father thinks my grandfather is soft and swears if it wasn't for him taking over Du Ponte Enterprises, the business would've failed.

He's probably not wrong, but while the business has thrived, his family life is a complete failure. He's a lonely sixty-five-year-old man who never settled down after my mom left him and thinks having a gorgeous younger woman on his arm proves he's made it in the world. It's pretty fucking embarrassing if you ask me.

I've only taken a couple more bites of my food when another email comes through, this time from my brother.

Ryder,

I know you've been through a lot recently, but with me announcing my candidacy for president in the upcoming election, it would mean a lot if you could please attend the annual picnic. All eyes will be on us, and it will help to have a united front, especially after everything that transpired last year.

Sincerely,

Eric

"Let me guess," Julian says. "Your brother emailed you."

"Of course he did."

I love my brother, and he's never done anything wrong—just the opposite, he's as perfect as it gets—but because of the ten-year age difference, we aren't close. He lives in Austin since he's the governor of Texas, so we don't see each other often, and ever since Nora left, I've made it a point to hide from the public so I can deal with my shit in private.

Going to this picnic will mean putting myself, as well as my daughter, back in the limelight. People are going to want to know where her mother is and why she isn't in the picture anymore. Even if Eric wasn't a public figure, the Du Pontes are one of the wealthiest families in Texas, having owned and sold over one hundred thousand miles of pipeline years ago. Our family is still heavily involved in oil, among other things, and it was only a matter of time before I'd have to step out of the shadows.

"Knock, knock." Ana pops her head in, grins, and then walks in. "Am I interrupting something important?"

"Never," Julian says, pulling her into his arms on the couch we're sitting on and eating our lunch. "Are you heading home?"

"Soon," she says, giving Julian a kiss. "I need to grab Kingston from childcare first. Speaking of which ..." Ana glances my way. "I'm not sure what to do. Julian and I have decided to hire a nanny instead of Kingston returning to childcare after the baby is born. And since Britney moved up to the older age group, that only leaves Addie with Kira."

"And ... what's the problem?" I ask, refusing to let the mention of her name get to me.

I've done a good job of pretending she doesn't affect me every time I drop off and pick up Addie when the truth is, I can't get the woman off my mind. I'm only around her for maybe a total of ten minutes, three times a week, yet she's managed to somehow get under my skin.

Her laughter, her smile. The way she genuinely

cares about my daughter. Last week, Addie was teething and cranky, and Kira handled it with such patience and kindness. She doesn't have a mean bone in her body. And don't get me started on her looks. As if her blue eyes and dimple weren't enough, her body is damn near perfection with curves for days and breasts I imagine would fit perfectly in my palms. I'm ashamed to admit the number of times she's starred in my fantasies in the past month.

"Well, technically, it's not a problem," Ana says. "And we can afford to pay her, but since nobody else is pregnant or planning to use the corporate childcare in the foreseeable future, we'll be paying Kira to only care for Addie. I just wasn't sure if you wanted to consider getting a nanny ..."

"Addie likes her. I don't want to force my daughter to get used to another person."

"Okay, then she stays," Ana says, standing. "I'm actually glad you want that because she needs the job, and I dreaded having to let her go. We can probably have Kira join the other daycare workers, so she and Addie don't feel isolated. I'll talk to them tomorrow."

The rest of the afternoon flies by, and before I know it, I'm heading to the second floor to pick up my daughter. It's Friday, and I'm looking forward to the weekend. With Addie now walking, she loves to go to the park, and when it's too hot, we take a drive to the beach. She can play in the sand for hours.

"Hey, Ryder," Kira says with a warm smile. "How was your day?"

She asks the same type of question every time I pick up Addie. The first time she asked, I simply replied with, "Okay," hoping to quickly make my escape, but when she scrunched her nose up and said that wasn't a good enough answer, I elaborated, and we talked for a little while. It was nice to talk to someone who wasn't Julian or Ana.

Each time, our conversations have gotten more in depth. We discuss the kids and the plans we have for the weekend. We've even talked about our favorite books and music. If I were at a place in my life where I was interested in dating, Kira would be someone I'd want to get to know on a deeper level. She hasn't mentioned being in a relationship, and she only ever talks about her and her daughter, which leads me to believe she's a single mom.

But I'm not looking for love. My only focus is my daughter, and the last thing I want is history repeating itself. Addie already had a mom who walked away, and isn't the woman who birthed you supposed to be the one person who loves you the most? If I wasn't enough for my mom to stay and Addie wasn't enough for Nora to stay, how can I expect some woman who has no ties to us to stick around? Getting involved with a woman will only lead to one thing—heartbreak. And I've been there, done that, and I got the shirt to prove it.

"It was long," I admit truthfully, answering her question. "I was thinking about heading to the beach with Addie this weekend. Any plans?"

"That will be fun," she says, handing my daughter over to me. "Violet has been into bugs recently, so I was thinking of taking her to the science museum."

"Nice. The one in Houston?"

"Yep. Have you been?"

"Many times." My nanny used to bring me every summer, and then last year, when my brother and his family visited, we went back. "Make sure she checks out the fossil exhibit. She'll love digging for treasure."

"Thanks for the tip." She hands me my diaper bag, and I sling it over my shoulder. "Bye-bye, Monkey," she says, using Addie's nickname that she dubbed her without even knowing I called her Chunky Monkey.

When I asked where she'd heard it, she said she made it up because Addie loved to hang all over everything, like a spider monkey. And she was shocked to learn I called her the same name.

"Have fun at the beach. Build me a sandcastle."

"Bye!" Addie waves as we head out.

We're almost to my car when I get a text from Julian, asking about a budget report I promised him. Realizing I never saved it so I have no way of grabbing it from the cloud, I throw the diaper bag into the car and then run back up to my office to send it to him.

I'm walking back to my car when I see Kira and

Violet walking toward their SUV. They're too far, so I don't bother calling out to them. I strap Addie into her car seat and then round my vehicle so we can head home.

I put the car in reverse and start to back up when I notice the SUV is driving in the wrong direction. There's only one exit, yet Kira is heading toward the top of the garage.

My first thought is that she must've gone in the wrong direction by accident and she'll make her way back down soon, but as I sit and wait to see her vehicle drive by, it never appears.

Afraid something is wrong and not wanting to leave without knowing they're okay, I drive up the same way they went, circling around the four-floor garage. By the time I get to the third floor, I've convinced myself I was seeing shit and she left, but when I arrive at the top level and find her SUV parked in the corner, I know I wasn't mistaken. Now, the question is, why the hell is she parked up here?

I pull in next to her SUV, and leaving my car running so Addie has AC, I get out to make sure Kira's okay. Only instead of finding her in the driver's seat, she's sitting in a folding chair while her daughter is lying on the ground on a blanket.

"Hey," I say, making my presence known. "Are you ..." My question trails off when I notice the back seats are lying flat, and there's an air mattress spread out across the entire area with a couple of pillows and blankets.

Kira's eyes widen in shock, and she immediately stands. "What are you doing here?"

"Hi, Ryder!" Violet says, waving to me like it's perfectly normal for them to be hanging out at the top of a parking garage. It's then I notice she's not just lying on the ground, but is also coloring in a coloring book.

"Is Addie with you?" Violet asks.

"Yeah, sweetheart, she's in the car," I say, glancing at Kira, who looks a mixture of horrified and embarrassed. "You want to go say hi to her?" I suggest, my eyes not leaving Kira's.

"Mommy, can I?" Violet asks.

"Yeah, that's fine," Kira chokes out.

As soon as Violet is out of earshot, I step toward Kira, praying what this looks like isn't what it actually is.

"This isn't what it looks like," Kira says as if she can read my mind.

"No? Then, tell me what I'm looking at." I point toward her vehicle. "Because it looks like you're living out of your vehicle and using the Kingston parking garage as your temporary resting spot."

"Okay," she breathes. "That is what you're looking at, but it's not forever. I'm so close to getting enough money to rent a place. Please," she begs, tears of desperation filling her lids, "you can't tell anyone. If they find out, they'll take her away from me."

"Kira," I say, closing the gap between us, "I can't possibly let you and that little girl of yours sleep in your SUV."

"Yes, you can," she rushes out. "Please, just pretend you didn't see us. Get back in your car and drive away. We're okay. I'm not a bad mom."

Her words crack at the end, along with my heart. How could I have spent the past month talking to this woman and not known she and her daughter were homeless?

"I swear, it's only for a short time," Kira sobs. "It's not permanent."

"Hey, hey." I pull her into my arms, and even though she's freaking out, she lets me. "It's going to be okay."

I don't know what I'm going to do to fix this, but there's no way I'm letting her handle this alone.

"I'm so close," she cries into my chest. "She's taken care of, I promise. You can't turn me in. She's my entire world. I'm all she has and …" She hiccups the last part, and I pull back so I can look her in the eyes.

"Shh," I say, wiping her tears. "I'm not taking her away from you. I know you're a good mom. I see the way you care for my daughter and yours. But I can't let you guys live in your vehicle."

"Okay." She nods emphatically. "I'll get a room in a hotel, I promise."

"You're not staying in a hotel."

If she could afford one, she wouldn't be sleeping in

her damn SUV.

"Then, what do you want me to do?" she cries.

"Come home with me." The words are out of my mouth before I can stop them, but I can't find it in me to regret them.

I don't know this woman's story, but I know enough about her to know that she's kind and sweet and caring, and if she's living in her fucking car, there's a damn good reason why.

"What?" She steps back. "No, I can't."

She shakes her head, looking at me like she's a rabid animal I'm trying to corner and capture. Whatever happened to her is enough that she'd rather sleep in her car than get help from me.

"Yes, you can. I have a big home with too many damn rooms," I say, trying to assure her. "You can trust me. You've known me for over a month now. You and your daughter will be safe in my home."

"But…"

"But nothing," I argue. "Come home with me and get a good night's sleep, and tomorrow, we'll figure this out. I'd bet your little girl would love to have a nice shower and sleep in a comfy bed tonight," I add, not above guilting her into listening to me because there's no way in hell I'm leaving them here to sleep in their vehicle another night.

She stares at me for several seconds. Then, her shoulders slump, and her panicked features morph into defeated acceptance, telling me she's going to give in.

"Okay," she whispers. "We'll go home with you."

KIRA

"Mommy, where are we going?" Violet asks as I drive out of the Kingston parking garage, following Ryder.

After I agreed to go to his house, he took the phone Ana had given me and input his address into the GPS.

Sensing my hesitancy, he looked at me and said, "Don't run, Kira. If you do, I'll have to chase you."

And since I could tell his threat wasn't empty, I agreed.

"Ryder invited us to have a sleepover at his house with Addie. Doesn't that sound like fun?" I ask, keeping my voice light even though I'm freaking the hell out on the inside because he knows my daughter and I are homeless and living out of our SUV.

I begged him to leave it alone, to forget he saw us,

but he insisted on us staying with him, and I could tell he wasn't going to stop until I gave in, so I did—right after I cried in his arms like a crazy person.

Sigh. This is not how I thought today would go.

I guess I should be thankful he didn't turn me in. When he pulled up and got out, I thought for sure that everything I'd done up until now was for nothing.

Oh God, speaking of everything I've done ... what is Ana going to say when she finds out? Will she fire me for using their parking garage? Will she think less of me once she knows *living around the corner* didn't mean in an actual home, but in a vehicle? I shove the fear away, needing to get through tonight. I'll deal with the fallout later.

"Does Addie have a pool?" Violet randomly asks.

"I'm not sure, Vi, but we're just sleeping there for tonight. Ryder said we can shower and sleep in a bed."

"Okay," she says, always going with the flow. "But if they have a pool, can we swim in it?"

"Probably not," I tell her, not wanting to get her hopes up.

"Are we still going to see bugs tomorrow?" she asks after a few minutes of silence.

Shoot, I forgot all about the trip to the museum I'd promised her. I don't know what will happen once we get to Ryder's, but there's no way he'll prevent me from taking my daughter to the science museum. I let one man dictate my life, and I'll never allow that to happen again.

"Of course we are," I tell her as we pull up to a massive guard's gate.

Ryder stops ahead of me and rolls down his window. He speaks to the guard for a couple of minutes and then pulls forward. I follow, waiting for the guard to stop me, but he only nods, indicating that I'm good to go.

As we drive through the streets of his neighborhood, I glance at the homes in shock and awe. I'm no stranger to living in a nice neighborhood—I lived in one for over a year—but these homes are on a completely different level. Like, there's rich, and then there's *rich*. I figured Ryder makes a good living since he's the CFO of a multibillion-dollar company and drives a newer BMW, but, holy shit, this is insane.

When we pull up to what must be his home, Ryder waits for the wrought iron gate to open—because he apparently has another gate despite his neighborhood being guarded—and then we drive up a long driveway.

When we turn the corner, we're met with the most beautiful mansion—yes, mansion because it would be an insult to call it anything less. To the left is a three-car garage. Ryder must press a button because one of the bay doors begins to rise. He pulls in, and the door shuts behind him.

And because I have no idea what to do, I stay in my seat, staring at the exquisite home in front of me, wondering what the hell I was thinking, following

Ryder here.

To most, the idea of wealth is a turn-on. I've witnessed how envious and jealous women can be of other women—of the house she lives in, the car she drives, the designer bags she totes around, and the clothes she wears. I must admit, I was one of those women ... *before*.

Now, it sickens me. Because while money has the potential to do good—to cure diseases and feed and house the homeless—it's rarely ever used for things like that. Instead, it's wielded around like a deadly weapon, those having it being able to do and get away with damn near whatever they want while leaving those without it in its wake.

And judging by the ridiculously expensive home in front of me, Ryder has a lot of money. I hate to lump him into the same category as *other people*, but I've learned the hard way that giving people like Ryder the benefit of the doubt only leads to devastation. And I would be stupid not to proceed with caution.

Just as I'm considering taking my chances and bolting, Ryder emerges from out of nowhere. As he saunters my way, I can't help but notice how good-looking he is with his bright hazel eyes, which are always aware and assessing, and his chiseled jawline, which is more prominent today due to his neatly trimmed beard. His brown hair is freshly cut, and his suits always fit him like they were made for him, showcasing his broad shoulders and muscular thighs.

He's one hundred percent sex personified from head to toe, and him sporting a diaper bag on one shoulder with his daughter on his hip only adds to his appeal. There is nothing sexier than a man who puts his child first. I don't know what happened with Addie's mom, nor is it my business, but from what I've seen, Ryder's best feature is how good of a dad he is.

I'm so lost in my thoughts that I don't realize that Ryder's standing right in front of my window, waiting for me to roll it down.

When I do, he bends slightly, and his eyes find mine. "You can park here for tonight," he says. "If you have laundry, bring it in so you can wash it."

I nod, but make no move to get out. His intentions seem pure, but then again, so did *his*. I fell for the white-knight routine once before, and he turned out to be nothing more than a villain, hidden under Armani.

As if sensing my hesitancy, Ryder sets Addie down, who toddles toward the front door, and leans in closer, giving me a whiff of his scent.

Jesus, even the smell of him is sexy and masculine.

"You okay?" he asks, his voice calm and patient.

"Hey, Ryder!" Violet says. "Mommy said we're having a sleepover! Can we go swimming?"

Before I can tell her again that it's probably not happening, Ryder answers her, "Sure. How about we order a pizza and have it by the pool?"

"Yes!" Violet flings her seat belt off and pushes the door open, running over to where Addie is trying and failing to open the front door.

"Hey," he says, forcing me to look back at him. "You're safe here, I promise."

If only he knew that those words do nothing to calm my pounding heart. If anything, they scare the hell out of me because I know all too well how easy it is for a man to fling promises around and not mean a single one of them.

"I'd better grab our stuff," I mutter, turning the vehicle off and getting out.

After gathering our dirty clothes and sheets so I can wash them—because I would be an idiot not to take advantage of having a free washer and dryer at my disposal—I follow Ryder and the girls inside.

The inside is just as beautiful as the outside, but I'm surprised to find that it looks lived in. While the living room furniture is clearly high-end, it's all been baby-proofed, and there's an entire corner dedicated to Addie, complete with a princess carpet, a child-sized reading chair, and a bookshelf filled with children's books.

"The washer and dryer are this way," Ryder explains, guiding me to the massive laundry room. "I'm going to order the pizzas and get Addie into her bathing suit. Do you guys prefer any toppings on your pizza?"

"Pepperoni, please!" Violet exclaims.

"I'm good with pepperoni as well," I tell him. "Thank you."

While I throw a load into the washer, Violet talks my ear off about how excited she is to have a sleepover even if Addie is a baby who doesn't talk—her words, not mine.

"Oh no!" Violet gasps when Ryder and Addie come down in their bathing suits. "We don't have bathing suits." She glances at me, her brows furrowed. "How are we gonna swim? My bathing suit is at—"

"It's okay," I tell her, cutting her off before she can spill our business in front of Ryder. "You can go swimming in your shorts and shirt."

She pouts. "But ..."

"I can't get you a suit tonight. It will be fine."

"Okay," she relents. "But will you come in with me?"

I wasn't planning on it, but the way she's looking up at me, not wanting to be the only one swimming with her clothes on, I can't say no.

"Sure."

After I've changed into a pair of cotton shorts and a tank, leaving my bra on, we follow Ryder through the living room and family room and out a pair of French doors that lead to the most exquisite backyard I've ever seen. His home is situated on what looks like several acres of land, and with the privacy shrubs and trees surrounding his home, you can't even tell he has any neighbors.

When we step outside, to the right is a state-of-the-art outdoor kitchen with a bar and a table and chairs that seat eight people. To the left is a beautiful stone fireplace with comfy-looking patio furniture.

"Mommy, look at the pool!" Violet yells. "Can I jump in?"

"Can she swim?" Ryder asks as he removes his shirt and flings it onto the lounge chair.

I'm about to answer when my eyes lock on his shirtless chest—with the perfect amount of hair—and six-pack abs and then slowly descend as I follow the happy trail toward the defined V that disappears into his board shorts. I knew the man was fit, but I had no idea he looked like that underneath those perfectly pressed suits. As if being rich and successful weren't enough, he has to go and look like one of the guys on the cover of *GQ*. Without a tattoo in sight, his tanned skin is smooth and flawless.

A throat clearing shakes me from mentally snapping pictures of him to save for later when I'm alone, and when I look up, I find Ryder smirking. *Shit!* He just caught me checking him out.

"I'm sorry, what?" I choke out and then flinch when I realize I sound as turned on as I am.

Thankfully, Ryder doesn't call me out on it. Instead, he says, "I asked if Violet could swim."

Oh, right! He did ask that ... and then he took off

his damn shirt, and I lost all train of thought.

"Yes, she can swim like a fish."

She's always loved the water, even when she was a baby. I taught her at an early age how to swim since the apartment complex we lived in with my mom had a community pool. She probably swims better than most adults.

"Go ahead," I tell her, following her to the infinity pool that overlooks the bay.

When I step out from under the overhang, glancing up, I see a second-story balcony. On one side is a set of stairs, and on the other is ...

"Is that a pool slide?" I gasp, refusing to look at Ryder because I know exactly what I'll see if I do.

He chuckles. "It is."

"Can I go down it?" Violet asks.

"Go for it," Ryder says.

He steps into the water, and I focus on Addie as he places her in her cute little float.

Violet wastes no time racing up the steps and running across the balcony that houses several lounge chairs.

"Ready?" she calls down.

"Yep," I say back.

She plops onto her butt and slides straight down and into the water. A few seconds later, she pops up, laughing hysterically. "That's so cool!"

She swims back to the steps and gets out to do it

all over again.

"No running," I remind her since she's now wet, and the last thing I need is her slipping and cracking her head open.

"You coming in?" Ryder asks as he pushes Addie all around the pool while she giggles and splashes the water.

"She is!" Violet calls down just before she slides down again.

"I guess I am," I say with a small laugh.

Of course, the water is warm, so I glide in with ease, watching as my daughter heads back up to the slide for round three.

She goes up and down several more times while Ryder plays with Addie, and I watch everyone around me, feeling a sense of peace for the first time in a long time.

"Pizza's here," Ryder says when an alarm chimes. "Can you watch her while I go grab it?"

"Of course."

"Dada!" Addie yells as Ryder gets out of the pool.

"He'll be right back," I tell her, pushing her wet hair out of her eyes while trying and failing not to look at Ryder as he walks away with his muscular back on display, droplets of water trailing down his body. I've never been jealous of water until now …

Once he disappears inside, I take a deep breath and vow to get my shit together. I have too much going on to be thinking about him sexually. It doesn't matter that I've gone over six months without sex—and even longer without *good* sex. I need to focus on what's important—Violet and our future.

A few minutes later, Ryder returns with the food and drinks—and thankfully has a shirt on. We eat, both of us focusing on the kids, and even though it should be awkward, it's not. Violet fills the silence with talk of the museum we're going to visit tomorrow while Ryder acts like it's the coolest place in the world.

"You wanna go?" Violet asks him, making me damn near choke on my drink.

"I think it's just you and your mom going," he says.

"Yeah, but you can go too. Right, Mommy?"

"I'm not sure Addie will have as much fun as you, but they can go if they want." I shrug.

"You wanna go?" Violet repeats to Ryder, who smiles warmly at her.

"Sure," he says.

"Okay! Can I go swimming again?"

"Go ahead," I tell her since I'm done with my food anyway. "But first, what do you say to Ryder for buying this pizza?"

"Thank you," she says. "It was yummy!"

Then, she takes off like a bat out of hell toward the steps.

"Thank you," I tell him.

"You're welcome," he says, wiping Addie's face.

So she didn't feel left out, he cut up some of the crust so she could munch on it, along with her dinner.

We make our way back to the pool, both of us sitting on the steps while Addie sits between Ryder's legs, splashing in the water.

As Violet flies down the slide for the millionth time, her giggles fill the air, and I inhale a breath of fresh air. The sun is setting, and the orange backdrop is picturesque. The past couple of months have been rough, and I don't know what the future holds, but right now, my daughter is happy and laughing, we have a roof over our heads, and our bellies are full.

I can't ask for much more than that.

Six

RYDER

"What do you mean, she's homeless?" Ana shrieks over the phone, telling me everything I need to know—she had no idea that Kira and Violet had been living out of their SUV. Had she known, we'd have been having an entirely different conversation.

"She's been parking at the top of the garage, and they've been sleeping in their vehicle."

"Oh my God. I didn't know," she cries. "How did you find out?"

Even though I'm in my office, which is nowhere near where the girls are situated in their room and taking showers while Addie sleeps soundly in her own room, I speak low, not wanting to risk Kira overhearing me.

I tell Ana how I needed to run back up to my office to send a budget report over to Julian that I forgot to save, and when I came out, I saw Kira and Violet heading to the car. I go into detail about finding them camping out at the top of the garage like they were in a camper and not a fucking SUV and her freaking out because she thought I was going to turn her in and have her daughter taken away.

"What are we going to do?" Ana breathes. "We can't let them keep sleeping in their vehicle."

"I know. But Kira is too proud to take a handout."

"So, what should we do?"

"I was thinking I could hire her as my live-in nanny."

I've been thinking about how to fix this since I found them, and it's the only solution that I can come up with that will give them a safe place to stay while Kira works.

"You'd do that?" Ana asks. "I thought you didn't want to hire a nanny."

"You said it yourself. With Kingston staying home with you, it only leaves Addie for her to care for. She might as well do it from the comfort of my home."

If there were any other solution, I'd be all over it, but handing her money would be a slap in her face. She doesn't want to be a charity case. If she did, she wouldn't have been coming to work every damn day, surrounded by wealth, with a smile on her face and working her ass off, all while living out of her vehicle. She would've asked for help already, which she hasn't. Hell, even after I found out, the only thing she asked was for me not to turn her in.

"Did she agree to that?" Ana asks.

"I haven't asked. I wanted to run it by you first. It would mean removing her from Kingston's payroll since she'd be working strictly for me."

"As long as Kira's okay with it, I am. If we need to hire someone else in the future, we'll worry about it then. I can't believe they've been sleeping in their freaking car and we never knew."

We talk for a few more minutes, and when I hear someone padding down the stairs, I let her know I'll update her with Kira's decision tomorrow.

I step out of my office just as Kira's rounding the corner. She doesn't notice me at first, so when she does, she shrieks, clutching her chest.

"Sorry," I say with a chuckle. "Didn't mean to scare you."

"It's like you came out of nowhere," she breathes, glancing around like there's a trap door hidden somewhere.

"This is my office."

I open the door behind me that looks like it's part of the wall when it's closed, and she peeks in curiously. With her body so close to mine, I catch a whiff of her scent—coconut with a hint of vanilla. Her arm brushes mine, and I stiffen in response, overwhelmed by her scent and touch hitting me all at once.

I've made it a point to avoid getting too close to Kira,

knowing nothing good can come from my attraction toward her—and seeing the way she practically eye-fucked me by the pool when I took my shirt off, I have no doubt she's just as attracted to me—which is why it's even more imperative that I keep my distance from her, especially if she's going to be living here. Boundaries are going to need to be set to ensure lines aren't crossed.

"I was going to get a bottle of water," she says, stepping back. "If that's okay …"

"You don't need permission to go anywhere in this house," I tell her, closing my office door and walking to the kitchen with her following. "Is Violet asleep?"

"Out like a light," she says with a soft laugh as she has a seat at the island. "With how many times she went up those stairs and down the slide, I'm surprised she stayed awake long enough for me to give her a bath. Addie asleep?"

"She did in fact fall asleep while I was bathing her," I say, handing her a bottle of water from my fridge.

"Thank you," she says with a watery smile. "I didn't realize how badly we needed this."

She closes her eyes and shakes her head, and it takes everything in me not to round the island and pull her into my arms. Every day I see her at the childcare, she always looks so put together, dressed professionally with her hair and makeup done. But right now, dressed in a pair of pajamas with her wet hair up in a messy bun and no makeup on, she looks utterly defeated. Still beautiful, but defeated.

"How long have you been living in your car?" I ask, sitting next to her.

"Almost three months," she admits, turning toward me. "But we sleep at a motel occasionally to do laundry and shower. I've almost saved enough to rent an apartment, and then we won't have to sleep in the car anymore."

"You're not sleeping in your car again."

"You don't understand," she starts but immediately closes her mouth.

I wait several seconds for her to explain, but when it's clear she's not going to, I set my hand on top of hers and lock eyes with her. "You're right. I don't understand. But what I do know is, you wouldn't be sleeping in your vehicle unless you had no other choice. If and when you're ready to tell me what's going on, I'll be here. But until then, I want you and Violet to stay here."

"What?" she gasps, shaking her head. "No, we couldn't—"

"You can," I argue. "I need to hire a nanny, and I'd like to hire you."

"But I work for Kingston."

"Taking care of Addie," I point out. "Ana's decided she's going to work from home for a while after the baby comes, which means the only baby you'll be caring for is my daughter. I spoke to Ana, and she's agreed."

"She knows?" she whispers.

"I had to tell her." I squeeze her hand comfortingly, ignoring how soft her skin is. "But nobody is judging you or thinks any less of you. You're a wonderful mother, and I would love it if you came to work for me. I don't trust a lot of people with my daughter, but I trust you."

And that's the truth. For the past month, I've watched her take care of Kingston and Addie and the other kids at the childcare as if they were her own. She not only takes care of them, but she also cares about them. I see it in the way she speaks to them and interacts with them.

"I don't know what to say," she murmurs, removing her hand from my touch to wipe her eyes that have filled with tears.

"You and Violet would have your own rooms and bathrooms. Addie's and my rooms are on the west wing of the second floor, so you guys can have the entire east wing to yourselves. As you saw tonight, my home is plenty big enough for all of us. Your hours would be eight to five, Monday through Friday. With Addie getting older, it's harder to work from home with her. On the days you're not needed, you'll still be paid. Nights and weekends are yours, aside from the occasional evening I might need you, but I'll give you plenty of notice."

"Ana was paying me in cash," Kira says. "I don't have a bank account…"

Ana told me as much, which should've been a clue

that there was more to her story than met the eye, but Ana just chalked it up to her being new in town and not having had time to open a bank account yet.

"I'll pay you two thousand a week in cash."

Kira's eyes widen in shock. "That's—"

"Eight thousand a month."

"Too much."

"It's what I would pay any nanny I hired. I do have one stipulation though."

Her body stiffens as she prepares herself for the other shoe to drop because she doesn't trust me yet. And something in me wants her to trust me. I don't know what she's been through, but seeing as it's just the two of them, something tells me that there's a reason there's no man in the picture. And my guess is, since she doesn't have or want a bank account, she's hiding out from him. That's something we'll have to discuss eventually, so I know what we're dealing with and how to make sure they're safe. But for right now, I need to take it one step at a time so I don't scare her off.

"I want you to sign a one-year contract to live here and work for me. Anywhere you rent will be a drive to where I live, and I want someone here since my hours are all over the place. The company has a lot going on during the summer, and with the holidays, I'm going to need you quite a few nights. I want Addie to have consistency in her life, and it will be easier this way."

Most of what I just said is bullshit, but it's the only

excuse I can come up with to convince her to stay under my roof, where I know they'll both be safe, instead of her renting an apartment on the other side of town.

"Okay," she agrees, shocking the hell out of me. I thought for sure she'd argue about the one-year contract. "But I think we should have a probationary period, just to make sure it works. Ninety days, and if we're both happy, then I'll sign a nine-month contract. If we're not, then at least I'll have enough to get my own place, and since Violet is turning five in July, she'll be able to start kindergarten in the fall."

"Sounds good," I tell her. "I'll have the papers drawn up. Since the phone you were using belongs to Kingston, I'll have to get you a new one. Do you want to keep that number?"

"It doesn't matter," she says. "I only use it for work."

"Okay, get some sleep." I pat her hand and stand. "We have a busy day ahead of us at the museum tomorrow."

She opens her mouth, having obviously forgotten about our plans, but I leave the kitchen before she can argue or try to change them. I don't know what it is about this woman, but I'm drawn to her, and for the first time, I'm looking forward to Addie and me spending the day with someone other than Julian and Ana.

"GOD, THAT SMELLS LIKE HEAVEN," A FEMININE VOICE behind me breathes, shocking the hell out of me.

When I spin around, I find Kira standing in my kitchen, her hair messy from sleep and a small, unsure smile on her face.

"Sorry," she says. "I didn't mean to sneak up on you."

"It's all good. I'm just not used to people who can get out of bed on their own joining me this early in the morning," I say with a laugh.

She steps farther into the kitchen and nods toward the espresso machine. "Looks like we have the same idea."

"It's the only way to get through the morning with a toddler," I half joke.

"If I could, I'd have it directly injected into my veins," Kira jokes back, having a seat at the island. "I think the smell lured me out of my sleep and down here."

"How do you take your coffee?"

"Usually with caramel-flavored creamer, but really, it doesn't matter as long as it has caffeine."

I chuckle. "Give me a second." I grab some milk and sugar and pour it into the cup then hand it to her. "I don't have any flavors but try this."

She brings the cup to her lips and inhales deeply. "It smells so good," she sighs and then takes a sip. "And it tastes even better." She sets the cup down. "Thank you. I haven't had coffee in months."

"I don't think I could go days without coffee, let alone months," I admit, then immediately mentally chastise myself when I think about *why* she's gone months without it—she can't afford it.

"Don't do that," she says. When I raise a questioning brow, she adds, "Don't watch what you say. I don't need or want your pity."

I nod in understanding.

After making myself a cup of coffee, I sit down next to her, and for several minutes, we sit and drink in silence, both of us relishing in the quiet moment before our daughters wake up and our day officially starts. It's weird, not sitting here alone, but it's also kind of nice.

When Kira finishes her drink, she takes both of our cups to the sink. While she's washing them, the baby monitor I keep on hand goes off, indicating there's movement, followed by my daughter's babbling, letting me know she's awake.

A second later, tiny feet padding down the stairs hits our ears, followed by, "Mommy!"

Kira turns around and smiles. "Let the day begin."

"Are you sure this is a good idea?" Kira asks as I transfer her daughter's booster seat to my car. "Now that I'm working for you, we should probably keep things professional."

"Technically, you don't start working for me until Monday," I tell her. "And we're going to the children's science museum, not to a club, so I think we're safe from either of us behaving unprofessionally. Although"—I smirk at her—"I have been known to get down with the turtles. They might look tame, but inside, they're partying hard."

She rolls her eyes and groans. "You're such a nerd. I bet you were in the math club when you were in school."

"Damn straight," I admit proudly. "And the chess club and science club."

"Figures," she mutters.

"What?" I ask, driving down the driveway.

"Nothing." She shakes her head. "I was just thinking that maybe if I stuck with nerds, I wouldn't be in the position I'm in."

"Let me guess ... you were a cheerleader and dated the quarterback."

Her cheeks turn an adorable shade of pink. "Not my smartest decision," she murmurs, glancing back at her daughter. "But I can't find it in me to regret it."

She doesn't say she's talking about Violet, but as one single parent to another, I can read between the lines.

I nod. "Same."

She glances over at me, and for a moment, our eyes lock, a silent understanding passing between us. Our circumstances might be different, but one thing is the same—we're both single parents who would do anything for our kids, and despite what led us here, we wouldn't change it for anything.

Seven

KIRA

"*I know you're cheating on me! Admit it! Admit you're a slut!*" *Before I see it coming, his palm connects with my cheek.*

The slap to my face has me sitting up as I take in my surroundings.

My heart is thumping against my rib cage.

My forehead is damp with perspiration.

My hands are clammy.

I glance over to the spot next to me and find it empty. I'm about to scream for my daughter when I remember she's sleeping in her own room.

She's okay.

I'm okay.

We're safe in Ryder's home. *At least for the time*

being ...

As much as I wanted to share a room with Violet, when Ryder mentioned her having her own room, she got so excited that I couldn't argue. Besides, with my stupid nightmares that keep me from sleeping all night, it's for the best. When we slept in the SUV, I would wake her up many nights, and I could see the worry in her eyes. At least now, she'll sleep soundly.

I glance at the phone Ryder bought me and see it's only ten thirty. *Great.* Since I won't be falling back asleep anytime soon, I climb out of bed and go pee and then head downstairs to make myself a cup of tea.

It's been a week since we moved into Ryder's house, and I'm honestly shocked this is the first time I've woken up from a nightmare. I was hoping they were gone for good, but I should've known that it was too good to be true.

I pad downstairs, assuming Ryder's asleep, but stop in my tracks when I find him sitting on the couch, reading a book.

"Hey," he says, laying the book on his lap. "Are you okay?"

From the look in his eyes, he heard me. Violet had told me that I was loud in my sleep, so I assumed I screamed during my nightmares, but it wasn't confirmed until now.

"Yeah," I choke out, plastering on a smile. "I'm just going to grab some tea."

He nods, thankfully not pressing the issue.

When I have my warm tea in my hands, I take a deep breath and inhale the relaxing scent and then head back through the living room. But before I make it through, Ryder stops me.

"If you want to hang out down here, you can."

I freeze in my spot. I didn't want to go back to my room, but I also don't want to put myself in a situation where Ryder asks me questions that I'm not prepared to answer.

As if he can hear my thoughts, he adds, "No conversation needed."

I sigh in relief and then have a seat on the couch across from him. After I take a sip of my tea, I ask, "What book are you reading?"

His cheeks turn a soft pink, and I don't understand it until he lifts the book to show me the cover. There's a man and a woman in a sensual position.

"Are you reading romance?"

"What if I am?" He laughs.

"I'm not judging. I'm just a little shocked. What made you pick romance to read?"

"I enjoy reading, but after working with numbers all day and taking care of a toddler, I needed something…"

"Mindless."

"Yeah. Since I don't have a romantic life of my own, Ana bought me a romance novel as a joke, telling me I can live vicariously through them. I picked it up one night out of boredom, and it was actually damn good."

"So, this isn't your first?" I ask, completely enthralled by this conversation.

"Nah, I've read several. Then, I got conned into joining her stupid online book club." He rolls his eyes teasingly, making me laugh. "This is the book of the month."

"What's it about?"

"A single mom who hasn't had sex in years because she was focused on school. She meets a guy, and they hook up, and she ends up pregnant."

"No! Ugh, that would be my luck. I haven't had sex in, like, six months."

The second the words are out of my mouth, I immediately regret them. My face heats with embarrassment, and I wish for the floor to open and swallow me up.

But before I can think of something to say or a way to make my exit, Ryder says, "I haven't had sex in two years."

I'm taking a sip of my tea when he says this, and without meaning to, I spit my drink out, making him chuckle.

"Two years?"

"Yep," he says, "not since the weekend Addie was conceived."

"Holy shit."

"I got my ex pregnant twice in a three-month time

period. I think I'll stick to books for now since I don't have the best track record."

I choke out a laugh at his admission, and he glares playfully.

"I'm sorry. I didn't mean to laugh, but ..."

"Yeah, yeah." He waves me off. "Laugh it up. At least I know I'm not knocking any more women up while reading these books."

"True." I think about what he said, and before I can filter my thoughts, I ask, "What happened to the other baby?"

His smile morphs into a thin line, and I instantly backtrack. "I'm sorry. It's not my business ..."

"It's okay," he says. "She miscarried. We had only been dating for a short time, and I wasn't feeling it. But when she said she was pregnant, I tried to do the right thing and proposed. We were planning the wedding when she lost the baby."

"I'm so sorry." I can't imagine losing a baby.

"I was torn between relief and sadness," he admits. "Nora lost it. Though, looking back, I have to wonder if it was all an act so I wouldn't end the engagement."

My features must convey my shock because he further explains, "I told her I didn't want to try again for a while, hoping once she felt better, I could call off the engagement, but before that could happen, she begged me to go away with her. We were drinking, and instead of being smart about things, I let my dick lead the way."

"It happens to the best of us," I say, taking a sip of my tea.

"Yeah, but what I didn't know at the time was that she was trying to trap me. She was monitoring when she could get pregnant and timed it perfectly. I used protection, but she tampered with the condoms."

I gasp at his words. "Why would she do that?"

"Because I'm worth billions," he says casually. "She knew it was the only way to keep me."

"That's horrible."

"It's life. We got married, and she had Addie. But life with me wasn't what she had expected, and she quickly regretted her decision. She hated being a mom and being married to me. When Addie was four months old, she signed her rights over and walked away."

The sadness in his eyes and defeat in his voice have my heart dropping into my stomach. I've only known Ryder for a short time, but he's one of the most selfless, caring men I've ever met.

Maybe there's more to it, my subconscious screams. *You thought Brian was a good guy, and look how he turned out.*

I swallow down the lump of emotion clogging my airway, pushing my thoughts away. I refuse to judge Ryder because Brian was an asshole. Just because one man was a piece of shit doesn't mean every man is. Besides, it's not like I'm emotionally or physically involved with Ryder. I'm simply his nanny.

"You're a good dad," I tell him. "She might not have a mom in her life, but she has you, and that's all she needs."

He nods, but the look in his eyes tells me he doesn't agree.

"So, the book?" I say, changing the subject. "What happens once she finds out she's pregnant?"

"I could tell you, but it's better when you read it." He smirks.

"You suck." I poke my tongue out. "Just read me one part," I say, hoping the distraction will help my nightmares disappear and sleep to come a bit easier. Otherwise, tomorrow is going to be rough. I enjoy taking care of Addie, especially since it allows me to also spend my days with Violet while getting paid, but taking care of a toddler on almost no sleep can be brutal.

"Fine."

He flips through the book, and I take another sip of my tea and then lie on my side, snuggling into the pillow.

"I think I'll have to start from the beginning," he says, "Otherwise, it won't make sense."

"Okay."

"It's the prologue, and her name is Sophia."

He glances up at me momentarily, and I smile at him, thankful he's entertaining my request.

"'*Three redheaded sluts*,'" he begins.

"I drop the shot glasses onto the bar top, and the three women thank me.

"'To redheaded sluts,' one woman—a brunette—yells over the blaring music. 'And may they all burn in the pits of fiery hell.'

"I feel ya, sister."

I chuckle at the way the book starts, remembering the time I came across the redheaded woman on Brian's phone.

"What?" Ryder asks.

"Nothing. I just … feel the same way about redheads."

The meaning behind my words must be clear because Ryder simply nods, his lips thinning, and then he continues to read.

"The other two women—both blondes—cheer in agreement as they lift their glasses, clinking them against each other before they tip them back and swallow down their shots in one fell swoop."

I close my eyes as he reads, getting lost in the story and the comfort of his voice. Instead of reading in a monotone voice, he sounds like he's narrating the story. I laugh at the parts that are funny, and my heart clenches in my chest when it turns sad.

And before I know it, I'm waking up in my bed, having no clue how I got there. I think back to last night … Ryder sharing some of his story with me. I must've fallen asleep while he was reading to me. *Did he carry me to bed?*

I glance at my phone and see it's already almost nine in the morning. *Shit!* I overslept. *Why the hell didn't my alarm go off?*

I throw my blankets off me and rush down the hall, not bothering to brush my teeth or pee. When I find Violet's bedroom empty, I race down the stairs. The kitchen is devoid of people, and so is the living room.

My heart pounds in my chest at all the possibilities. And then I hear the screeching sound of a toddler. I follow it down the hall and into Addie's massive playroom, where I find the girls and Ryder sitting at the round table with plates of food and drinks. The girls are wearing princess dresses and tiaras on their heads.

When I glance at Ryder, he's also wearing …

"Are you wearing a tiara?" I choke out through a laugh.

"Got a problem with it?" he asks, quirking a single brow.

"No." I shake my head.

"Mommy, we're having a princess tea party!" Violet exclaims. "Sit down!"

She gets up and grabs another tiara from the box of play clothes. I sit in the open seat, and she puts it on my head.

"There! Now, you're a princess too."

"Why, thank you." I smile up at my daughter and then glance at Ryder. "Sorry about this morning. My alarm didn't go off. You should've woken me up."

"I turned it off," he says nonchalantly.

"What?"

"It looked like you could use the sleep, and I'm working from home anyway."

Butterflies fill my belly at his gesture. I can't remember the last time anyone gave a shit about whether I had enough sleep.

"Thank you. If you want, I can take it from here."

"And miss out on this amazing tea party?" His eyes, filled with mirth, meet mine. "I'm good."

"Here's a princess cupcake," Violet says, setting one of the cranberry muffins I baked yesterday on my plate. "It's magical."

As I take a bite of my muffin and then a sip of my milk, I look around at the people sitting with me. Violet is talking animatedly while Addie watches her, absorbing everything she's saying. I stop on Ryder, who's smiling at my daughter, discussing which princess movie was the best and why, and I thank whatever god or fate that he came into our lives. It's because of him that my daughter and I are no longer sleeping in our car and are safe. I have a job and can save money for our future. I don't know what the future holds, but in this moment, everything is okay because of him.

"What's up?" he asks when he catches me looking at him.

"Thank you," I murmur.

It's only two words, and it doesn't feel like nearly enough for what he's done for us in such a short time, but it's all I've got.

Eight

RYDER

"It's a girl," Julian says over the phone.

When I saw him earlier at the office, he said Ana was having some contractions, but it wasn't enough to go to the hospital. I guess they progressed.

"Congratulations, man."

"Thanks. Her name is Emilia Helen Parker, named after Ana's mom and mine," he says.

He goes over the labor and delivery, her height and weight, and how proud he is of Ana. I'm so happy that my best friend found love, and when I listen to him talk, it gives me hope that maybe, someday, I'll find that too.

"Let us know when you're home and situated, and we'll come by and visit. And let Ana know I think she's superwoman. Oh! And tell her that if she's not up for running the discussion in our book club, I can do it for her."

Julian chuckles. "Will do."

After hanging up with Julian, I email my assistant to have her send a baby gift to Ana and Julian at the hospital. As I'm clicking Send, a scream echoes through the house, and I flinch, wishing there were something I could do. Since Kira and Violet moved in, the screams happen every few nights. The first time I heard it, I freaked out and ran straight to Kira's room, only to find her fast asleep. The second time it happened, she came down, and I ended up spilling my past to her and then reading to her until she fell asleep.

I debated on whether to carry her to bed, but I had fallen asleep on that couch and woken up with a crick in my neck and didn't want the same for her.

The past few times it happened, she either stayed asleep or didn't come down. As I wait to see what she'll do tonight, I scroll through my phone, checking my emails. But when the creak of the door sounds, followed by footsteps on the stairs, I grab my book to make it look like I'm reading so she doesn't think I heard her.

"Hey," she says softly.

"Hey."

I set my book down to give her my attention. Her hair is up in a messy ponytail, and her face is natural. She has tiny black circles under her eyes from her lack of sleep, but even still, she looks beautiful. Her blue eyes are darker, missing their usual brightness, and I wish I could fix whatever is causing her nightmares, so they'll go away. I was hoping after I told her my story, she would open up about hers, but it's been a little over a week, and she hasn't said a word.

"Still reading the same book?" she asks, sitting on the couch across from me and lying against the pillow.

"Yeah. I've been busy with work." The truth is, I'm almost done with the book, but I don't tell her that.

She nods in understanding and then says, "Can you read me some more?"

Since I dog-eared the page I stopped on when I read to her the last time, I find it quickly and start reading again. I feel her eyes on me as I read page after page, but I don't look up or stop reading. When I get to the sex scene, it takes everything in me to read it out loud. It's detailed, and even though we're both adults who have obviously had sex, there's something intimate about reading the words to someone else.

When the heroine orgasms, I glance up and find Kira staring at me, her eyes bright and her legs pressed together. She's wearing a flimsy tank top, and I can't help but notice the way her nipples are poking through it.

Fuck, she's turned on. And I would be lying if I said I wasn't.

"Well, keep going," she says, her words coming out breathy. "I need to know what happens next."

I chuckle and continue, "*'Shit! Pull out!'*

"His eyes go wide, and he jerks back. His dick springs at attention, and ropes of cum shoot out across my belly.

"'I'm so sorry,' he breathes. 'I've never gone without a condom.'"

Kira snorts out a laugh, and I glance back up at her.

"Typical man." She rolls her eyes. "That's exactly what Raymond said to me the night I got pregnant with Violet."

I'm shocked she's opening up to me, so I don't say anything, letting her talk.

"A month later, I found out I was pregnant, and he pulled the whole *I'm not ready for that kind of commitment* shit." Another eye roll. "He told me having kids wasn't in his plans and asked why I wasn't on birth control. One, I was. But I was a college student and sucked at remembering. That's what condoms are for."

She sits up and flails her arms, and I hold back my laughter at how adorable she is when she's worked up. Usually, Kira is calm, cool, and collected. I've never seen her so much as raise her voice at me or the girls.

"Anyway," she continues, "he dumped me and said to let him know when the baby was born and he would sign over his rights." Her anger morphs into sadness as she says, "I was hoping he'd see her and change his mind. I was raised without a dad because mine walked away, and I didn't want the same for my daughter." She sighs. "He wouldn't even come to see her. He had his attorney file the paperwork, and I never heard from him again. I hate that, one day, I'll have to tell her that her dad didn't want her."

This obviously happened years ago since Violet is almost five, so this can't be where her nightmares stem from, which means something else must've happened more recently.

"It's for the best," I tell her honestly. "Better for him to sign his rights over than be a deadbeat dad. Trust me, I've seen it firsthand."

"With Nora?" she asks.

"Her and both of my parents," I admit. "My mom walked away because she wanted a normal life instead of being the wife of Henry Du Ponte, Texas royalty."

I say his name and title in a mocking tone, and Kira laughs.

"You do look good with a tiara on." She smirks, reminding me of the other day when I was having a tea party with the girls and Violet insisted that I wear a princess tiara.

"Ha-ha, very funny." I try to glare at her, but it only makes her laugh harder.

Her eyes light up, and her cheeks turn a lovely shade of pink. There's nothing more beautiful than watching Kira laugh.

"Anyway," I say once she's stopped laughing, "instead of fighting for me, my mom let my dad get full custody, which meant I was raised by a nanny because my dad cared more about winning than raising me."

"I'm sorry," she says, her smile disappearing. "That sucks. My mom isn't the most responsible or successful, but she's always had my back. I can't imagine having no one."

"I learned family isn't just about blood. It's a choice. I have Addie and Julian and Ana. My brother and I aren't close because of our ten-year age difference, but we get along. And my grandfather and I have a good relationship."

"That's great that you have people," she says with a sad look in her eyes.

"You do too," I tell her. "You have me."

"I appreciate that," she says with a nod. "And just so you know, you have me as well."

I smile at her, thankful that she came into my life. I hate whatever it is that she went through to get here, but she and her daughter are growing on me.

"Should I keep going?" I lift the book.

"Yes!" She beams, lying back on the couch and cuddling the pillow. "I can't wait to find out how he reacts to her being pregnant."

"How do you know she's even pregnant?" I ask.

"Oh, c'mon," she scoffs. "It's romance. She's totally knocked up again," she says, referring to the heroine who is also a single mom.

I chuckle at her and then continue to read. When the heroine announces she's pregnant, Kira laughs, her adorable dimple on her right cheek popping out, and says, "I told you so."

I keep reading until a soft snore fills the air, and then just like last time, I dog-ear the page and carry her up to bed. As I watch her sleep, her features soft and carefree, my heart clenches in my chest, and I know I'm in trouble. Because despite my best efforts, I'm slowly falling for my damn nanny.

"WHAT ARE YOU GUYS UP TO TODAY?" I ASK AS KIRA, carrying Addie on her hip, and Violet appear in the kitchen.

Violet is in her bathing suit, and Kira and Addie are both wearing pink cover-ups.

"I got my new suit!" Violet says, pointing at her bathing suit that's covered in flamingos and half-eaten doughnuts.

Since they didn't have bathing suits and we have a pool, Kira ordered them online and had them delivered to the house.

"I see that. Are the flamingos eating all the doughnuts?" I joke.

"No!" Violet laughs. "Flamingos don't eat doughnuts, silly. Only people do!"

"Oh," I say with a chuckle. "In that case …" I pretend like I'm going to snatch the doughnut off her belly, and she jumps back with a giggle.

"No, don't eat my doughnuts!" She covers her belly. "Eat Mommy's!"

She reaches over and lifts Kira's cover-up, exposing the same pattern Violet has on. She only gets the material up a tiny bit, and I can't help noticing the doughnut that's conveniently located right above her—

"Don't even think about it." Kira glares as if she can hear my thoughts.

"What?" I say innocently.

"You know what."

"I have no idea what you're talking about, but that's cute." I nod toward her now-covered-up suit. "You have doughnuts and flamingos on your bathing suit."

"Violet wanted matching suits."

"Addie got one too!" Violet exclaims, lifting my daughter's cover-up to show me her matching bathing suit. "See? We all got one!"

I glance from Addie to Kira, and something in me shifts. She's struggling to make ends meet, and she was living out of her car. Yet when I paid her for the first time, she didn't just buy Violet and herself bathing suits. She also bought one for my daughter. She never asked me for the money or even mentioned it. She did it so Addie wouldn't feel left out even though she's only a year old and she probably wouldn't care.

But Kira cared. The way a mom is supposed to care. The way I wanted my mom and Addie's mom to care.

But Kira isn't her mom.

She's her nanny.

I look at Addie, completely comfortable in Kira's arms, and wonder if maybe I made a mistake. She's young and vulnerable, and she's already getting attached. What happens in few months if Kira decides she doesn't want to continue to work for me? Or if she does and signs the nine-month contract, what happens once it ends? She'll have more than enough money to move out on her own, and Violet will be in school. The chances of her wanting to stay here and work for me are slim.

She'll leave.

Just like my mom left.

Just like Nora left.

And Addie and I will be left heartbroken.

"I hope that's okay," Kira says slowly, as if she can sense me mentally freaking out. "I probably should've asked first."

Ignoring the fact that I included myself when I thought about being left heartbroken, I shake my head. "No, that's okay," I choke out. "I appreciate you including her."

I take Addie from Kira and set her in her high chair. With Kira here now, our routine has changed, and even though it's a lot calmer, I kind of miss Addie's and my crazy mornings.

"You sure?" Kira asks.

"Yeah."

I feel her eyes on me, but I refuse to look at her,

afraid she'll see what I'm trying to hide—I'm falling for a woman I have no business falling for.

"So, what's on the agenda today?" I ask, keeping myself busy by making Addie a cup of milk while Kira makes the girls breakfast.

"I wanted to go to the water park, but Mommy said no," Violet whines.

I glance at Kira, confused. I gave her my card and told her she could do whatever she wanted with the girls and that money was no object.

"Why can't you go?" I ask.

Kira's facing away from me, but her back stiffens. "As I told Violet, we'll go another time. Today, we're going to the pool."

"You said that last time," Violet argues.

"Violet," Kira says, using what I'm assuming is her mom voice because I've never heard her tone that serious before. "If you don't want to go to the pool, then you can sit out." She raises a single brow, making it clear that what she said is final.

Violet pouts, but doesn't argue.

While Kira finishes cutting up fruit for the girls, I think about the past couple of weeks that she's been here, wondering if I've made her feel like she can't go places with the girls. I gave her my card and thought I was clear that I was okay with her taking them wherever they wanted. It's the summer, and they should be out, having fun, yet now that I think about it, they haven't left once. Not unless I've gone with them.

"Hey, Kira," I say. "Can I talk to you for a minute?"

"Um ..." She glances at the girls, who are eating their jelly toast and fruit, and I could be wrong, but I think she's trying to come up with a reason to say no, but she can't find one.

"Now, please," I insist.

She sighs and gets up, following me into the living room. We're close enough that we can see the girls eating, but far enough away that when I speak softly, they can't hear.

"Is there a reason you haven't left the house?"

Kira diverts her gaze, and I know immediately that something is up.

"Talk to me, please," I tell her, tipping her chin so she'll look at me.

"I can't drive anywhere," she whispers.

"What?" That doesn't make any sense. I've seen her drive.

"I was parked in the parking garage to hide my vehicle," she admits, "because it doesn't belong to me."

"What?" I repeat, rearing back in shock. "Did you steal it?" I hiss.

"No." She shakes her head. "Well"—she swallows thickly—"kind of."

Fuck. I knew there was more to her story, but have I been aiding in car theft?

"You're going to need to explain," I grit out, trying

to remain calm when, inside, I'm freaking the hell out. If it ever got out that I was housing a stolen vehicle, the media would have a fucking field day.

My brother has announced his candidacy for president, which means everyone in our family is being watched under a microscope. It helps that I live in a small town and have stayed off the grid, but getting caught stealing would definitely place me in the spotlight.

"It was my husband's," she admits, glancing at the girls, who are still eating. "He bought it for me, but kept it in his name. When I left, I had no choice but to take it."

Holy shit, there's so much to unpack here, starting with …

"You're married?"

She nods once. "Not by choice."

Suddenly, the pieces start coming together—her nightmares, having no phone or money … living in a vehicle that's stolen.

I'm about to ask her to explain when Addie shrieks, "Up, up!" letting us know she's done and reminding me that the girls are awake and I need to go into the office today.

"Mommy, I'm done!" Violet announces. "Can we go in the pool now?"

"*Poo!*" Addie parrots.

"The girls need me, and I'm sure you need to go to

work," Kira says, as if reading my mind.

The uneasiness in her eyes makes me want to stay here so we can figure this all out because something is wrong, and I hate leaving it unresolved. But she's right—the girls need her, and I do need to go to work.

"Okay," I tell her. "We'll finish this later."

I give Addie a kiss on the top of her head and then take off. But I'm not even out of the neighborhood when I change my mind and turn around, something inside me telling me that I need to be home today. Whatever is going on with Kira needs to be discussed, but more importantly, as her nervous features replay in my head, I think she needs me.

When I walk back through the house, I find her doing the dishes while Addie and Violet play on the rug and watch a show.

"Dada!" Addie squeals, jumping up and toddling over to me.

I lift her into my arms and give her a kiss, then set her back down just in time to see Kira spin around, her eyes widening in ...

Is that fear?

"What's wrong?" I ask, walking over to her.

"Why are you back?" she asks, answering my question with a question.

"I asked you a question first. *What's wrong?*"

"Are you going to fire me?" Another question instead of an answer.

"What?" I rear back. "Why the hell would you—" And then it hits me. She thinks I'm mad about what she told me. "No, I'm not going to fire you," I hiss.

"Then, why are you back?" she asks, wrapping her arms across her chest in a defensive move.

"Because," I say, stepping toward her, "it felt like this was where I needed to be."

"Because you don't trust me?"

She looks up at me with the saddest eyes, and I shake my head.

"No, Kira. I trust you," I tell her honestly.

At first, was I worried about the stolen vehicle coming back to bite me in the ass? Yeah. But once everything started coming together, my only concern was for her.

"I came back because I need to know what happened so I can help you."

Her eyes fill with unshed tears as she darts her gaze over to Violet, silently telling me that whatever is wrong, she doesn't want to talk about it in front of her daughter.

I nod in understanding. "It's been a heavy morning. How about we play hooky today?" I smirk, hoping to lighten the mood. When her eyes lighten a shade and her frown disappears, I know it's worked. "We'll take the girls to the water park, and once they're passed out from exhaustion, we'll talk."

Her shoulders sag in relief. "Okay."

"Hey, Violet," I say, my eyes staying trained on Kira. "If I can convince your mom to go to the water park, can I have a doughnut?" I waggle my eyes at Kira, nodding toward where I know she's sporting doughnuts under that cover-up.

The corner of her lips quirks in the beginning of a smile.

"You're so bad," she mutters, just before Violet yells through her giggle, "They're not real!"

"Hmm," I say, raking my gaze down Kira's body, knowing I'm playing with fire. "I think I might need to find out for myself," I murmur so only Kira can hear me.

Her cheeks warm at my insinuation, but she rolls her eyes to play it off. "Very funny, Ryder." She gently shoves me out of the way as she saunters past me, not glancing back at me until she's in the living room. "Go get your bathing suit while I get the girls ready to go."

"What, no doughnut suit for me?" I pout playfully.

Kira shakes her head. "No doughnuts for you."

Nine

KIRA

As we drive to the water park in Houston, my head spins from everything that transpired this morning. I'm usually good at organizing my thoughts and dealing with one situation at a time, but so much has happened that I don't even know where to start.

I glance over at Ryder, who's driving. He changed out of his work suit and into a T-shirt and board shorts. He's wearing a baseball cap low on his forehead, and his sunglasses are covering his eyes. His fingers are tapping to the beat of the song that's playing, like he doesn't have a care in the world. As if he didn't just flirt with me not even thirty minutes ago. I watched how he raked his gaze over my bathing suit, his hazel eyes darkening like delicious, warm caramel apples, and the way he waggled his brows and smirked playfully, turning my insides to mush.

It was probably innocent fun, and I'm most likely making something out of nothing, but it was a side of Ryder I'd never seen before. He's always been nice—I mean, the guy literally gave my daughter and me a place to live—but he's never crossed that line, and I'm not sure how I feel about that.

On one hand, the way he looked at me and flirted made me feel good. It's been a while since I've felt wanted and desired by the opposite sex. But on the other hand, the want and desire always come with a price. A price I've learned the hard way I can't afford to pay. The last time a guy looked at me like that, it ended with a restraining order.

Which reminds me ... Ryder knows my car is stolen. And since he made it clear we'd be discussing it later, that means I'm going to have to be honest, and once he finds out everything, there's a chance Violet and I will be homeless again. Luckily, since I've worked for Ryder for a couple of weeks now, I have a good amount of money saved, so if he does decide my situation is one that he doesn't want to deal with, I'll be able to find a place for Violet and me.

Of course, that will mean I'm jobless again.

"Hey," Ryder says, snapping me from my thoughts. "Whatever's going through that head of yours, push it to the side. We're going to have a great day at the water park, and tonight, we'll talk." He reaches over and squeezes my hand. "Whatever's going on, we'll figure it out together."

I wish I had as much faith as he does, but my experience has caused me to become more jaded than I'd like to be. The problem is, when you've been hurt so many times in your life, eventually, your body starts to form scar tissue over the wound so thick that nothing can penetrate it. It protects you, but in doing so, it also isolates you from letting any potential risk—or happiness—in.

When we get to the ticket booth, I keep the girls busy while Ryder pays our entrance fees. Once he's done, he guides us toward a cabana that's situated right in front of the main kiddie pool and near the lazy river.

"This is for us?" I ask when we step inside.

There's a television hanging in the corner, a mini fridge, an L-shaped couch, four lounge chairs, and a fan in each corner to keep us cool.

"Yeah, I figured the shade would help if the girls got hot or tired."

"This is perfect. Thank you."

I rifle through my bag, trying to find the sunscreen. I pull out several baggies of snacks—which the girls snag—a first aid kit, a pacifier Addie uses when she's super cranky, a couple of diapers, and a pack of wipes.

"Aha!" I pull out the can of sunscreen. "Got it."

"That purse reminds me of the Mary Poppins bag," Ryder says with a chuckle, checking it out.

"It's probably just as old," I joke. "I can't even imagine what I'd find if I were ever brave enough to clean it out."

Brian bought me a nicer purse when we were together, but I left it, along with everything else he'd bought me, at his house, not wanting anything that came from him. I found this purse at Mom's house, tucked away in my closet. It's the purse I used when Violet was little, and while it's old, it reminds me of *before*.

"But I love it," I add.

After a waitress comes by to take our drink order, I slather the girls with sunscreen. I'm spraying myself when Ryder comes up behind me.

"Here, let me help." He takes the can out of my hand, and I lift my hair, tying it into a ponytail.

He sprays me down, and then his hands are on me, rubbing the liquid along my neck and back. His touch is innocent, yet my body reacts as if it were anything but.

And then he drops to his knees and rubs the back of my calves and thighs, and I have to hold back a moan that's threatening to come out.

He stands back up and leans into me from behind. "All done," he murmurs, his warm breath hitting my ear and sending electric currents straight to the area between my legs.

I turn around, ready to tell him to stop messing with me, but when I do, my hands hit his chiseled chest, and our eyes lock, leaving me momentarily speechless.

"Do me?" he asks.

And because my brain is filled with some kind of sexual fog, like a dumbass, I say, "You want me to do you?"

Ryder chuckles. "As good as that sounds, I meant, can you put sunscreen on me?"

He lifts the can and shakes it while I wish the ground would open up and swallow me whole.

Since I have nothing to say that will defend what I just said, wordlessly, I take the can from Ryder and spray him down. As I'm running my hands along the ridges of his abs, I realize he could've done the damn front himself.

"Turn around," I choke out, trying and failing not to be turned on by his fit body.

He does as I said, and I spray his neck and back and then rub the liquid into his naturally tanned skin. He's smooth and flawless, not a scar or tattoo in sight.

Brian was good-looking too, my subconscious reminds me.

"All done," I breathe, taking a step back.

"Thanks." He turns around and smiles warmly at me. "What should we do first? Pool or lazy river?"

"River!" Violet yells.

"Yay!" Addie adds, having no idea what we're talking about but excited nonetheless.

"Lazy river it is," Ryder says.

We spend the day swimming and playing in the

water areas, and then we have lunch brought to us by the waitress who's assigned to our cabana. It's the most fun Violet and I have had in a long time, and when we're leaving and she thanks us a dozen times for bringing them, I'm glad Ryder convinced us to go.

Violet has had a bad hand dealt to her, thanks to my shitty choices, and she deserves to have some fun. Which means I'm going to have to be honest with Ryder and hope he meant it when he said we'd figure it out together. I hate the thought of putting my trust in another man, but something tells me that Ryder is different. And that trusting him won't be a mistake.

"Addie fell asleep the second I laid her down," Ryder says when he walks into the living room and sits on the couch across from me. "Do you think she's ready for a bigger bed? She looks like she's outgrowing her crib."

"Violet was about her age when I got her a toddler bed," I tell him, thankful for the small talk. Soon, I'm going to have to pour my heart and soul out to this man, and I'm nowhere near ready to do so. Though, to be honest, I'm not sure if I'll ever be ready.

"I'll have to check them out." He lifts his leg, placing his ankle on the top of his knee, and looks at me, his hazel eyes warm and soft. "Is Violet asleep?"

"Yeah. She had a wonderful day. Thank you."

"I did too," Ryder says. "The truth is, since you and Violet moved in, I find myself having quite a few wonderful days."

I swallow nervously at his admission, unsure of what to say in response. Thankfully, he continues without expecting me to say anything.

"What I insinuated earlier, regarding the doughnuts, was inappropriate," he says, shocking the hell out of me. "I got carried away in the moment ... *in you*," he admits. "But that's no excuse for what I said this morning. I shouldn't have flirted with you. I'm your boss, and you deserve to feel safe in this home, and I promise it won't happen again."

His apology is filled with so much sincerity that a ball of emotion gets lodged in my throat. So many men would've made excuses, tried to blame the woman, but without me even asking, Ryder took full responsibility.

"I don't want you to quit," he says softly, remorse etched in his features, "but if you feel it's best, I'll pay you for the rest of your ninety days and help you find a place to live."

"What? No." I shake my head. "I don't want to quit."

If I'm honest, I might not have flirted with Ryder, but I've checked him out and fantasized about him. The only difference between the two of us was that he voiced his attraction by flirting.

"You're right though," I add. "I work for you, and

flirting isn't the best idea. Even if it's innocent. Besides," I say with a self-deprecating smile, "once you hear my baggage, you'll realize I'm not the person you want to be flirting with. Hell, I wouldn't blame you for letting me go."

"That's not going to happen," Ryder says, his voice strong like steel. "But I do need to know everything so I know what we're dealing with and I can help you."

I release a harsh sigh and nod. "I guess it's best if I start from the beginning."

Ten

RYDER

"When I was growing up, my mom would read me fairy tales. She wasn't the best mom, but she loved me—she still does," Kira says with a soft smile. "She grew up poor, and when she was old enough, she started working the streets. She was beautiful, and wealthy men would pay a lot of money to be with her. She learned how to use her body to get what she wanted.

"The problem was, no matter how much they wanted her, at the end of the day, she was still a hooker, and while she was a good lay, she wasn't wife material."

The sadness on Kira's face makes me want to get up and go over to her, pull her into my arms and hold her, but I remind myself that she just forgave me for my momentary lapse in judgment this morning, and the last thing I want is to do something inappropriate to push her away.

"My sperm donor was a married man with an entire other family who made my mom think he wanted more," she murmurs. "Or maybe my mom was delusional, hoping he would choose her. Regardless, when he found out, he threw money at her and told her to get rid of me."

She pushes out a harsh breath. "I never wanted that for my life. I did good in school, participated in clubs and cheerleading, and got into a decent college. I continued the same way in college … doing my best to create a life for myself.

"I met a guy I thought was good. He came from a respectable family. He got decent grades and had his future mapped out. We had fun together, and he made me laugh and smile. But then I got pregnant, and everything changed." She shrugs. "As you already know, he didn't want any part in the pregnancy or being a dad."

"He was a fool," I tell her, wishing I could say exactly what I'm thinking—that I would give anything to find a woman like her.

She's sweet and kind and so selfless. She's not only a damn good woman, but she's also a wonderful mom, and any guy who gets to call her his would be stupid not to cherish and worship her and do everything in his power to keep her.

"It was for the best," she says. "I would never want

someone to stick around who doesn't want to."

"I get that. But it doesn't make it any easier."

"No, it doesn't," she agrees. "After Raymond left, I focused on being a mom. After graduation, instead of starting my teaching career, like I had planned, I got a job at a bar because my mom could watch Violet at night instead of me putting her in day care.

"And then I met Brian."

She visibly shivers, and I know whatever she's about to say isn't going to be good.

"He was charming. He would come in every night and flirt with me. I was a lonely single mom, and he gave me the attention I craved. I could tell he had money. It was evident in the expensive drinks he ordered, the suits he wore, and the way he carried himself. I refused to give in, not wanting to make the same mistake my mom and I had both made, but eventually, he wore me down. He promised me the happily-ever-after, like the ones you read about in romance books, and I fell for it."

A single tear slides down her cheek. "At first, it felt like a fairy tale—massive house, nice vehicle, a man who worshipped the ground I walked on."

When another tear escapes, I can't help but wish I could be next to her, wiping her tears. Seeing Kira sad does something to me. It makes me want to make her happy all the time so I never have to see her cry.

She smiles sadly at me. "I can't pinpoint the moment Brian changed. Maybe it gradually happened, and I wasn't paying attention. He asked me to quit working at the bar, and at first, I refused, not wanting to give up my independence. But then he got upset and threw a tantrum, and I gave in, choosing to believe he was doing it because he cared instead of admitting what it really was—possession."

She glances down at her hands before she speaks her next words. "One weekend, he was out of town for a conference, and a couple of friends asked me to go out with them. I didn't know he was tracking my phone. Although I should've suspected it since, at that point, he was so controlling that I couldn't do anything without his approval."

She looks up at me, and it's like she's not even here anymore. Her usually bright blue eyes are so dark that it's as if she were lost in the deepest part of the ocean, and I would give anything to save her and bring her back to shore.

"He showed up at the club and dragged me out," she murmurs, sounding far away, like she's back in that moment, recalling what happened. "Accused me of cheating on him, called me every name in the book. When we got home, he beat the crap out of me, saying I was unappreciative of everything he'd given us, pushed me down the stairs, and then he left me for dead."

"I'm going to kill him." The words are out of my mouth before I can stop them, but I can't find it in me to regret them.

I'm not a violent guy, but a man putting his hands on a woman is my breaking point.

I'm busy thinking about how I can go about finding this guy and all the ways I can end his life when Kira places her hand on mine.

"I appreciate that, but I won't be the reason you go to jail … and you would because Brian is an attorney—and a damn good one. So good that after he left me for dead, I called the ambulance before passing out, was taken to the hospital, and pressed charges after being told by a police officer and an attorney that Brian wouldn't get away with it, and he managed to get away with it."

"What the fuck do you mean, he got away with it?"

"I had two black eyes, a split lip that required stitches, a broken wrist, two cracked ribs, and a concussion."

"Come here, please," I plead, needing her to be closer. Across the room, on separate couches, is too far away. I need to hold her, comfort her. More for me than her because fuck if she isn't the strongest woman I've ever met. But I don't want to go to her because I want it to be her choice. I want it to *always* be her choice.

She crosses the room and sits next to me, and I take her hand in mine, craving the connection. She could've died that night, but she survived. She's a survivor.

"The prosecutor's office said he would get years in jail with assault and battery and attempted murder," she continues, staring down at our linked fingers.

I already know there's a *but* coming because if he had gotten convicted for all that, she wouldn't have been living out of her car.

"While we were awaiting trial, he was out on bail. He would harass me from afar, calling and making threats. But he never once crossed the line. I just kept telling myself that, soon, he would be put away, and Violet and I would move forward with our lives, lesson learned."

At the mention of her daughter's name, I still. "Did he ever …"

She shakes her head. "He never laid a hand on her. Until that night, he never laid a hand on me. Had he done so, I would've left sooner. I was already preparing to leave him as it was. It was hard because he had gone from Prince Charming to the villain so quickly that I didn't even see it coming. One minute, he was charming me and proposing, offering me and my daughter a great life, and the next, he was cutting me off from the world and locking us up in a gilded cage."

"Where is he now?" I ask, needing to know how this ends so I can start figuring out how to take care of it.

"He took a plea bargain," she says with a sigh. "Aggravated domestic assault—Class A misdemeanor. Sounds good in theory, like he would get some major time behind bars. Nope, he got a four-thousand-dollar fine and thirty days."

Jesus, fuck, and people wonder what the hell is

wrong with our country.

"I'd heard him tell me a million times how a guy he'd defended got six months and was out in thirty days. Once, a guy got sixty days, and then he walked in and then walked right back out due to overcrowding. I couldn't risk it," she says, meeting my eyes. "I left the courthouse and went straight to my mom's to get Violet. Because he had cut me off and wouldn't let me work, I had little money. A couple thousand saved that I'd been slowly stealing from him."

She blows out a harsh breath. "I knew without a doubt that he would come for me, restraining order be damned, so I had to cut all ties with my mom and leave my phone behind. I had no choice but to take the SUV he had given me since it was my only form of transportation. I stopped at a mechanic shop that a friend owned, and he made sure it couldn't be tracked, and then we took off."

"How did you end up here?" I ask since her license plate says California.

"I started driving and didn't stop until I felt like I was far enough away. I love flowers, hence Violet's name, so when I saw a sign for Rosemary, I felt like it was fate."

"I'm glad you came here."

"I am too," she breathes out. "But I didn't realize that I'd picked such an expensive town." She chuckles. "The cost of hotels added up quickly, and before I could find a job, I was almost out of money, which is why you found us living out of our car."

"What can I do?" I ask, needing to do something to help Kira.

She's been through so much, none of which she deserved.

"You're doing it," she says, palming the side of my face. "You gave me a job and Violet and me a safe place to live."

"You can't run forever," I tell her, hating that I need to point out the obvious, but I'm a realist. I deal with facts and numbers.

"I know," she says, swallowing nervously and dropping her hand from my face. "But I'm hoping, with time, he'll move on."

"You're still married to him. You're driving a vehicle he bought you."

Speaking of which…

"How are you paying for the insurance?"

"I'm not," she admits sheepishly. "Because he kept it in his name so I would be forced to be dependent on him, I couldn't get insurance on my own."

Fuck. "That's why you were hiding it in the parking garage and don't drive anywhere."

"Yep. I'm sure he's reported it stolen."

"And you're still married…"

"Only until I can figure out how to divorce him without him coming after me. And I don't know how that's going to happen when he's a damn attorney with money and connections. My only saving grace is that I never let him adopt Violet." She glances down and shakes her head. "I feel like the biggest fool for falling for him. I should've known it was all too good to be true."

"Hey," I say, lifting her chin so she'll look at me. "You're not a fool. And not all men with money are like that. He's a piece of shit who's going to get what's coming to him. Not only will I make sure you get your divorce, but he's also never coming near you or Violet again."

"How can you promise that?" she whispers.

"Because money talks and I'm filthy fucking rich."

"Ryder," she gasps. "I can't ask you to do that for me."

"You didn't ask. But I'm going to handle it all the same."

"And what do you want in return?"

"I want you to have a choice. I want you to be safe and free. You won't owe me anything, but the promise that you'll live your life how you want. That you won't let guys like Brian or your or Violet's sperm donor taint you or your perception of the world. I know it's hard to believe since you've been surrounded by so many shitty men, but not all of them are like that. I promise."

"I'm beginning to see that," she says with a sigh, leaning into me and resting her head on my shoulder.

Without thought, I turn my face and kiss the crown

of her head. "It's all going to be okay," I murmur. "I'm going to make sure of it."

She nods in understanding, and then after a few minutes of silence, she says, "Can you read another chapter to me? I'm dying to find out what happens now that she's found him."

I chuckle and grab the book from the end table. "What do you think is going to happen?" I ask as I turn back to where I left off the other night.

I've already finished the book, so I know how he acts, but I'm curious about her thoughts.

"It's romance, so at some point, he's going to sweep her off her feet and confess his undying love to her, but it's only the beginning of the book, so it's too soon for that. Which means he's probably going to freak the hell out."

I chuckle, knowing that's exactly what happens, and then say, "Let's find out."

KIRA

"You know you don't work on the weekends, right?"

I turn around and find Ryder standing in the kitchen, leaning against the wall. He's in a pair of basketball shorts and a white T-shirt, stretched taut across his chest. His brown hair is messy from sleep, his eyes still slightly hooded, and when he rubs his stomach, his shirt rises, showing off that goddamn happy trail that has starred in quite a few of my fantasies as of late.

"I know," I tell him, spinning back around to focus on what I'm doing. "But eating has nothing to do with working."

"I meant you waking up and taking care of Addie for me."

I shrug him off and turn back around, grabbing the

bag of chocolate chips. "I was up anyway. Changing a diaper and feeding one more child breakfast isn't a big deal." Especially not after everything Ryder's done for me.

I think back to our conversation last night. The way he listened and then promised to help me. When I went to bed, it was the first time in a long time that I truly felt like maybe everything would be okay. And it was because of him. Sure, there's a chance that he's full of shit, and it won't be the first time I've been wrong about a man, but something about Ryder makes me feel like I can trust him. And if I'm wrong about him, it's not as if I gave him my heart or anything.

As I pour the chocolate chips into the batter, I feel his warmth behind me, and when I glance back, he's standing over me, his masculine scent enveloping me.

He reaches around, and for a second, I assume he's about to wrap his arms around me—and crazily, nothing in me even thinks to stop him.

But then his finger dips into the batter, and he brings it to his lips, moaning, "Damn, I love your brownies."

The girls and I made brownies the other day, and Ryder damn near ate the entire pan himself after everyone went to bed. The next morning, he told me with a teasing smirk that I wasn't allowed to make them anymore because he couldn't control himself.

So, that day, we made a cake. And after he ate several slices, he told me I should open my own bakery and that I was banned from baking in this house anymore.

"Get out of here!" I playfully scold. "These aren't for you."

Ryder slides around next to me and leans against the counter. "Who the hell are they for?" He pouts like a petulant child, making me laugh.

I've learned the past couple of weeks that Ryder is as immature as he is mature. He's got many sides to him—the serious businessman, the doting and loving father, the sweet and caring confidante, and the side I'm seeing more and more of ... the playful friend. And the more I get to know him, the more I like every part of him.

"Ana," I tell him. "In case you forgot, you're going to visit them today. I'm making a couple of dishes for you to bring over. The lasagna is already done."

I remember how hard it was to juggle everything after I had Violet. I'm sure they have plenty of help, but nothing beats a homemade comfort meal. So, after I made the girls breakfast, I got to work on making lasagna and brownies for Ana and her family.

"Thank you. She'll love it."

He leans over and gives me a quick kiss on my cheek, which does something to my insides that I refuse to acknowledge.

"Any plans for today?" he asks, opening the fridge and grabbing a water bottle.

"Nope. I'm sure Violet will beg to go in the pool."

I glance back at him and roll my eyes. "Wherever we move will have to have a pool. Living here is spoiling her."

I expect Ryder to laugh, but instead, he frowns. "Are you planning on leaving?"

"What? No. I mean, not unless you decide not to extend my contract after the ninety days are up."

"That's only for you," he says, encroaching on my space. "To make sure you're comfortable. I'll gladly sign a contract for however long you want."

"I think twelve months is good." I go back to mixing the batter. "And obviously, if anything changes and you want to break the contract, as long as you give me a little bit of notice, I'll understand."

"Why the hell would I want to do that?"

"I don't know." I shrug. "What if you meet someone and decide you don't want Violet and me crashing your mansion anymore?" It's supposed to come across like a joke, but the humor gets lost in my words.

"That's not happening," Ryder says. "And there's nothing wrong with Violet being spoiled by my pool. For too long, it never got used."

"Dada!" Addie calls. "Up!"

Ryder lifts her into his arms and gives her a kiss on her forehead. "Morning, Chunk."

"Mommy, can I have a brownie?" Violet asks.

"No, these aren't for us," I tell her, pouring the batter into the pan and then popping it in the oven.

"But you can lick the spatula."

I hold it out for her, and she runs over, her eyes lit up in excitement.

"Thank you!"

"Me! Me!" Addie squeals.

"Okay," I tell her with a laugh. "You too."

I grab a spoon and swipe a small amount of batter from the mixing bowl onto it, then hand it to her. Addie pops it into her mouth, and the look of awe and wonder on her face at having tried brownie batter for the first time is so adorable that I have to snap a picture.

"More, more!" She thrusts the spoon my way. "*Pease*," she adds.

"Okay, one more," I tell her, swiping a tiny bit more and handing it to her.

She pops it back in her mouth and grins, in chocolate heaven.

"I think someone likes chocolate," I say to Ryder with a wink. "Like father, like daughter."

Ryder chuckles. "Great. Soon, I'll be fighting over those addictive brownies with another person. At this rate, I'm going to have to bribe you to make me my own batch."

"Dramatic much?"

I take the spoon from Addie and drop it into the sink with the bowl and spatula that Violet licked clean before running back into the living room to watch another show. Addie wiggles around, and Ryder sets her on the floor so she can toddle back to Violet.

"You and Violet should join us," Ryder says, coming up next to me at the sink.

"What?"

I start rinsing the dishes and fill the dishwasher.

"To see the baby," he clarifies. "Ana asks about you all the time. I'm sure she'd love to see you. When she found out that you were living in your car, she felt horrible for not knowing."

"I don't want anyone's pity," I murmur, focusing intently on the dirty dishes.

"Nobody's pitying you," he says. "It's called caring. There's a difference."

When I don't say anything back, he tries again. "Come with us to their house. It'll be fun. They're hanging out by the pool, so Violet can go swimming. And you said you were dying to meet the baby."

"I don't want to crash."

"You wouldn't be. But if it'll make you feel better, I can text them and make sure they're up for two more people."

"That'd put them on the spot," I argue, shaking my head even though I'd love to see the new baby. I mean, who doesn't love holding a newborn and sniffing their newborn scent? "No, we'll stay here. Maybe another time."

"All right." Ryder sighs. "But if you change your mind, text me. I can come get you guys anytime. They don't live far."

"Thank you, but we'll be fine here. Promise."

I pour the soap into the dishwasher, close it, and press Start. "The brownies will be ready in about thirty minutes."

While they're baking, I throw in a load of laundry and then run up to my room to get my suit on since I already know Violet will beg me to join her. I'm grabbing my suit from the drawer when my phone goes off with an incoming text. Since Ryder's the only one who knows and uses my number—since he's the one who bought me the phone after hiring me and I can't contact my mom in case her phone is somehow being monitored by Brian—I glance at it, expecting to see a text from Ryder.

Instead, I find a message from Unknown.

> Hey, Kira! It's Ana. Ryder gave me your number after he called Julian to let him know he'll be over soon and said you and Violet aren't coming. Then, when I asked him to please invite you, he said you would think he conspired it and it was a pity invite—which, by the way, is ridiculous. So, now, I'm texting you to let you know that I'm inviting you to come over with him. I thought it was a given since you and Violet live with him, but I shouldn't have assumed. Please come over. I'd love for you to meet the newest Parker and catch up with you.

I sigh after reading her text, knowing I'm going to have to go whether it's a pity invite or not since it was so heartfelt and I would look like a complete bitch if I said no.

ME

> Hey, are you sure you're up for so many people? You did just have a baby ...

UNKNOWN

> I am more than sure. I'm lying on the couch, relaxing with Emilia. Kingston and Julian are about to go swimming. Because we were in the hospital on Kingston's birthday, we're celebrating today. We would love for you guys to join us.

ME

> Okay, but if it gets to be too much, we can leave anytime.

UNKNOWN

> See you soon!

After creating a contact for Ana, I grab my bathing suit and cover-up and then go to the girls' rooms to pack for them. Once everything is ready to go, I head back downstairs, just in time to take the brownies out of the oven.

"Mommy, can we go swimming now?" Violet asks.

"Change of plans," I say, glaring at Ryder, who

doesn't look the least bit concerned. "We're going to see Ana, Julian, Kingston, and their new baby."

"Oh, yay!" Violet exclaims. "I love babies!"

"Oh, you decided to join us after all?" Ryder asks with a smirk.

"You know exactly what happened," I mutter.

"I have no idea what you're talking about," he says nonchalantly.

"Oh, yeah? Well, it looks like I have *no idea* how to make you any more brownies," I volley.

"You wouldn't dare." He glares.

"We'll see." I shrug, sauntering past him.

Because my back is to him, I don't see him come up behind me and grab me by my waist. I shriek in surprise when he lifts me off my feet and drops me onto the couch, and then I start to half scream, half giggle when he proceeds to tickle me. Of course, the girls think it's hilarious and immediately join, helping him to tickle me.

"Stop!" I beg through my peals of laughter.

"Take it back," he says, tickling me under my armpit. "Tell me you'll make me all the brownies I want, and we'll stop."

"Yes!" Violet agrees. "I want brownies."

"No," I hiss defiantly. "No brownies for you!"

The tickling doesn't stop.

"That's the wrong answer," Ryder says with a smirk. "Agree to make us brownies, or it's only going to get worse."

He glides his fingers down my body and then squeezes my knee, eliciting a loud shriek from me, which only makes the girls laugh harder.

And because I'm damn close to peeing my pants, instead of telling him to go fuck himself, like I want to, I nod in agreement.

"Fine! I promise, I'll make you brownies."

"Pinky swear?" he replies.

"Yeah!" Violet, the damn traitor, agrees. "Pinky swear!"

"Okay!" I breathe. "I pinky swear I'll make you all the brownies."

Ryder stops tickling me, and the girls thankfully follow suit.

While they're running around, chanting, "Brownies," repeatedly, Ryder extends his hand to help me up.

I take it, allowing him to pull me into a sitting position, and when our faces are only inches apart, our lips only just not touching, I murmur, "Just remember, payback's a bitch."

His eyes widen in shock, and for a moment, I wonder if I took it too far. Until his hazel eyes shimmer with mirth and he throws his head back with laughter, exposing his throat—which I shouldn't imagine running my nose along and inhaling his scent, but I do.

Once he's calmed himself, he shoots me a flirty wink and then says, "I can't wait to see you try."

Game on.

Twelve

KIRA

"Where are we going?"

I've never been to Ana's place, but I can't imagine they live in the middle of downtown.

"Coffee." Ryder glances over at me and grins. "You haven't been over here?"

"Nope. With me not driving and there being no public transportation, we tended to stick to the places near Kingston."

Ryder nods in understanding. "Well, over there"—he points to the left—"is a nice park. And over there"—he points to the right, just across the street—"is the public library. It's three stories, and it has an entire floor for children."

"I wanna go to the library!" Violet squeals. "Can we go?"

"Not today," I tell her, "but I'm sure we can go one day."

My little girl loves reading. Before we had to leave our old house, we used to spend a lot of time at the library. We pull up to a cute coffee shop with a pink-and-white awning in the front and the name *Coffee Addict* written across the top.

"They make the best coffee," Ryder explains. "Only downside is, they don't have a drive-through." He parks and then turns to me and asks, "You want your usual?"

My usual is an iced caramel latte that I make using his Nespresso machine, but since we're here …

"I want to see what else they have."

"Can I see too?" Violet asks.

"Me!" Addie adds, making Ryder shake his head.

"Okay," he says, unbuckling. "I guess we're all going in."

"Yay!" Violet exclaims, undoing her seat belt.

I end up ordering an iced salted caramel latte, to which Ryder playfully rolls his eyes. We get the girls each a chocolate milk with whipped cream, and Ryder gets his usual boring coffee—strong with a drop of milk. We're walking back to the car when Ryder stops short, and I almost run into him.

"You okay?" I ask when I notice he looks like he just saw a ghost.

"Yeah," he chokes out. "Just thought I saw someone."

"Who?"

"Nora," he whispers.

I follow his line of vision, curious to see what Addie's egg donor looks like, but there's so many people that I don't know who he's referring to.

"I doubt it was her," he says with a shake of his head. "I was probably just seeing shit."

The drive to Ana's is quiet, and I can tell Ryder's stuck in his own head. I'm not sure if he's upset that he saw her or if maybe seeing her made him realize he misses her, but I don't ask, not wanting to open a can of worms in front of the girls. Addie might be too young to understand, but I don't want to chance upsetting Ryder in front of her.

When we arrive at Julian and Ana's house, I take in the cozy vibe. Unlike Ryder's massive house, this home is smaller—still big, but it's not a mansion—with a softer feel to it.

"What are you thinking?" Ryder asks, snapping me out of my thoughts.

"I picture you in a house like this," I say truthfully. "Your house is beautiful, but—"

"It's ostentatious," he finishes for me. "Nora picked it out," he admits. "And since I was already settled in, after she left, I stayed."

"Mommy, can we get out?" Violet asks.

"Yep," I tell her.

She immediately flings off her seat belt and clambers

out.

"You grab Addie, and I'll get the food," I tell Ryder, who nods, still obviously lost in his own head.

I wish we were alone so we could talk, but since we're not, I grab the dishes and leave my thoughts and worries in the car for later.

"MY GOD, WOMAN, THESE SMELL HEAVENLY." ANA audibly sniffs the brownies one more time and then sets them on the counter, next to the pan of lasagna. "Thank you." She smiles warmly at me and then shocks me when she pulls me into a hug.

"You're welcome," I choke out, wrapping my arms around her in return, unsure why I'm suddenly so emotional.

Maybe it's because I've been on my own with Violet for the past few months or because, aside from Brian demanding to *get laid* a few times a week, I've essentially been alone, craving the affection one can only get from another person.

Ana backs up slightly but remains close, her glassy eyes meeting mine.

"What's wrong?" I ask, worried something happened.

"Nothing." She shakes her head. "I'm just ... a bit emotional. Having a baby will do that to you." She laughs lightly. "And also … why didn't you tell me you were living out of your car?"

More tears fill her lids, and my heart drops.

"I would've helped you," she mutters. "Every day, you came into work, happy and smiling, all while living in an SUV."

"It's okay," I tell her, placing my hand in hers, knowing she's reacting this way because, as she mentioned, she gave birth recently and her hormones are all over the place.

"No, it's not," she argues, her tears now streaming down her cheeks. "But I'm so glad Ryder found you. Is he being good to you? If not, we have plenty of room here."

"He's amazing. I promise, we're good," I tell her honestly, my heart swelling with how sweet she is to even offer us a place to stay. "I owe you guys everything."

Before she can tell me that I don't, I keep speaking, needing her to know how much I appreciate everything they've done for my daughter and me.

"You gave me a chance when I was at my lowest, and then Ryder took us in and not only gave us a roof over our heads, but what he's paying me …" I shake my head, overcome with emotion. "You guys have given me a sense of security that I haven't felt in a long time. I don't know how I'll ever repay either of you."

"You don't owe anyone anything," Ryder says, appearing out of nowhere.

"Ana." Julian rushes in and goes straight for his wife. "What's wrong, Red?"

"Nothing. I'm fine." She half laughs, half cries. "I'm just a little emotional." She swipes at her eyes. "Sometimes, I just can't help crying."

"And apparently, it's contagious," I add with a laugh of my own, wiping my tears away.

"Emilia is waking up," Julian tells her. "Why don't you go grab her, and I'll put the food in the fridge?"

"Okay." She kisses the corner of his mouth. "But the brownies are coming with me." She grabs the entire pan with one hand and then mine with the other. "Come meet Emilia," she says with a watery smile. "But be warned. She's so precious that you might get baby fever."

"That is not happening," I say through a laugh. "There's a reason babies are so cute … to get us through the sleepless nights."

Ryder chuckles and nods in agreement. "I feel that deep."

"Mommy, can we go in the pool now?" Violet asks when we walk into the living room.

"In a few minutes, Vi," I tell her while Ana goes to the bassinet and scoops up her daughter, who's stretching her arms and legs as she attempts to wake up. "Want to see the new baby?"

"I already saw her. She's too little to play with us." Violet pouts, making the adults laugh.

"She is little," I agree, taking Emilia from Ana so

I can hold her.

Her eyes are closed once again, and she's sucking on her pacifier, curled up like she's still in the womb.

When I sit down, Violet comes over and leans against me, gently stroking the baby's hair.

"I remember when you were this little," I tell her, glancing over at her.

"Was I boring too?" she asks, looking at me seriously.

"Nope," I say with a laugh. "You hated sleeping, so you kept me very busy."

"Sleeping is boring," she mutters.

"It is," I agree. "But we need it so we can grow. That's why babies sleep a lot—so they can grow."

"Can I go in the pool now?" she asks. "Addie and Kingston want to go in the pool too. Right, guys?" She looks over at the toddlers, who are playing in the pretend kitchen and couldn't care less about going swimming. "Addie! Pool?"

"Poo!" Addie agrees, toddling over and pulling up her cover-up to show off her bathing suit.

"Ugh, fine," I groan, not wanting to give up the precious baby yet.

"I've got them," Ryder says with a chuckle. "Come out when you've had your baby fill." He winks at me and then says to the girls, "Who wants to go swimming?"

Both girls squeal in delight.

"All right, let's go."

Ryder lifts both girls into his strong arms and carries them out the back door with Julian and Kingston following behind.

Once they're gone, Ana glances at me with wide eyes and whispers, "What was that?"

"What was what?" I ask, leaning in and sniffing the baby's sweet scent.

God, I miss that smell. It was what got me through the weeks of sleepless nights. I would rock Violet for hours, smelling her scent.

"Um, hello? That!" Ana points in the direction of the pool, but before I can ask her again what the hell she's talking about, the doorbell rings, and she gets up to get it. A moment later, she returns with another woman.

"Kira, this is Paige," Ana says, pointing to a beautiful woman with brown hair and blonde highlights that are swept off her neck in a messy bun.

Her blue eyes meet mine, and she smiles warmly.

"It's nice to meet you," she says, coming over and sitting next to me. "Oh, and aren't you just the sweetest little thing?" she coos to Emilia, who's still sleeping in my arms.

"She must really like you," Ana says with a smile. "This is the longest she's gone without eating."

"Well, the feeling is mutual," I say, glancing back down at the baby.

There was a time when I imagined having an entire

household of little ones running around. Until I became a single mom and then dreaded the thought of getting pregnant by Brian. I'm still young, and I know anything can happen, but at this point, I've accepted that Violet might be my only baby.

"Where's John?" Ana asks Paige.

"He had an emergency at work. I told him if he gets done soon to come by." Paige looks at me. "John is my workaholic boyfriend." She rolls her eyes playfully. "He's trying to prove himself at the company he works at, so he's become their *yes* man."

"Hopefully, once he renews his contract in September, he'll allow himself to breathe a little bit," Ana says to Paige. Then, to me, she explains, "John moved here from the UK on a one-year contract. He's managing the division he works in, and as long as he's doing well, they're planning to make it permanent."

"Oh, are you from the UK?" I ask Paige.

She doesn't have an accent, but anything's possible.

"Not originally. My dad is a pilot, so we moved all over. We lived in London for a while and then I moved back after college to get my MBA and stayed when I accepted a job at Benson Liquor. That's where I met Ana," she says, smiling at her friend. "Last year, John was offered a promotion, but it meant moving to the States, and since it was in Houston and so close to Ana, I moved with him."

"She's our chief marketing officer," Ana explains.

"And one of the best people I know."

"Damn right I am." Paige lightheartedly bumps Ana's shoulder. "Speaking of which, where's the wine?"

"What does wine have to do with anything?" Ana laughs.

"Um, everything," Paige deadpans. "Friends don't let friends stay sober for too long."

Paige shrugs, and Ana giggles.

"That's definitely not how the saying goes," Ana says as Emilia starts to whine.

With one last inhale of her sweet scent, I hand her over to Ana, who grabs a blanket from over the couch and drapes it across her front so she can feed her daughter.

"Kira, white or red?" Paige says, standing.

"Oh, um, none for me, but thanks."

"Fine," Paige groans. "Guess I'm going to be solo drinking."

"You might want a drink," Ana says to me. "There's nothing worse than hanging out with a drunk Paige while you're sober."

"You're such a cheeky bitch," Paige calls out behind her while Ana cackles.

Their close friendship is evident, and it makes me miss my mom. Our relationship isn't as comfortable and easygoing as theirs, but she's always been my person. Someone I could talk to and confide in. She's never judged me, and she's always had my back.

"Hey, what's wrong?" Ana asks as if she can hear my thoughts.

"Nothing. I just …" I take a deep breath, questioning if I'm ready to put myself out there, knowing once I do, there's no going back. "I recently got out of a relationship where he was … possessive," I say, giving her a half truth. "He pushed all my friends away … at least the ones I had left after having a baby when the rest of my friends were still in the partying stage of life. Watching and listening to you two reminded me of how much I miss that."

Ana sobers, then places her hand on my leg. "You're not alone anymore. You know that, right? You have Ryder and me …"

"And me," Paige says, sauntering back into the living room, obviously having had heard us. "I got you a drink anyway," she says. "Figured you could use it."

"Thanks." I take a sip of the white wine. It's crisp and fruity and refreshing. "Sorry, I didn't mean to be a downer."

"By opening up?" Ana shakes her head. "That's what friends are for. And to be honest, I don't have many."

"Same," Paige agrees. "I moved too much to make any real ties … until I met Ana."

Ana lifts her daughter onto her chest and burps her, then moves her to the bassinet that's right next to the couch. She whines for a second and then falls back asleep.

"You know what we need?" Paige says.

"No, but I'm sure you're going to tell us," Ana deadpans.

"A girls' night!"

"Um, in case you forgot, I just gave birth." Ana points from her stomach to the sleeping baby.

"Not at a club," Paige clarifies. "A stay-at-home girls' night ... like a slumber party! We can watch cheesy rom-coms, eat junk food, gossip about boys, and drink." Before Ana can argue, Paige adds, "You can pump and dump for one night."

"Okay. That actually sounds like fun," Ana says after a moment, her face lighting up. "What do you think?" she asks me. "You up for a girls' night?"

"Oh, I don't know." I shake my head. "I have Violet and ..."

"Julian can watch her," Ana says. "What's one more kid?" She laughs.

"Maybe ..." It's not that I don't want to, but ... "It would have to be on the weekend."

"What would have to be on the weekend?" Ryder asks, strolling into the house in nothing but his board shorts. His hair is wet, and a few droplets of water are lingering on his shoulders and chest as several slide down his muscular torso, disappearing into his—

A throat clearing breaks me from the thoughts, and when I glance up, I find Ryder smirking and both Ana and Paige grinning.

"Huh?" I ask, having no clue what was said.

The women crack up laughing while Ryder chuckles, and I can't help but feel like I'm missing something.

"What?" I ask in confusion.

"I asked, what would have to be on the weekend?" Ryder says with a smirk.

"Our girls' night," Ana answers for me. "We're going to have a slumber party."

"With alcohol, junk food, and lots of gossip," Paige adds.

"Sounds like fun," Ryder says with a chuckle. "As long as you're not discussing this month's book without me." He glares teasingly at Ana and Paige.

"We wouldn't dream of it," Ana says. "Don't forget, it's your turn to pick the book for next month."

"And it'd better be spicy," Paige adds, waggling her brows.

"I already know which one I'm picking," Ryder says, then looks at me. "You should join us since you're reading the book as well."

He winks at me, and I swear my panties nearly combust. I don't know what's sexier—a man who reads romance or a man who is so unashamed that he's part of a book club.

"Oh, you're reading the book?" Ana asks me.

"Yep," Ryder says, "and she's loving it."

"Then, you definitely have to come! We have an online book club, but this month, we're going to discuss it live with the group."

"Sounds like fun," I tell them, not mentioning that I don't have any social media.

Brian would give me shit about it, to the point that it was easier to just delete it than deal with him.

"Now, what were you saying about your girls' night?" Ryder asks.

"I was telling Kira that she can bring Violet and Julian can keep an eye on her," Ana says. "We have plenty of beds ..."

"What?" Ryder glances at me in confusion. "Why the hell would Julian need to watch her? She knows me a helluva lot better than him. She can stay with Addie and me and sleep in her own bed."

"You wouldn't mind?" I ask despite the fact that he sounded almost offended that I hadn't asked him to begin with. But I don't want to assume.

"Why would I mind?" he asks incredulously.

"I don't know." I shrug. "I mean, I work for you. It's my job to watch your daughter, not the other way around."

"Are you serious?" he says, stepping closer to me. I'm sitting on the edge of the sofa, so he kneels in front of me, his eyes locking with mine. "You might work for me, but I'd like to think there's more to us than just *that*."

"Like what?" I breathe, the air surrounding us suddenly thick with tension.

"Like ... *more*."

The word is simple yet confusing at the same time. Because *more* can mean so many things.

"More ... like friends?" I throw out, then hold my breath, waiting for his response, unsure if I want him to agree or tell me what's happening between us is *more* than that.

Ryder stares at me for several seconds before he nods once.

"Yeah," he agrees. "Like friends."

My stomach sinks, and I realize in this moment that I was hoping for a different answer from him. But it doesn't matter because despite his flirting, he only sees me as a friend. Which is for the best because the last thing I need is anything *more* anyway.

"Friends," I parrot, plastering on a smile.

"Friends," he repeats.

"Well, now that we've established we're all *friends*," Paige says, reminding me that Ryder and I were having this entire conversation in front of an audience, "can you watch Kira's daughter so we can have a girls' night?"

"Of course," Ryder says, standing.

"Awesome. What about the weekend after next?" Paige suggests, looking at her phone. "Next weekend, I'm attempting to pry John away from his job to go to a bed and breakfast, just the two of us." She looks up and rolls her eyes, but I can hear it in her tone that she's worried about their relationship, and my heart goes out to her. There's nothing harder than being the only person in the relationship fighting for it.

"I'm down," Ana says.

I glance at Ryder, who's looking at me with an unreadable expression.

"Can you watch Violet?" I ask.

"Absolutely," he says with a small smile.

"Yay!" Paige exclaims. "Girls' night!"

Ryder shakes his head and chuckles, and it's then that it hits me—he's in here with me without our daughters.

"Are the girls okay?" I ask him.

"Yeah." He nods. "Julian is keeping an eye on them. I came in here to make sure it's okay for Violet to have ice cream before lunch."

"Sure," I tell him. "If she gets to be too much …"

"We're good," he says. "Enjoy your girl time."

With those words, he heads back out, leaving me staring at the cords of muscle that make up his back.

Once he's gone, Paige says, "Ho-ly shit. What was that?"

"What was what?" I ask, turning to her in confusion.

"*That*," Ana says with a smirk, "was two people living in denial."

Paige laughs. "It is the longest river in Egypt."

"What are you talking about?" I question.

"You and Ryder," Ana says.

"Totally having the hots for each other," Paige

finishes.

"Did you not hear him?" I ask. "We're just *friends*."

Paige and Ana both snort out a laugh.

"Okay, keep telling yourself that," Paige says. "But the heat in his eyes when he looked at you was hot enough to damn near set this room on fire." She fans herself.

"I think you're seeing things," I mutter.

"Sorry, girl," Paige says with a laugh. "My eyesight is twenty/twenty, and I know *exactly* what I saw."

"And what's that?" I ask, too curious not to take the bait.

"A man," Paige says with a smirk, "who is falling hard."

"And what a sight it is," Ana adds with a smile. "I've been worried about Ryder." She glances at me. "But it seems I no longer have to be."

"I can't wait for our girls' night," Paige says with a glimmer in her eye. "I'll bet you're going to have *a lot* to share."

I lift my glass of wine to my lips and down it in one shot as I wonder if what they're saying could be true. Does Ryder want more with me? And if so, am I capable of giving him that?

Thirteen

RYDER

Friends.

I've never despised the word until it slipped past Kira's pouty lips. Now, I wish it didn't fucking exist.

Friends.

It's not that I don't want to be friends with her. In the short time I've known her, I'd like to think we've forged a friendship that goes beyond employer and employee. And I'm not ignorant enough to believe that every relationship shouldn't be based on friendship. Hell, it's what Nora and I were lacking.

No, what makes me despise the word is the thought that it's the most we could ever be. That what we have right now is all I'll ever be lucky enough to have with her. When the truth is, I want more. I want her laughter, her smiles. I want to be the reason that sexy fucking dimple pops out of her right cheek. I want to be the reason she turns an adorable shade of pink when she gets caught eye-fucking me. I want to be the man she turns to when she's had a good day or bad. I want to be the person she reaches for when she's had a nightmare. Hell, I want to be the reason she never has another nightmare again.

Friends.

Fuck that shit. I have enough friends. I want more with Kira, and I could've read her wrong, but based on the disappointed look she gave me when I agreed that we were friends, I'd say she wants more as well. Now, I just need to figure out how to get her on the same page.

"Thank you for today," Kira says when I pull into the garage.

"You don't have to thank me. But I'm glad everyone had a good day."

I look back at our daughters sleeping soundly in the back seat. They ate, swam, and played the day away. I doubt anything will wake them up until tomorrow morning.

"Good night," Kira says once we're inside and about to head in opposite directions, both of us carrying our daughters to bed.

"Sweet dreams," I say back, hoping she doesn't have any nightmares even though I selfishly enjoy spending time with her when she comes down after having one. My hope is that, one day, she'll come down on her own and not just because she can't sleep.

As I'm putting Addie to bed, I get an alert on my phone from my calendar letting me know that tomorrow is Mother's Day. Because of my mom not being in my life, and Nora walking away, I haven't had a reason to pay attention to this holiday, but now I do.

"Hey, you're still awake?"

I glance up from my laptop I was working on and take in Kira's sleepy appearance. Her eyes are half lidded, and her hair is up in her signature messy knot. She's wearing a pair of blue-and-white striped pajama shorts and a thin tank top. She looks sexy without even trying.

"Nightmare?" I ask as she scurries over to where I'm sitting, grabs the blanket from the back, and snuggles up on the couch next to me so she's close, but not touching me.

"Actually," she says, shyly looking up at me through her lashes, "I had some stuff on my mind, and I wanted to talk to you."

"Okay." I turn so I'm giving her my full attention. "What's up?"

"Earlier, when you thought you saw Nora, I couldn't tell if you were upset that you saw her or if you were upset because you miss her. I know it's not really my business but—"

"I hate her," I say, not needing her to finish her thought. "I know I shouldn't because she means nothing to me. When I told you I never loved her, I meant it. She was someone I was dating, and then she got pregnant, and it all spiraled.

"I tried like hell to convince myself to feel something for her, anything, but I couldn't. But the day she walked out on Addie for five million dollars, I finally felt something for her … hate. Hate for creating a child she never wanted, just to trap me. Hate for abandoning a baby who will one day wonder where her mother is. Hate because she chose money over the person I love the most in the world."

I release a harsh breath and then continue, "This morning, when I thought I saw her, I was pissed because she'd agreed to disappear, and I thought maybe she wasn't holding up her end of the deal. If it wasn't for Addie, I wouldn't give a shit where she lives, but the idea of Addie one day running into her makes me feel sick.

"Right now, she's too young to understand, but just like you, one day, I'm going to have to explain to my little girl that her egg donor didn't want her. And the only way to protect her is to make sure she never has to see her unless she chooses to."

Kira nods and edges closer, taking my hand in hers.

"You're such a good dad," she says softly. "Addie is so blessed to have you, and ... I know you're not Violet's dad or anything, but I'm glad while we're living here, my daughter can see what a good man and father looks like."

"Thank you," I say, refusing to focus on the part where she mentioned *while we're living here* because if I have it my way, she and Violet will never move out.

"Can you read to me?" she asks, thankfully changing the subject.

As much as I don't mind talking about anything with her, the topic of Nora tends to ruin my mood.

"Of course." I pull out the book I've been reading to her and turn to the page I left off on.

I read for several minutes with her snuggled into my side. She laughs at the funny parts and sniffles when it gets emotional.

"I want a love like this," she says when the hero confesses his love for the heroine.

Since I'm at the end of a chapter, I bookmark the page and close the book. When she lifts her head off my shoulder, I glance down at her, my eyes tracing her beautiful features—her button nose and the smatter of freckles that goes across the bridge of it and the tops of her cheeks. Her lips are naturally plump and pink, and I often wonder what it would feel like to run my tongue along the seam of them and then suck her bottom lip into my mouth. Would it feel as pillowy soft as it looks?

"Ryder," Kira whispers after several seconds of me staring at her.

I imagine her saying my name the same way when I stop kissing her as I move my lips to her neck and then to her breasts.

"What are you thinking?" she whispers, her eyes not leaving mine.

"I'm thinking"—*that you've rocked my world and turned it upside down, made me feel again, and given me hope of a future where I don't feel quite so alone*—"that I don't want to be just friends with you," I blurt out.

Her eyes widen. "What does that mean?"

"That means"—I lean in and pinch her chin with my thumb and forefinger—"that I want to kiss you." My gaze descends to her lips as her tongue slides across them, leaving them glistening wet. "Tell me that you want me to kiss you," I murmur, meeting her eyes again, begging, pleading, needing for her to tell me yes.

After several long, grueling moments, she nods, but I need more than that.

"Say the words, Kira."

"Kiss me," she breathes out, and I do.

With my hands framing her face, I lean in and press my mouth tenderly against hers. I trace my tongue along her top lip and then the bottom, tasting her sweetness, feeling her softness. I've fantasized about kissing this woman dozens of times, but not a single fantasy comes anywhere close to the reality.

She exhales softly, her body sinking into mine, and I slide my tongue between her parted lips, coaxing hers. She tastes like everything good in this world, and I know that one kiss won't be enough. I've only just gotten a taste, and I'm already addicted.

Gliding my hand around, I cup the back of her neck and deepen the kiss. Her lips are as soft as I imagined, and her tongue moves in perfect sync with mine, as if we were made for each other.

Kira moans into my mouth, and the sound sets me off. I slide my hands down her backside and, grabbing her ass, lift her into my lap. We continue to kiss, our tongues stroking and caressing one another. It's like the entire world ceases to exist and all that's left is Kira and me.

Until a whimper comes through the baby monitor that I have on the end table, reminding us that we're not alone.

Kira pulls back slightly, breaking the kiss, but neither of us moves, our foreheads resting against each other as we work to catch our breaths.

"Kira..." I begin, but I'm cut off when Addie cries out for me, forcing me to set Kira on the couch so I can go make sure my little girl is okay.

"I'll be right back," I murmur against her mouth, wishing I didn't have to go, but knowing if anyone understands what it's like to be a single parent, it's her.

When I come back downstairs from getting Addie

back to sleep, Kira has retreated to her room. I'm tempted to go knock on her door, not wanting to leave things unfinished. But if she's asleep, I don't want to wake her. And I imagine after that kiss, we both have a lot to think about.

So, instead, I shoot her a text.

> To be continued ...

I stare at my phone for several seconds, hoping she'll text back. And I'm about to give up, assuming she's asleep, when she hearts the text I sent. It's not much, but it's enough to give me hope ... for more.

KIRA

"Yum! Yum!" Addie shrieks.

"Shh …" Ryder says.

"Mommy's gonna love this," Violet adds, attempting and failing to whisper.

As I listen to the voices, wondering what the heck is going on outside my room, I grab my phone and glance at the time, shocked that Violet hasn't woken me up yet since it's already eight thirty in the morning.

"Okay, open the door," Ryder says.

A second later, the door swings open, and Violet runs into my room. "Happy Mommy's Day!" she squeals, jumping on my bed. She crawls over to me and thrusts a bouquet of purple flowers my way that I immediately recognize as violets.

Addie toddles over to the side and lifts her arms.

"Me!" she shrieks. "Pick me up!"

I lift her onto the bed, confused as to what is going on until she pushes a piece of paper my way and I read what must be Ryder's handwriting.

Happy Mommy's Day!

"I made you one too!" Violet says, handing me her card. "See? It says, *Happy Mommy's Day. I love you.*"

I glance up at Ryder with tears in my eyes. He's standing off to the side with a tray in his hands.

"Happy Mother's Day," he says, walking over and setting the tray across my lap.

"I put the chips in," Violet tells me, referring to the chocolate chips in the pancakes on my plate.

"You did?" I choke out. "Thank you." I lean over and kiss Violet's forehead and then Addie's. "Thank you so much."

"Why are you crying?" Violet asks, reaching out and wiping a tear that I didn't realize had fallen.

"Because I'm so happy," I tell her honestly.

I look at the cards the girls made—their handprints traced with flowers sprouting out of each finger, obviously done with the help of Ryder—and I cry harder.

I've been a mom for four years, and this is the first time it's ever been celebrated. The first Mother's Day I became a mom, I went out and bought myself a small cake to celebrate getting through almost a year of being a single mom since my mom isn't maternal like that, but the years following, I didn't bother. I always get my mom a card, but I've never had the money to do anything more for her.

When I was with Brian, aside from him wishing me a happy Mother's Day and mentioning, "Hopefully, by this time next year, you'll be pregnant," he barely acknowledged the fact that I was already a mom.

I figured it was because Violet wasn't his. But as I sit here, surrounded by so much love that Ryder is responsible for—despite Addie not being mine and Violet not being his—I can see the difference in the type of men they are.

I mean, I already saw the difference, but this moment right now solidifies what I already knew but was afraid to admit—Ryder is nothing like Brian. And that scares the hell out of me because, now, what reason do I have for keeping my growing feelings for him to myself?

"Eat," Ryder says, snapping me out of my thoughts.

"Thank you," I tell him, cutting into my pancakes and taking a bite. "Have you guys eaten?"

"I had three pancakes," Violet says, holding up three fingers.

"Me!" Addie adds, holding her hand up.

While I eat, Violet explains the cards the girls made me in full detail, and once she's done, she looks at Ryder and says, "Can we give her the gift now?"

"A gift?" I question. "Breakfast and cards and flowers are the best gifts I've ever gotten," I tell her, leaning over and kissing her cheek. "I don't need anything else."

"I'll be right back," Ryder says, taking the tray from me.

"I want to go!" Violet scrambles off the bed and runs after him, leaving Addie and me.

Since the tray is gone, she climbs onto my lap like the little monkey she is, and I cuddle with her until Violet and Ryder return.

"A gift for you!" Violet drops the wrapped box onto the bed.

"What is it?" I ask in shock and awe.

"You have to open it," Ryder says with a chuckle, taking Addie from me so I have my hands free.

She squirms to get out of his arms, and once on the floor, she toddles right back over to me.

"Up, up!"

Before Ryder can grab her, I reach down and lift her back onto the bed. She crawls into my lap, and I kiss her forehead, loving how clingy she is.

"Open the gift, Mommy," Violet insists.

With my arms on either side of Addie, I rip the paper off, exposing an orange-and-blue box with the words *Louis Vuitton* written across the top.

"Ryder," I hiss when I open the box and find a gorgeous leather bag. "When did you find the time to do this?" I lift it up and admire it. It's big enough to be a diaper bag, but it's way prettier. "This is too much."

I glance up at him, and he shakes his head.

"You love and care for our daughters every day. You give them every part of you. And even though Addie isn't your blood, you treat her like she is. Today is about moms, and you're one of the best damn moms I know. This stuff"—he waves his hand toward the cards and flowers and bag—"is the least of what you deserve. Besides," he says with a smirk, "that bag you carry around is ready to be retired, no matter how much you love it."

I glare playfully at him even though he's not wrong.

"Thank you," I whisper, wiping the tears from my eyes.

I went to bed, thinking tomorrow would be like any other day, and woke up, feeling more love than I'd ever felt.

"You're welcome," Ryder says with a soft smile. "So ..." he says slowly. "I was thinking, if you wanted the day to yourself, I could watch Violet for you."

"I appreciate that," I tell him, "but Violet and I actually have plans today."

"Mommy and I are going to the zoo," Violet tells him.

"That sounds like fun," he says.

"We go every year. It's become a tradition."

I didn't think it would happen this year since I

didn't even have the money to provide a roof over our heads. But thanks to Ana taking a chance on me and then Ryder hiring me and moving us in, I have more than enough money to take Violet to the zoo.

When Ryder simply nods, I add, "Would you guys want to go?"

"We don't want to intrude," he says, reaching over and grabbing Addie.

"You definitely wouldn't be intruding," I say as Addie tries to reach for me again. "The girls are practically inseparable."

And then it hits me. Brian hated going to places like the zoo. Anytime I asked him to join us, he'd say he had work to do.

"But if you don't want to go, I can take them."

"Really?" He raises a brow. "And how are you going to get there?"

"By ordering a car." It will cost a pretty penny, but it will be worth it.

"That's not happening," he scoffs. "C'mon, Violet. Let's give your mom time to get ready. We're going to the zoo."

"Yay!" Violet cheers, flying off the bed. "I'm gonna wear my princess dress!"

I shake my head as she runs out, not bothering to

argue with her. Some battles aren't worth taking on.

"Mommy, look at the giant monkey!" Violet runs over to the gorilla exhibit and jumps onto the rocks, smashing her face and hands against the glass.

"Those are gorillas," I explain. "It says she recently had a baby."

"Up, *pease*!" Addie raises her arms, and I lift her up, setting her on the rocks while staying behind her so she won't fall.

"Oh, look," Ryder says, coming over next to us. He points toward the corner, where the baby is lying in the grass, playing with his feet.

"That's the baby!" Violet says. "He's so cute."

A moment later, another gigantic gorilla comes around the corner, joining the other two.

"It's the mommy, daddy, and baby," I explain to Violet, not realizing my mistake until she glances at me, her eyes curious.

"Where's my daddy?" she asks.

"Um ..."

"Addie has a daddy, and so does Kingston and baby Emilia," she continues. "The baby gorilla has a daddy. Why don't I have one?"

She stops talking and waits patiently for me to answer her, as if she were asking about the damn weather, while I try to think of what the hell to say to my daughter.

I always told myself I would never lie to my little girl. And that was easy because she's always been home with me and, I guess in a way, sheltered. I don't have a dad, and my mom doesn't bring any men around. Even when I was with Brian, which wasn't long, she just called him Brian. But now, she's older and been exposed to other family dynamics, so it makes sense that she's curious.

"Everyone's family is different," I explain carefully since the zoo isn't exactly the right place to have this conversation. "Some have mommies and daddies, and some only have a mommy or a daddy."

She thinks about this for a moment before she says, "Can Ryder be my daddy? He's a daddy, and we live with him."

Oh Lord.

"Ryder is Addie's daddy," I say through the lump in my throat.

"Well, where's mine?" she asks, annoyance laced in her tone because she's not getting an answer.

"You don't have a daddy," I tell her truthfully.

Maybe it'd be better to tell her that he's not here, but then, what if she asks where he is? I hate this for my little girl, but I need to be honest with her—even if it hurts.

"Why not?" she asks.

"Because not every family has a mom *and* a dad," I say. "Kingston has a mommy and a daddy, Addie has a daddy, and you have a mommy. I don't have a daddy either," I tell her. "But you know what?" I palm her cheek, hating my ex for creating a baby and then walking away. I know it's for the best because I wouldn't want him resenting her, but it sucks, having to be the person to explain that the man who was supposed to be her dad didn't want her. "I love you so much, Violet. More than all the stars in the sky."

When she was a baby and colicky, I would take her for walks at night around the neighborhood to help her sleep. Sometimes, when I was beyond frustrated, I would hold her close and look up at the starry night, praying for the patience and strength to get through it. Then, I would take a deep breath and tell her I loved her more than all the stars in the sky.

"I love you more than the stars and the moon," she says back. Then, because she's hell-bent on getting answers, she looks at Ryder and says, "Do you have a daddy?"

"I do," he says, "but he's not very nice. I'd rather have a mom like yours. She makes the best brownies ever."

He rubs his stomach to emphasize his point, and Violet laughs.

"I love brownies!" She glances back at me. "Can we make brownies?"

"We sure can," I agree. "Which animal do you want to go see next?"

Violet taps her chin thoughtfully for several seconds and then says, "The panda bears!"

"Holy shit," Ryder says once she's out of earshot, running ahead toward the panda exhibit. "That was rough."

"Tell me about it," I groan. "I hate it for her ... not having a dad. I know exactly how she feels since my dad wasn't around either. I think that's why I gave in to moving in with Brian so quickly. I wanted to give her the family I'd never had. Of course, with how shitty he was, we would have been better off alone."

"I get it," Ryder says. "Both of my parents are worthless. I stayed with my ex in hopes that we would give Addie the loving family I'd never had." He wraps his arm around my shoulders and tugs me into his side while I push the stroller. "It's a shitty situation to be in, but you handled her questions well. And I meant what I said." He looks over at me. "You love that girl enough for ten people. She might not have a dad, but the only person she needs is you."

"Same," I say, nodding toward Addie, who's toddling behind Violet, trying to keep up. "You're the dad I wish Violet and I had."

"Oh, yeah?" He smirks. "If you want to call me daddy"—he waggles his brows playfully—"I could be down with that."

"Oh my God," I choke out. "Don't ever say that again."

"What?" he says with a laugh. "Lots of women like that."

"Really? You have a lot of women calling you daddy?"

"No." He laughs. "But they say it a lot in romance books. Especially in bed."

"Well, I can promise you that I will *not* be calling you daddy in bed."

When he doesn't say anything, I look over at him and find him grinning.

"What?" I ask.

"You said you won't call me daddy in bed."

"Okay, so?"

"So, that means you plan to be with me in bed. And who knows?" He smirks devilishly. "Maybe I'll satisfy you so good, like in those books, that you'll be calling me daddy."

"That is not happening." I choke out a laugh.

"Okay, fine." He winks. "I'll settle for you just calling out my name."

Before I can argue, he takes off after the girls, leaving me visualizing what it would be like to be with Ryder in bed, calling out his name.

Fifteen

KIRA

"My feet hurt," Violet whines as we walk toward the exit of the zoo.

Today has been a great but long day. Of course, Ryder wouldn't let me pay for a single thing, using the excuse that it's Mother's Day, while he spoiled the girls with rides and treats and stuffed animals.

"Addie's sleeping in the stroller," I tell her even though she can see it for herself.

When she started to get tired, I told her to get in the stroller—it's a double-seated rental from the zoo—but she insisted she was a big girl and didn't need a stroller. Addie fell asleep, sprawled out across the two seats, and there's no way I'm waking her up even if that means I have to carry Violet despite the long walk we have.

I'm about to ask Ryder to push the stroller so I can

pick her up when Ryder says, "Wanna piggyback ride?"

"Yes!" She runs over, and he kneels so she can jump onto his back.

She yells, "Giddyup," and he goes along with it, making the sounds horses make.

Violet giggles the entire way to the exit, and my heart that I've kept hidden and protected feels like it's been removed from my chest and placed on my sleeve for all to see.

AFTER WE'RE HOME AND BOTH GIRLS ARE ASLEEP IN their beds, I take a quick shower to rinse the day off. When I get out, I find a text from Ryder, asking me to meet him in the garage.

When I walk outside, I immediately notice my SUV has been replaced by another vehicle.

"Hey, did you move my car?" I ask.

I wouldn't dare drive it unless it was an emergency, but the thought of having no vehicle has me damn near hyperventilating.

"It's gone," he says, closing the gap between us.

"What?" I whisper. "Ryder ..."

My vehicle is the only way for me to escape. I might have some money saved, but it's nowhere near enough to buy a new car.

"I had it taken care of," he explains like that will

make me feel better when it's only making shit worse. "Nobody will be able to find it, let alone your ex."

"But..."

"This is for you."

He takes my hand in his and guides me over to the gorgeous metallic-gray Mercedes SUV. I know nothing about cars, but even I know this SUV costs a cool six figures.

"I can't afford this," I choke out.

"It's paid off," he says. "And in your name. The insurance has been paid for the year as well."

"What?" I whip my head around to look at him in shock. "Ryder, the purse was too much. This ... this is ..." I shake my head, unsure of how to voice what I need to say. "This car is a lot of money," I whisper.

"Not for me," he says matter-of-factly. "I'm worth billions." He shrugs like he's discussing the weather. "The truth is, I only work because I love numbers and wouldn't know what to do with myself if I didn't have a purpose."

"That doesn't mean you have to buy me a car that's equivalent to the cost of a house!"

"Your safety is my priority, and this vehicle is damn safe." He reaches out and rests his hands on the curves of my hips, pulling me toward him. "You don't need to worry about how much it cost because you don't have to pay a dime. It's in your name, and it's yours to drive. If you decide to quit tomorrow, it goes with you."

"Why would you do that?" I whisper, having a feeling I know exactly why he did it but needing to hear him say it.

"Because you were reliant on your ex and that will never happen again. You hid out in fear of someone finding the vehicle. But now, you own it. Nobody, including me, can take it away from you. I also spoke to my attorney, and he recommended someone who can help you. We have a meeting with her next week."

"Ryder," I whisper, having no clue what to say to the man who swooped in and saved me and my daughter. *Thank you* is the right answer, but those two words don't feel like nearly enough.

As if he can hear my thoughts, he says, "You don't have to thank me, Kira. It's the least I can do after the way you've helped take care of my little girl. There's also a double stroller in the trunk for when you take the girls out, and a car seat and a booster are set up in the back seat."

I frame the sides of his face and then lean in, pressing my mouth against his, hoping to convey without words how much he's come to mean to me in such a short time. He's not just my employer. Ryder Du Ponte has become my friend, and if I'm honest, I'd like for him to be more.

With his hands on my hips, Ryder pulls me toward him, his arms encircling my waist. His tongue finds mine, and we explore each other's mouth, getting to know one another on a deeper, more intimate level. His lips are strong yet soft, just like him. And he kisses me the same way he approaches everything he cares about—passionately—giving me his full attention.

"Go out with me," he murmurs against my mouth, making me back up slightly, breaking the kiss and our connection.

"What?" I ask, wondering if the kiss has gone to my head, leaving me out of sorts—because did he just ask me out?

"I want to take you out on a date."

"Ryder, I don't ..." I shake my head, at a loss for words.

On one hand, I'm attracted to him, and I would love to go out with him, but on the other hand, I'm—

"I know you're scared," he says, pulling my thoughts straight from my head before I can even think them, let alone voice them.

He tucks a wayward strand of hair behind my ear and then palms my cheek.

"I am too," he admits.

His green-and-brown eyes bore into me. They're particularly bright right now, reminding me of the grass and soil after a fresh rain, soaking up the nourishment and preparing for a fresh start. I can't help but cling to that metaphor as he opens his heart and soul to me.

He backs up, giving me space, and I'm shocked by how much I hate it. I want back in the comfort and warmth of his arms.

"I don't want to let my past win," he says. "I don't want to push you away, and I'm hoping instead of running, you'll stay and fight our demons alongside me."

He holds out his hand, and I get why he let me go. He wants me to come willingly.

"I'm not going to hurt you, Kira. In fact, I'm going to do everything in my power to keep you and Violet safe."

I stand in my place, staring at his hand, thinking about everything that's happened. Falling for Raymond and assuming he was right there with me. Rushing into things with Brian and realizing too late the type of person he was. Running when I knew he wouldn't stop until he dragged me back.

My past might've caused me to think twice, to look closer and take things slower, but I won't allow it to win, to ruin any type of future I can have. To prevent me from finding happiness. Ryder was in the same boat with his ex, but here he is, extending his hand and willing to put his heart back on the line for a chance at finding love.

And I'm willing to as well. Maybe in the end, he will hurt me—after all, we can't predict the future—but I don't believe for a second that he's anything like the men from my past. Ryder has a good, pure heart, and I want nothing more than to be on the receiving end of his love. It's scary, giving someone your heart and hoping they don't break it, but Ryder is worth the risk.

Reaching out and taking his hand, I entwine our fingers and step closer to him. "I want to stay and fight with you," I tell him, knowing he needs to hear those words.

His mom never fought for him, his dad—from what he's told me—was barely around, and Addie's mom didn't give a shit about either of them. If my biggest fear is being hurt—emotionally and physically—then his is not being worth sticking around for.

I take another step into his space and glide my knuckles down his cheek, wanting all the connection I can get with him. "I want to go out on a date with you."

The smile Ryder gives me is equivalent to fireworks going off on the Fourth of July. It's beautiful and magical and breathtaking. It's a smile he usually reserves for his daughter, but right now, it's all for me. Because I've agreed to go out with him.

He tugs me into him, so our bodies are flush, and then his mouth descends on mine. And as our lips mold around each other, I can feel every one of his promises deep in the marrow of my bones. Now, I just have to hope that Ryder is a man who keeps his promises.

"C'mon," Ryder says when the kiss ends. "Let's go inside. We have a book to finish."

When he sits on the couch, like the last several times he's read to me, I snuggle into his side, resting my head on his shoulder. He opens to the page we left off on, where the heroine's ex is causing problems for the heroine, and the hero's promising he'll handle it.

He reads page after page, and I stay awake, engrossed in every word. I feel like I've started on a journey with this woman, and I'm invested in finding out what happens, if she'll get her happily ever after.

When Ryder reads the final page, happy tears slide down my cheeks.

"I always thought romance was cringy," I admit, sitting up and wiping my tears.

"And now?" he prompts.

"I felt like I could relate to so much of that story. Being a single mom, wanting to find love ... finding it in the wrong place and then being overly cautious when she met the right guy."

"Oh, yeah?" Ryder shifts in his seat. "Does that mean you think you've found the right guy?"

"My heart is telling me it's definitely a possibility," I tell him honestly. "I guess we'll have to wait and see."

"I guess we will," he agrees.

He closes the book and sets it on the end table, and I sigh, already missing the couple.

"What's wrong?"

"I feel like I know them," I say, nodding toward the book with a laugh. "I'm going to miss them. I know that sounds crazy but—"

"No, it doesn't. I know exactly what you mean. When a book is filled with emotions, it's easy to feel like the people are real. Their love and situations and heartbreak are real."

"Yeah," I agree. "Now that it's over, I'm like, what do I do with my life?"

I bark out a laugh, and Ryder smiles.

"We start the next book." He shrugs.

"There's another book about them?" I whisper-yell, not wanting to wake the girls.

"Not them, but their kids. The first book is about their son. I picked that book for the book club next month."

"Oh my God, yes! Where do I get it?"

"You're in luck," he says, pulling me into his arms. "I already own it."

"Can we start it now, or do we have to wait until next month?"

"Technically, we should wait until after we discuss the first book, but if you don't tell, I won't."

He shoots me a panty-dropping wink, and then after a tender kiss to my lips, he pulls out the book and starts reading.

Sixteen

KIRA

"Mommy, can I get whipped cream on my milk?" Violet looks at me with hopeful eyes.

"Sure."

I push the stroller into the coffee shop that's conveniently located near the local park that Ryder reminded me about when he insisted that I get out with the girls after three days of not driving anywhere despite him buying me a beautiful, over-the-top SUV.

It's not that I didn't want to go anywhere or that I'm not appreciative, but it's hard to accept handouts, even with Ryder insisting there are no strings involved. I've always been independent, and after what I went through with Brian—allowing him to strip me of my independence—I never want to be that woman again.

"Oh, can I get apple slices?" Violet grabs a package

of apple slices and peanut butter from the cold case and holds it up to me.

"Yep, grab one for Addie and a salad for me."

Violet stacks the goodies into her arms and then drops them onto the counter.

I order myself a coffee and the girls each a chocolate milk with whipped cream and then pull my card out of my new purse to pay.

The barista directs us on where to go to pick up our drinks, and we head over to wait for them.

"Do you want to eat here or at the park?"

"Here, then go to the park," Violet says. "It's so hot out. I don't want my drink to melt."

I chuckle at my almost-five-year-old's dramatics and nod in agreement.

"Kira!" the barista calls, pushing our three drinks to the edge of the counter.

"Thank you."

I grab the girls' drinks, stick a straw through the lids, and hand them to them. As I'm grabbing my drink and turning, I run straight into another body.

"Oh my God! I'm so sorry," I say to her.

Luckily, my drink is iced and has a lid, but when I glance down, her drink is hot, and a bit of it has spilled out onto her canary-yellow shirt.

"It's okay," she says. "Accidents happen." She glances from me to the girls, and then her gaze lands on my purse. "I love your purse. Where did you get it?"

"Oh, thank you." I smile, happy she isn't pissed her shirt is now stained. "Honestly, I have no clue. I was given it for Mother's Day."

"Very nice," she says. "I'm Marie."

"I'm Kira. I'm sorry again about your shirt."

"It's no big deal." She looks back at the girls again and leans down in front of the stroller. "And who are you?" she asks sweetly.

"I'm Violet, and this is Addie," Violet tells her.

"It's nice to meet you," she says, standing again. "Are they both yours?"

"Violet is mine." I point to my daughter. "And I have the pleasure of taking care of this little one."

"Oh, you're a nanny," she says. "That's sweet."

Her words almost sound condescending, but since I don't know her, I don't want to assume.

"I am." I glance at the girls, who are getting restless. "Well, we need to get going. We have a busy day ahead of us."

"We're going to the park and then the library!" Violet exclaims.

"That sounds like fun," Marie tells her. "Have a good day."

Once the girls are done eating their snack, I purchase a couple of bottles of water to go, noting to buy some insulated cups to bring with us to the park in the future.

We spend a couple of hours playing on the equipment, and when I notice Addie is slowing down and rubbing her eyes, I let the girls know it's time to go. Since Addie is too young to really appreciate the library, she naps while Violet searches for books and signs up for the summer reading program we didn't know about. We hang out at the library, and once Addie wakes up, I let her run around, showing her the books for her age.

As we're checking out, I get a text from Ryder.

> We're going out on a date tomorrow night. And before you ask, Ana and Julian are watching the girls. It's only for a few hours, and they'll have their nanny to help as well.

Since he covered everything that I was going to bring up, I reply with an, **Okay. I look forward to it**, mentally trying to figure out what I should wear. Nothing I own is remotely nice enough to go on a date with Ryder, which means I'm going to have to go shopping.

Of course, since I'm new to the area, I have no idea where to go shopping, so I send a text to Ana, asking her for any ideas. Within minutes, she sends me names of several boutiques downtown and makes me promise to send her some pictures since she wishes she could go.

I'm on my way from one store to the next when I run into the woman from the coffee shop earlier. She spots me right away and stops.

"I know it's a small town," she says with a laugh,

"but I feel like this was meant to be. Shopping for anything special?"

"Actually, I have a date." I can't help the way my cheeks turn pink at the thought of going on a date with Ryder.

Many other guys would've taken advantage of the fact that we lived together and tried to jump straight into bed. But Ryder seems to be taking things slow, like stopping at a kiss and asking me out on a date. I like Ryder, and I'd like to explore the chemistry between us despite working for him, but I'm glad he's trying to go about it the right way.

"Oh," Marie says, her green eyes lighting up with interest. "Shopping for a new outfit?"

"Yeah. I haven't been on a date in forever," I blurt out.

"Well, it just so happens, I'm the queen of shopping. Want some help?"

"You sure?" I ask, stunned that this woman I don't know is willing to help me find an outfit, especially after I spilled coffee on her shirt—which I notice she's no longer wearing. I hope the stain comes out. "I imagine you have better things to do."

"I'll use any excuse to go shopping," she says with a laugh, flipping her brown hair over her shoulder. "Besides, us women need to stick together. C'mon. I'll show you my favorite stores."

We spend the afternoon shopping, and the girls do

great. It helps that Marie keeps them entertained while I try on various outfits. After several stores, I have a brand-new outfit that I'm happy to say didn't break the bank, so to speak—speaking of which, I need to ask Ryder about where I should open a bank account since I plan to stick around for a while and the cash that he's been giving me is starting to look a little suspicious, piling up in my underwear drawer.

"So, you never mentioned," Marie says as we walk back to the car, "who are you going on a date with?"

"Actually ... it's the guy I work for," I admit.

She stops in her place. "Ryder?"

"You know him?"

"You mentioned his name."

"I did?" I don't remember doing so, but things can get crazy with two kids.

"Yeah, earlier," she says. "Do you think it's wise to go on a date with your employer?"

This time, it's my turn to stop and look at Marie. I don't know her well enough to gauge her tone of voice, but she almost sounds offended.

"We've become friends," I explain. "And we both want to see where things go."

"And what happens when it doesn't go in the direction you want?" she snaps. "Will he kick you out?"

I jerk back at her tone.

"It's not like that," I say, going on the defense.

Her features immediately soften. "I'm sorry," she

says, her tone gentler. "It's just ... if a guy is willing to date his employee, what does that say about him? How well do you know this man?"

"I know that when Violet and I were struggling, he opened his home to us. He not only gave us a roof over our heads, but he also gave me a job."

"And you don't think maybe he's taking advantage?" she asks. "If you say no, where does that leave you ... back out on the streets?"

"No." I shake my head, refusing to believe Ryder is like that. "He wouldn't do that."

"How do you know?" she asks. "I'm not trying to rain on your parade, and I know we've only just met, but I've been in your position, and I don't want to see the same thing happen to you."

"What happened to you?" I ask.

"I thought he loved me and we were on the same page, but the second I didn't agree with him, he pushed me out the door, leaving me to fend for myself."

"I'm sorry," I say. "Are you okay now?"

"Barely," she says, tears filling her eyes. "But I will be." She smiles a watery smile. "Just be careful." Then, she pulls out her phone. "I know you mentioned you don't know a lot of people. I don't have many friends either. Take my number, and I'll give you mine. And if you need anything, please call or text me anytime."

While Marie seems a bit over the top, I feel like her heart is in the right place, and since the number of people in my corner are limited, I decide to give her the benefit of the doubt.

"Okay." I hand her my phone so she can put her number in it. "And if you need anything, I'm here as well."

"Thank you," she says, handing my phone back to me. "And, Kira, please think about what I said. I know it's easy to get caught up in the fairy tale, but what happens when he doesn't turn out to be your Prince Charming?"

Her words send a chill up my spine because not too long ago, I was thinking similar thoughts about Brian, and now, she's using the same analogy about Ryder.

The entire drive back to the house, I can't get Marie's words out of my head. While I like Ryder and believe he's a good guy, she does have a point. What if he changes his mind? Then, I'm out of a home and a job. Sure, I have money saved now so Violet and I won't be out on the streets, but I love my job. I've grown attached to Addie, and I care about Ryder. Then, there's the new friendships I've found in Ana and Paige. I'm looking forward to our girls' night and the book club get-together. Is the chance of finding love worth the risk of losing everything?

After giving the girls a bath and settling them on the couch to chill out since they're both exhausted from our busy day, I start dinner, my mind half on the food I'm cooking and the other half wondering if I should cancel my date with Ryder.

I'm taking the macaroni casserole out of the oven when Ryder comes up behind me, scaring the crap out of me. The heavy pan sways in my hands, but I thankfully get it to the counter before it hits the floor.

"You can't be sneaking up on people!" I hiss, turning around and glaring at him. "I could've burned myself or dropped dinner all over the floor."

Ryder raises his hands in a placating manner. "I'm sorry, but I did call your name three times."

"You did?"

"Yeah." He chuckles. "For a second, I thought you had noise-canceling headphones on."

"Sorry," I say, shaking my head. "I guess I was lost in thought. I didn't mean to yell at you."

"It's okay. What's going through your head that has you completely zoning out?"

I debate whether to lie and say nothing, but instead, I go with the truth. The last thing I want is to start a potential relationship off with a lie.

"I met a woman today ... well, more like I spilled coffee on her."

Ryder laughs. "Is she okay?"

"Yeah." I roll my eyes. "We ran into each other again later, and she helped me shop for a dress for tomorrow night."

At that, Ryder's face lights up. "Oh, yeah? I can't wait to see you in it."

I must frown because his brows dip.

"Do you not like the dress? You don't have to wear one ..."

"No, I do. I love the dress and heels. But, um ..." I swallow nervously, darting my gaze over to the girls.

Addie is playing with her doll, and Violet is immersed in the show she's watching.

"When she asked who I was going on a date with and I told her you, she was concerned."

"Why?" He steps closer to me.

"Because I work for you, and if something goes wrong, I'll be the one to lose my home and job. I mean, technically, this isn't my home but—"

"It damn well is your home," he growls, cornering me against the counter. "And what does *she* think is going to go wrong?" From the sound of his tone, it's clear he already doesn't like Marie even though he's never met her. And that was not my intention.

"It's not like that," I say since she's not here to defend herself. "She didn't say anything bad about you, but she's been in a similar situation, so she just wanted me to be careful."

"You just met this woman," Ryder murmurs, palming my cheek. "If Ana or Julian thought us dating was wrong, they would've said something. Yet both are rooting for us."

He rubs his thumb back and forth along my jawline, and I lean into his touch.

"You have nothing to fear with me," he continues. "I would never kick you and Violet out, and unless you did something to hurt Addie—which I know you never would—your job isn't going anywhere."

"Okay, but what if we go out and it doesn't work out? Will you really want a woman you dated living under your roof? And what if you move on and find someone else? The last thing I'd want is to be around to watch you date." Just the thought of Ryder with another woman makes me feel sick to my stomach.

"Kira," he says, "there are a million what-ifs in life. And I get where you're coming from because, like you, I put my faith in someone who fucked me over. I've spent the past year avoiding women because of it. But with you, it's different. You had me hooked from the moment I met you. First with the way you cared about Addie and then with the way you cared about me. I can't possibly know what the future holds, but if I wasn't serious about wanting something more with you, I wouldn't be pursuing this with you."

He closes the gap between us so our bodies are almost flush, and then he wraps his arms around me so I'm looking up at him. "I'm scared shitless to open my heart up. To let someone else in. But if there's anyone who's worth taking a risk on, it's you. I don't want to hurt you. I want the chance to be with you. To protect you, to love you."

"I'm scared," I admit. "Every time I thought I'd

found myself a prince, he turned out to be the villain. And for the first time, I feel like I've finally saved myself. I want to let you in, but I'm scared because if you turn out to be like every other guy, I don't know if I'll have it in me to save myself again."

"You're so fucking strong," Ryder murmurs. "Stronger than you give yourself credit for."

He leans down and brushes his lips against mine. It's not a long kiss, but it's enough to remind me of the connection we share.

"I have no doubt that if you got knocked on your ass, you would find a way to get back up," he says. "And the fact is, even if everything goes perfectly with us, there's no guarantee that life won't still knock you down."

He releases me, and with one hand, he tenderly glides his knuckles down my cheek. "But the difference between those other guys and me is that if you fall, I'll be there to catch you. And if I can't, I'll be right there on the floor with you."

"Ryder," I whisper, my heart swelling in my chest at his words, making it hard to breathe. I drop my head and close my eyes, needing a moment to think.

There's a chance everything he's saying is a lie, and it won't be the first or second time a man has screwed me over, but I refuse to live my life scared.

Marie made valid points, but the problem is, she doesn't know Ryder. She doesn't see the way he looks at me, the way he reads to me when I can't sleep. How he treats my daughter like his own. And even though this isn't our home, he's made us feel more welcome in the short time we've been here than I've felt anywhere else in my entire life.

"Kira," he says after several seconds. His fingers settle around my throat, and he tips my face back up to look at him. "It's okay to jump, baby. I got you."

I inhale a deep breath and then exhale. "Okay. I'm going to jump, but if you don't catch me, I'm going to be seriously pissed," I half joke.

The second I finish my sentence, Ryder's lips descend onto mine, and he kisses me deeply. Like every time, butterflies take flight in my belly, and my lady parts tingle, begging to be given some attention as well. My arms wrap around his neck, and he lifts me onto the counter, parting my legs so he can stand between them. I'm so lost in Ryder that I forget where we are until Violet calls out my name, reminding us that we're not alone.

I shove Ryder back and jump off the counter so fast that I lose my balance, but before my ass hits the ground, Ryder catches me.

"You see, baby? I won't let you fall," he whispers into my ear. "I like your ass too much to let it get bruised."

Seventeen

RYDER

"Holy shit."

When I suggested I drop the girls off at Julian and Ana's, I did it so that I could pick up flowers and come to the door like a gentleman. And I'm so glad I did because as I stand in the doorway, staring at Kira—with her hair straight, makeup done, and dressed in a stunning little black dress—I'm glad the girls aren't around right now.

"You like?" Kira asks, twirling around in place.

The top of the dress goes up to her neck and is long-sleeved, but it's sheer with a polka-dot design, so I'm able to make out her black bra. The bottom half of the dress is solid black with a layer of the same sheer material on top, showing off her tanned thighs. And the tall heels she's wearing wrap around her ankles and make her legs look a mile long.

"Like?" I choke out. "More like *love*. In fact, I love it so much that it's taking everything in me not to lift you into my arms, wrap those sexy legs around me, and fuck you up against the wall while your heels dig into my back."

When Kira's eyes widen, I curse myself for being too forward. This is our first date, for fuck's sake, and the last thing she wants is me acting like a damn perv.

But then her cheeks tinge a light pink, and her eyes darken to a midnight blue, as if she's imagining what I just said happening.

Setting the flowers I bought for her on the entryway table, I eat up the area between us, snagging her around the waist and turning us so her back is pressed up against the wall.

"Is that what you want, gorgeous?"

I palm the side of her face, careful not to mess up her makeup, and she swallows thickly, then runs the tip of her tongue along the seam of her lips before drawing her bottom lip into her mouth.

"You want me to fuck you against this wall and make you come on my cock?"

Her mesmerizing eyes lock with mine, and then she nods slowly. And I swear to God, I'm so damn hard that it could be used as a fucking weapon.

Needing to taste her, I run my thumb along her lip to pull it out from the confines of her teeth, and then I lean in and kiss her. She tastes like the sweetest addiction, and with every swipe of her tongue and brush of her lips, I crave more of her. It would be so easy to lift her dress and yank off her underwear and fuck her right here in my foyer. But instead, I pull back, wipe the corner of her mouth where her lip gloss smeared a bit, and take a step back.

"You … you don't want to …" she asks, letting the rest of her question trail off since I know exactly what she's asking.

"Of course I do," I tell her. "But I'm not going to because, for one, we have a date I want to take you on, and two, when the time comes for us to be together, while it's going to be quick since I haven't had sex in two years, it won't be in my damn foyer."

She chokes out a laugh, and I shrug.

"It'll be rough," I admit. "I'll probably come in, like, two seconds flat, but I promise to make it up to you with multiple orgasms," I say with a wink, making her cheeks and neck flush. "But right now, I want to take you on a date and get to know you without our little girls distracting us."

I walk over to the table and pick up the vase of orchids I bought and then hand them to her. "For you."

"They're beautiful."

"I looked them up, and they have a few meanings behind them, but one that caught my eye was strength." I rest my hand on the curve of her hip. "You're one of the strongest people I know."

"Thank you," she murmurs, her eyes turning glossy.

She steps out of my touch and walks over to the dining table, setting them down since the vase already has water in it. Then, she grabs her purse and comes back over to me.

I kiss her on her cheek and then take her hand in mine.

"C'mon, beautiful. Let's get this date started."

"Oh my God, this filet is delicious," Kira moans. "Wanna try it?"

Before I can respond, she stabs a piece with her fork and brings it up to my mouth so I can take a bite. She's right. The steak is good, but the only thing I can focus on is how close she is. When we were seated, I was a little annoyed that we were given some weird U-shaped booth, but then Kira slid in and patted the seat next to her, and my complaint was completely forgotten.

She ordered a glass of wine, and I ordered a scotch, neat—Kingston Gold since I'm loyal to the company I work for. Then, we started talking. Until the food arrived, the conversation has flowed from one topic to the next, just deep enough to learn about each other but on the surface enough to keep it light.

"It's good," I tell her once I've chewed and

swallowed. "You want to try my salmon?"

She shakes her head, adorably scrunching her nose up. "Salmon is too fishy."

"I would hope so." I laugh. "It's fish."

"I love most fish—mahi-mahi, tilapia, cod—but salmon tastes too fishy. But I will have a bite of your potatoes." She nods toward my plate and waggles her brows.

I feed her a bite, and she moans in pleasure.

"So good."

The last date I was on was with my ex, and the vibe is like day and night. She ordered a bottle of the most expensive wine on the menu and a salad—requesting the bread be removed from the table because it was too tempting—and then barely ate it.

Unfortunately, in the circles I run in because of my family name, that's the norm for most women, and because of that, I've never experienced a woman like Kira.

She ordered her glass of wine based on the waiter's recommendation after she asked what was "light and fruity," ate half the bread in the basket, and then ordered the filet because she said she loved steak and hadn't had it in forever.

Every day I spend with Kira, getting to know her, has me falling harder. She's sweet and funny and warm. She listens when I speak, and she genuinely cares about what I have to say.

"You're going to have to grill us some steaks," she says, taking another bite of her food. "The girls can have hot dogs," she adds with a laugh.

"You got it."

Her phone goes off, and she puts her fork down. "It's Ana," she says. "Hey, is everything okay?"

She was worried about being away from Violet, but when she asked her daughter if she was okay with going, she was completely fine with it. And when I dropped the girls off, they didn't even say bye when I was leaving.

She speaks to Ana for a few minutes, and since I can only hear her end of the conversation, I have no clue what's going on.

Finally, she says, "Okay, thank you. If anything changes, just let us know." She covers the phone and says to me, "She's getting Violet. She wanted to say good night to me."

She talks to her daughter for a couple of minutes—who, from the sounds of it, is having a good time—and then says, "Okay, hold on." She extends her hand with the phone. "She wants to talk to you."

"Hey, Violet. How's it going?" I ask once I've taken the phone from Kira, having no clue why she wants to speak to me.

"Good," she says. "Addie was crying for you earlier 'cause she misses you, but I laid with her and sang her the sunshine song my mommy sings to me, and she's asleep."

Her words wrap around my heart and squeeze.

"Thank you," I choke out. "That was very nice of you. We'll see you guys soon."

"Mommy said we can sleep here."

"She did?" I glance at Kira. "Okay, well, then we'll see you in the morning."

"Night!"

She hangs up, and I hand the phone back to Kira.

"You are raising one sweet little girl. Addie was crying for me, and she sang to her until she fell asleep." I place my hand on Kira's thigh and squeeze. "Thank you. If half of your and your daughter's sweetness rubs off on my little girl, she's going to be so blessed."

"She's already blessed," she says, cupping my cheek. "She has you." She leans over and kisses me tenderly. "Now, eat before your fishy fish gets cold."

I chuckle and then remember ...

"You agreed for the girls to spend the night?"

"I hope that's okay," she says. "Ana mentioned you would be fine with it since Addie has spent the night there plenty of times, and Violet is okay with it. I guess she and Ana are going to watch the new princess movie that just came out."

"That's completely okay," I tell her, trying not to think about the fact that instead of having to get the girls after our date, we'll have the entire house to ourselves. All. Fucking. Night.

We eat the rest of our meal, and instead of ordering dessert, I tell Kira that we're going to have it somewhere else.

"There's more to our date?" she asks, raising a questioning brow.

"That was only dinner," I scoff. "There's plenty more to come."

"Are you freaking kidding me?"

Kira glances at me with what looks like a mixture of shock and awe on her features, and I know I made the right decision.

I debated which way to take the date. As a man with an unlimited amount of funds, I could've planned damn near anything for our date. At first, I considered doing a helicopter ride to the city and taking her to an expensive restaurant. But when I thought about it, I felt like it was too cliché for her. Sure, she'd have a good time, but that wasn't her style. So, I came up with something different.

When we first got home, I told her to change into something more comfortable, and she was confused since I told her there was more to the date. And for a second, I worried that maybe I should have gone with something more extravagant, like the helicopter ride. But seeing the look in her eyes now, it confirms that Kira isn't like the other women I've wasted my time with.

"Is that a blowup screen?"

"It is. We're watching a movie on it."

"This is"—she shakes her head, looking around at the backyard that I've had transformed into an outdoor movie theater, complete with popcorn and slushy machines, a candy counter, and inflatable lounge chairs—"amazing," she finishes.

"Are more people joining us?" she asks, pointing to the chairs.

"I rented it all for the week so the girls could enjoy it too."

"They're going to love it! What movie are we watching?" she asks, walking over to the food and drink area.

"I pulled a few strings and was able to get an early copy of the new Mila Kunis movie."

Kira mentioned she was her favorite actress, and since one of my best friends from college happened to produce the movie, he was able to hook me up.

Kira's eyes lock with mine. "You know, I wasn't planning to put out on the first date, but now, I'm seriously rethinking it."

It takes me a second to wrap my head around her words, but once I do, I throw my head back in laughter. Fuck, this woman is something else.

After selecting all our favorites, I hit play on the movie, and then we have a seat in the double lounger

I picked out so I could sit with her.

We spend the first half of the movie eating candy, drinking our slushies, and laughing at the movie. I'm not one for romantic comedies, but I must admit, the movie is hilarious.

The second half, Kira snuggles into my side, and I wrap my arm around her, inhaling her coconut scent that I've become addicted to, and run my fingers along her smooth flesh—across her collarbone and down her shoulder and arm. I can't help but touch her in some way. I've never been attracted to a woman the way I am to Kira.

At some point, Kira takes my hand in hers and threads our fingers together. She places them on the top of her thigh, and I glance down at our entwined hands, loving the way they look together. I've never been the kind of guy who notices shit like that, but with Kira, I notice everything.

After several minutes, she unthreads our fingers and glides my hand onto the top of her creamy thigh, and my attention diverts from the movie to her. Since it's warm outside, she's sporting tiny cotton shorts and a tank top that show off her gorgeous curves.

With her eyes trained on the movie, she parts her legs slightly and places her hand on top of mine, sliding our hands around to the inside of her thigh.

"You want something?" I murmur into her ear.

She glances up at me and nods. "Yeah, you."

And that's all it takes for my mouth to descend on hers.

I tried to be a gentleman, but who am I to stop her from having what she wants?

Eighteen

KIRA

I've never been the type to have sex on the first or even second date. Growing up, I watched my mom try to use sex to keep a man's interest, but it never worked. Instead, it would leave her feeling used and worthless. She would sink into a depression that would last for weeks before she finally pulled herself out of it. I love my mom, and she's always been there for me the best she could, but it was difficult to watch her be so desperate for a man's affection that she would put him above everyone and everything.

It's why I was selective about who I was intimate with. I was with my high school boyfriend for several months before I gave him my virginity. But that didn't stop him from cheating on me within weeks after he took off to a university an hour away.

I held off with Raymond until I felt we were serious. But he still walked away the second he found out I was pregnant with Violet.

And with Brian, I waited until we got married. I thought if I made him wait, I would know he truly loved me and was in it for the long haul. After all, every guy my mom had been with never put a ring on her finger. But it turned out that marrying someone didn't guarantee a happily ever after.

I told myself I was done with men for a while. I needed to focus on Violet and myself. And then I met Ryder, and everything changed. He's proven that some men are capable of being amazing dads. He's shown me how a good man is supposed to behave and treat a woman. And even when he gets frustrated, he handles it as a man should—with patience and understanding.

I told myself I wouldn't have sex on the first date, but here I am, straddling Ryder's legs in the middle of his backyard under the stars.

"I want to be with you," I murmur against his lips.

I've tried to do things the right way in the past, but I've learned the hard way that no matter what you hope for, no matter how much you try to do the right thing, you can't control the actions of others, and you sure as hell can't control the future.

I never could've predicted my high school boyfriend would cheat. I never imagined in a million years that Violet's sperm donor would walk away from his flesh and blood. And when Brian asked me to marry him, I couldn't see the monster underneath his facade.

So, I've decided that I'm going to go with what my heart is telling me, and that's that Ryder is worth taking a chance on. Sure, there's the possibility that this will blow up in my face, but if I don't open my heart, then I'll never know. And I refuse to allow myself to be jaded by my past heartbreaks at only twenty-seven years old.

"Are you sure?" he asks, looking into my eyes. "Because once we do this … once I'm buried deep inside of you, you're mine, baby."

His words cause a swarm of butterflies to attack my chest, and I frame his face, needing his full attention for what I'm about to say.

"I'm already yours. I've been yours since the moment Violet and I moved into your house and you gave us something we'd never truly had—a home," I choke out, not trying to ruin the moment by getting emotional, but needing him to know how I feel. "I've been yours since the first time you read to me when I couldn't sleep from the nightmares."

I inhale and then exhale a harsh breath. "I've been yours since the moment you treated my daughter like she was yours even though she's not and since you trusted me with Addie despite the fact that after what Nora put you through, you had no reason to trust a woman with your daughter."

"Kira," Ryder whispers, his eyes filled with as much

emotion as I feel.

"I've been yours since you showed me how a woman deserves to be treated," I continue. "Since you listened to me tell you about Brian, and instead of pushing me away, you pulled me in."

I lean down and connect my lips with his in a bruising kiss that I hope conveys every emotion I feel.

"I'm already yours, Ryder," I murmur against his lips. "Now, please take me and show me that you're *mine*."

"Fuck," he curses.

Then, grabbing ahold of my ass, he flips us over so I'm lying on the inflatable lounger and he's hovering above me. He rakes his gaze over me, starting with my face and ending at my feet, as if he's trying to figure out where to start, while I lie still, letting him take the lead.

I'm shocked when he takes my foot in his hand. Of all the body parts he could touch, I have no idea why he would choose my foot. Until he leans down and kisses his way along my instep and up my inner thigh. He spreads my legs, and I expect him to go straight to my pussy, but instead, he starts back at my other foot and kisses his way up my other thigh. He's clearly not in a rush, so I prop myself up onto my elbows and watch as he works his way back up my legs. His lips are soft, and his open-mouthed kisses send chills through me despite the warm evening.

When he gets to my cotton shorts, he glances up

at me, silently asking for my permission to remove them. I nod once, and he grins like he won a prize at the fair as he tugs my shorts and underwear down my legs, then tosses them to the side.

He spreads my legs once again, then leans in and kisses the hood of my neatly trimmed pussy. And then, once again, he confuses me when he trails more kisses up my torso, stopping to give attention to the stretch marks I bear from having Violet. I run my fingers through his hair, and he glances up at me.

"So fucking strong," he murmurs. "I bet you were beautiful when you were pregnant."

I choke up, hating that our exes hurt us but so thankful that our pasts have led us here because there's nowhere I'd rather be than right here, being worshipped by Ryder Du Ponte.

Ryder gives my belly one last kiss and then continues his way up my body. When he gets to my tank top, I take it off for him, exposing my breasts since I'm not wearing a bra. With my boobs being on the smaller side, I only ever wear bras when I leave the house. Brian used to make comments that I should get plastic surgery to enhance them, making me feel slightly insecure about their size.

But as Ryder gets on his knees and climbs up my body, his eyes filled with heated desire, I shove the bullshit Brian said out of my head and mentally capture the way Ryder's looking at my breasts like he wants to do dirty things to them.

As if he can hear my thoughts, he fondles one of my breasts and murmurs, "Fucking perfect," before he leans over and takes my nipple between his lips.

He sucks on it for several seconds, causing heat to spread throughout my body and go straight to my core. I clench my thighs in response, and he chuckles.

"When I'm done with you, you're going to have no doubt that I'm yours."

He takes my other nipple into his mouth, only this time, he bites on the hardened peak—not enough for it to hurt, but enough for me to feel the delicious sting.

My fingers delve into the messy strands of his hair, and I tug gently, craving more. He palms one breast, pinching my nipple, while he sucks and licks the other one.

I don't know if it's because I've dated selfish men in the past or maybe they didn't know what they were doing, but no man has ever given my body this much attention.

Ryder continues to play with my breasts, alternating between them, and when he bites down on my nipple once more, I swear I almost convulse without him even touching my pussy.

"I need you," I whimper, so wound up that I swear I'll implode if I don't find a release soon.

"You got me," he says, leaving my breasts and crawling further up so he can kiss me.

While his tongue massages mine, Ryder shifts slightly. A moment later, his fingers part my folds and then push into me. I'm already wet, so they slide right in, filling me in the best way possible. It's been too long since I've felt pleasure, and I'm soaking up every drop that Ryder's giving me.

Wanting to feel him as well, I reach between us and push his shorts down, wrapping my fingers around his hard length and pulling it out of its confines. I can't see it, but it's thick and smooth, and I can't decide if I want him in my mouth or pussy first.

As Ryder finger-fucks me, I stroke his cock, using my thumb to spread his pre-cum around the head and lube it up slightly. But it's not enough. I'm about to slide down so I can take him into my mouth and wet his dick properly when his thumb finds my clit and sparks fly.

"That's it," he murmurs against my mouth. "Come all over my hand, baby."

Between his fingers in me nice and deep and his thumb massaging my swollen clit, it doesn't take long for my orgasm to hit me hard. My legs shake, and I moan into his mouth as I come all over his hand, just as he demanded, every ounce of pent-up sexual tension leaving my body.

I'm still coming down from my climax when Ryder reaches behind him and pulls his shirt over his head. I've seen his body dozens of times between him going shirtless at the pool and walking around the house, but I'll never get sick of seeing it. He works out several days a week, and it shows. He might be pushing close to forty, but it's obvious he takes good care of his body.

With a teasing, knowing smirk, he twirls his shirt around his finger and then slingshots it at me, covering my eyes.

I bark out a laugh as I drag it off my face and toss it to the side, loving his playful side and that we're comfortable enough with each other to be silly with each other.

Ryder quickly pushes his shorts and boxers down and then drops his hands to either side of my head. His mouth brushes against mine, and as his tongue slides between my parted lips, I reach between us and guide his hard length into me. I wanted to taste his cock, get to know it on a more personal level, but that'll have to wait.

He pushes into me slowly, inch by inch, as if he's savoring every second, not wanting it to end, as my legs wrap around his backside, my ankles locking behind him.

"Kira," he breathes against my lips, shaking his head when I push on his backside, wanting him all the way inside me, "you're too wet and warm and goddamn perfect."

I encircle my arms around his neck and thrust my hips upward to push him in the rest of the way. When he bottoms out, his forehead rests against mine, his breathing accelerated.

"Fuck," he groans. "I'm never going to last."

"I don't care. Please," I beg. "It's okay if you don't last. I just want you to fuck me."

He nods in understanding, then cages me in with his strong arms. With our bodies connected in the most intimate way, he begins to move in and out of me with deliberate, controlled thrusts, hitting places deep within me I didn't know existed.

"That feels so good," I moan, tugging on the ends of his hair and bringing his mouth to mine.

He continues to move his body against mine in a slow rhythm, every thrust deep and sensual. And it dawns on me—Ryder isn't fucking me. He's making love to me. The thought causes my heart to swell with emotion because as many times as I've been fucked in my life, I don't think a man has ever made love to me. Until now.

I didn't plan or expect to climax again—hell, I was simply happy he made me come by his hand beforehand—but nonetheless, another orgasm works its way up, climbing higher and higher until I'm coming again, and, holy shit, this release is nothing like my last one. It's deep and intense, causing my entire body to tremble as I clench around Ryder's cock.

"Fuck," he chokes out, unable to hold back any longer.

His thrusts turn erratic and unrestrained, showing me what he's capable of. His arms tighten around my body, and he nuzzles his face into my neck, sucking on my heated flesh.

And then, with a guttural groan, he comes deep inside of me, coating my insides with his warm seed. I should care that we didn't use protection, but in this moment, with Ryder wrapped around me and in me, my only thought is how perfect this moment is.

Skin on skin.

Our hearts beating as one.

Our releases mixing with each other.

I've never been closer to anyone on such an intimate level, and it only confirms what I already knew—I've fallen in love with Ryder.

After several seconds of comfortable silence as we work to steady our breathing, Ryder lifts and kisses me tenderly before he pulls out and sits back on his haunches.

His eyes go straight to my pussy, where, I have no doubt, our arousal is dripping out of me. I should probably be embarrassed, but after two mind-blowing orgasms, I'm too satiated to even care.

"I came in you," he says, reaching out and swiping his finger through our joint release, as if he needs to feel it to confirm it's true.

I shiver at his touch and then sit up, climbing into his lap. He drops onto his butt, wrapping his arms around my waist as I encircle my arms around his neck and my legs around his torso.

"I'm clean," I tell him. "The second I got insurance from working at Kingston, I went to the doctor to get tested."

"I am as well," he murmurs, "but that's not what I'm worried about."

His eyes meet mine, and it hits me—he's scared that I could get pregnant.

"I'm on birth control." I cup the sides of his scruffy face, loving the feel of his trimmed beard beneath my fingers. "And unlike your ex, I actually mean that." I take his hand in mine and bring it up to my bicep. "Feel that?" I run his finger across a small metal bar beneath my skin. "That's the implant. I got it less than a year ago, and it's good for three years, so we're good."

I smile at Ryder, and he sighs in relief.

"Thank you. It's not that I wouldn't want to have a baby with you ..."

"I know," I tell him. "We're not there yet. And there's no rush. When Brian and I got married, he knew I was on birth control and demanded I got off it, wanting to start a family. It rubbed me the wrong way that he didn't include Violet as part of that family, but I thought maybe he just needed time.

"When things between us began to deteriorate, I started to freak out at the thought of getting pregnant, so I went behind his back and got the implant. I couldn't risk having a baby with him and being tied to him forever. Having a baby is a big step, and my hope is that the next time I make that commitment with someone, it's with the man I plan to spend my life with."

He nods in agreement. "I got so caught up in the moment that I didn't even think about using protection. Your pussy is like magic, making me lose my damn mind."

I choke out a laugh. "I feel you. Your dick is like a magic stick."

I wink playfully, and Ryder chuckles.

"FYI," he says once he's sobered, "if you did get pregnant, I wouldn't be upset about it. I should probably be traumatized as fuck after what Nora did, but when I'm with you, it's like all that bullshit is left in the past, and all I can see is a future with you and our daughters."

Unable to say anything, thanks to the huge lump of emotion lodged in my throat, I lean in and kiss Ryder. His fingers delve into the back of my hair, deepening the kiss, and with my body wrapped around his, he lays me back on the lounge chair and proceeds to make love to me all over again.

We're both sweaty and sticky, but neither of us gives a shit. The only thing on our minds is being together.

And as we both find our release, I whisper the three words against his lips I wanted to say earlier, but couldn't get out. "I love you."

His body stills, his cock buried deep inside me,

and as he looks into my eyes, his own filled with so much raw emotion, I can feel the words before he says them back.

"I love you," he murmurs. "More than all the stars in the sky …"

My stomach tightens at his words. I love that he pays attention to even the small things.

He kisses the tip of my nose. "More than the moon shining down above us …" He kisses the corner of my mouth. "More than all the planets and the entire solar system."

His lips connect with mine, and as he pours every ounce of emotion into the kiss, it flows through my veins and goes straight to my heart, filling every crack and fissure with his love, making it feel whole once again.

Nineteen

RYDER

ANA

> I hope you guys had a good night. No rush getting the girls, but we're making breakfast if you want to join.

I glance over at a sleeping Kira, and the only thing I want to eat is her.

So, I type back,

> Thank you again for watching them. We'll be there soon, but don't wait on us for breakfast.

ANA

> I'm so happy for you both.

I set my phone down and roll back toward Kira,

who is wearing nothing but my dress shirt. After we showered and I refused to let her leave my room to get dressed, she got creative and snagged the dress shirt I'd hung over my chair. It's unbuttoned halfway down, showing off the swells of her perfect breasts.

I edge closer and separate her thighs, pushing my knees between them and rubbing against her pussy. She moans in her sleep, and my dick hardens at the sound.

Undoing another two buttons, I part her shirt and uncover one of her breasts completely. Her dusty-rose nipple is hard and begging to be licked. So, I lean in and flick my tongue across it.

Kira moans again and stretches, exposing her other breast. I take that one in my mouth, sucking on her nipple. Then, I pull back and softly blow on the wet tip.

"What are you doing?" she chokes out, her voice gravelly from sleep.

"Enjoying my breakfast."

She laughs, and the melodic sound has me feeling shit I've never felt.

Pushing her gently onto her back, I brush my lips against hers and then trail more kisses along her jawline and neck.

"Ryder," she breathes, cupping my face.

I hover above her and kiss her again. "Good morning, beautiful," I murmur against her lips.

"Morning," she says back, smiling as I slide down her body, pushing the cover off her.

Spreading her legs and pussy lips, I dip my head and lick up her center. Her body bows at my touch, and her hands go to my hair, tugging on the strands. I'm quickly learning that's her go-to when she's turned on, and I fucking love it.

Since I know she's going to want to get the girls soon, I don't draw it out. Instead, I go straight for her clit, massaging it in the way I know will set her off, while I push two digits into her warmth and finger-fuck her until she's screaming out my name as she climaxes all over my tongue and fingers.

I drink her in, memorizing her taste—the perfect mix of sweet and tangy and all fucking mine. And then, without giving her a moment to come down, I climb back up her body, her juices still coating my lips.

"You hungry, baby?"

She nods, her lust-filled eyes landing on my mouth. "Ravished," she breathes.

Pulling my face toward hers, she licks my top lip and then the bottom, tasting herself on me.

"Tastes delicious, right?"

"It's okay." She shrugs. "I prefer my breakfast a bit saltier."

I chuckle and shake my head, remembering the way she went to town on my cock last night in the shower after we went inside, swallowing every damn drop.

"That's going to have to wait. Right now, I need to be inside you." I lean in and kiss her once more. "Now, be a good girl and turn over on your hands and knees so I can fuck you from behind … and take that shirt off."

She nods eagerly and then scrambles to do as I asked. Once she's naked with her pert ass in the air, she glances back and waits patiently for me.

I could stare at her all day. At the way her hair is messy from us fucking after our shower. The way her smooth, tanned back curves. Just above her ass are two sexy-as-fuck dimples that remind me of the one on her right cheek.

She wiggles her ass, growing impatient, and I snap out of it, remembering that I don't have to resort to only looking. I get to touch.

I run my hand between her shoulder blades and down her spine, reveling in her creamy flesh. I stop at the twin dimples and lean over, swirling my tongue around each one. And then I brush my lips over the swell of her ass and give her left cheek a playful bite.

"Ryder," she groans, wiggling her ass again.

"Don't rush me, woman. I'm admiring your ass."

I slap the cheek I just bit, and she shrieks in surprise.

"Well, can you admire it later? I'd really like another orgasm."

I chuckle at her sassiness as I spread her cheeks apart with one hand and run my fingertip down her crack with the other. When I stop at her puckered hole, I press it gently, and she whips her head around to look at me.

"Have you been fucked here?" I ask curiously. As much as I don't want to think about her fucking other guys, it's stupid to pretend like either of us hasn't been with other people.

"A few times," she says, "but it wasn't really good."

"That's because he didn't know what he was doing," I muse, pushing my finger into the hole slightly, imagining how good it would feel to fuck her ass. "Would you let me fuck it?"

She thinks for several seconds and then nods, and it takes everything in me not to grab some lube so I can fuck her ass. But I glance at the time on my clock and remember we need to get the girls soon. Ana might've said it's no rush, but I don't want to take advantage of her and Julian's kindness.

"Another time," I tell her, pushing her legs further apart and then lining myself up with her pussy.

With my hands gripping the curves of her hips, I enter her as deep as I can go and then draw out slowly. I do this a few times until Kira completely loses her patience and starts to meet me thrust for thrust.

"Do you feel how perfectly my cock fits inside your pussy?"

"Yes," she moans, throwing her head back in pleasure.

Our reflections catch in my peripheral vision, and I realize I can see us from the bathroom mirror. Our bodies connecting, her ass jiggling with every thrust of my hips, her teardrop tits swaying back and forth. Her eyes are closed, and her mouth is open as she takes everything I have to give, giving it right back.

I reach around and find her already-sensitive clit, and it doesn't take much to send her over the edge. Her pussy clamps down on my cock like a fucking vise, and I know it won't be long until I'm filling her up. I thought I'd be thankful when she admitted she was on birth control, but instead, I found myself disappointed in the fact that no matter how many times I came in her, it wouldn't end in her carrying my child.

The image of her swollen with my baby has me gripping her hips tighter and fucking her harder, hoping against all odds that I'll fuck her so good that she'll get pregnant.

With that thought, my orgasm slams through me, and I keep going until I've drained every last drop into her.

"Open your eyes and look at us," I choke out, wanting her to see what I see. "Look how good we look together. Our bodies so close that you can't tell where I end and you begin."

Her eyes pop open, and she turns her head to the left, her mesmerizing blue eyes meeting mine. Her skin is damp with perspiration, her puffy lips parted as she tries to catch her breath. Her hair is a mess, she has no makeup on, and I've never found a woman to be more beautiful.

As I look at us in the mirror, it hits me how quickly I've fallen for this woman and how badly I want to claim her and make her mine in every way possible.

Starting with marrying her.

But in order to do that, she has to get divorced first, which means I need to find a way to handle her ex as soon as possible. And if there's one thing I've learned from being a Du Ponte, it's that when we want something, nothing and nobody can stand in our way.

Brian had better watch out because I'm coming for him, and I won't stop until Kira's mine and that piece of shit is out of her life for good.

Ryder,

I hope you are doing well. Margorie mentioned you haven't RSVP'd for the Du Ponte Enterprises picnic. I understand you have personal issues with our father, but please remember that we're brothers, and it would mean a lot to me if you attended. The media will be there, and it's important that we put on a united front. I don't ask a lot from you, but I am asking you for this.

Sincerely,
Eric

I groan at his formality, wondering if other families

are like this.

"What's wrong?" Kira asks, snuggling into my side on the couch.

After we picked up the girls, we spent the morning at the park and then came home for nap time. I wasn't sure how the vibe would be now that we'd made it clear that we were more to each other, but it feels easy and natural, and the last thing I want is to pop our safe little bubble.

"My family has an annual Fourth of July picnic every year. I didn't go last year because Addie was only a few months old and Nora had just left. The year before, I hadn't attended because we were dealing with the upcoming wedding. My brother is running for presidency in the upcoming election and is giving me shit about attending. It's a whole fucking ordeal, and I don't really want Addie in the media. I know it comes with our family name, but I've managed to keep her out of it so far."

"So, why don't you keep Addie here with me? I can stay with her for the weekend, and you can go and enjoy yourself. I know you're not thrilled about being around your family, but consider it a little mini getaway."

"What?" I shake my head. "That would mean you're not going."

"Well, I just assumed I wouldn't since I have Violet. It's not exactly proper nanny etiquette to bring my daughter along while I'm working."

"What the hell are you talking about?" I set my phone down—I'll email my brother back later. "In case I didn't make myself clear last night, you're mine, which means I'm not hiding you or your daughter from anyone, especially my stuck-up family. If I have to go, I want you and Violet there with Addie and me."

"That's sweet," she says with a sad smile. "But to be honest, I don't really want to expose Violet to your family. Brian's family was nasty to her because she wasn't his, and she felt their hostility. I don't want to put her in that position again."

Just another reason for me to wipe that asshole off the face of the planet.

"Do you believe I would ever let anybody treat you and Violet less than you deserve?"

"No, but—"

"No *but*s. If you're not ready to meet my family, I won't force you to go. But I meant what I said about keeping you both safe. And that's not just from Brian. It's from anyone who dares to hurt you and Violet, physically or emotionally. I would kill them before I let that happen."

Kira smiles softly and wraps her arms around my neck. "Why is hearing you threaten bodily harm such a turn-on?"

"I don't know, but if that's what gets you hot, how about this? If I ever see Brian, I'm not only going to murder him, but I'm also going to torture him until he's begging me to take him out."

"Damn, baby." She playfully fans herself. "I bet if you reach into my panties, you'll find them damp."

"Oh, yeah? How about we find out?"

I press a kiss to her lips, having missed kissing them all day. We haven't discussed how to act in front of the girls yet, so I've made it a point to keep my hands to myself. Addie's too young to care, but Violet is old enough to understand and be affected, and because of that, I'm leaving it in Kira's hands.

"Mommy! I'm awake!" Violet yells, running down the stairs.

Kira and I quickly pull apart, but we're too late because Violet stops in front of us and says, "Why were you kissing my mommy?"

"Um," I choke out, having no clue how to answer that since I don't know what Kira wants her daughter to know.

"Because he's my boyfriend," Kira says, making me whip my head around and look at her.

"Does that mean you love him?"

"Yes," Kira says.

"And I love her," I add.

"Okay," Violet says with a shrug. "Can we go swimming?"

Kira laughs. "Sure. Go get your bathing suit on, and once Addie wakes up, we'll go."

"Okay!" Violet takes off, leaving Kira and me alone.

"I'm your boyfriend, huh?" I ask, pulling her back toward me. "Does that mean you're my girlfriend?"

I waggle my brows, and she rolls her eyes.

"I only said that because she saw us kissing and I don't want her to think it's normal to just go around and kiss random people."

"What the hell does that mean? I'm not your boyfriend?"

"Well, you haven't asked." She shrugs and then stands, but before she can get away, I pull her into my arms, her back against my front.

"Kira Miller, will you please be my girlfriend?" I whisper into her ear.

She visibly shudders, telling me she's affected by our closeness, but she plays it off when she shrugs again and says, "I'll have to think about it."

"Bullshit!" I growl into her ear and then turn her around so she's looking at me. "It sounds elementary as fuck, but you're mine, and I'm yours. And as soon as I handle this fucking Brian situation, I'm going to put a ring on your finger, and then you'll be my fiancée, and soon after that, I'm going to make you my fucking wife." I lift her left hand and press a kiss to the knuckle of her ring finger. "But until then, the terms *boyfriend* and *girlfriend* will have to do."

"You're such a romantic," Kira says, batting her lashes.

"I know." I palm the side of her face. "Now, let's

try this again. Will you be my girlfriend?"

"I think you've already decided for both of us," she taunts.

"Still wanna hear you say it."

"Yes, Ryder, I'll be your girlfriend."

Her eyes twinkle with mirth, and I vow to make sure she's always smiling and happy.

"Damn right you are." I kiss her quick and hard. "You know what that means, right?" I smirk.

"What?"

"We get to fool around under the bleachers."

She barks out a laugh and shakes her head. "Of course you were that guy. And since we both know you didn't play football, you can't even use that as an excuse."

I chuckle. "A make out under the bleachers kind of guy? Of course. Every red-blooded teenage boy was. An athlete? Hell no." I shake my head. "In the house I grew up in, that was unacceptable. Football players were worthless jocks, according to my father. My brother and I started playing golf at four years old. My dad said that was where all the deals and connections were made."

"Hmm." She taps her finger on her chin. "I think I can get down with dating a golfer. I was stuck watching a golf game once, and those guys are kind of hot in their polo shirts and—"

Before she can finish her sentence, I lift her off the

couch and over my shoulder, smacking her ass. "Don't be making fun of golfers."

"I'm not!" she shrieks through her laughter. "Now, put me down before—"

"Mom!" Violet yells, running back downstairs. "Are you okay?" Her face is serious, and it's clear she's worried about her mom, unaware that we were only joking around.

I immediately set Kira on her feet, and Violet runs into her arms.

"Don't you hurt my mommy!" she yells, glaring at me.

"No, no, sweetie." Kira hugs her daughter. "Ryder wasn't hurting me, I promise." She pulls back and looks into her daughter's glassy eyes. "We were playing around. I only yelled because I was laughing so hard. Ryder would never hurt me."

Violet nods in understanding despite not looking convinced. And I don't blame her. Kira told me she witnessed that asshole talking to her like shit, and a few times, he even pushed her around. She got out as soon as she could, but even once they were out, Kira would have nightmares. Violet might be young, but she's a smart girl, and she clearly saw and understood more than Kira was hoping she did.

"Hey," I say to Violet, bending down so I'm at her level. "I love you and your mommy, and I would never do anything to hurt either of you. I promise."

"Pinky swear?" she says cautiously, lifting her tiny finger.

"I pinky swear." I hook mine into hers. "Now, how about I go wake up Addie before she sleeps too long and refuses to go to bed later and we go swimming?"

"Yes!"

"Go grab a snack," Kira says. "And I'll meet you by the back door. Don't go out without us."

"Okay!"

Violet runs off, and I exhale a deep breath. "You okay?"

"Yeah," she says. "I think I'm going to take her to see a therapist."

"It can't hurt," I agree.

"We never finished discussing the Fourth of July picnic," she says, wrapping an arm around my waist.

"You're my girlfriend," I tell her. "I'm not having you watch my daughter while I go out of town."

"Ryder"—Kira laughs—"I'm still your nanny. That's literally my job."

"I don't like that." I pull her into my arms. "You're more than that."

"Well, I could drop the nanny label, but then you'd be pretty much paying me for sex." She smirks. "I'm not sure a prostitute is a better label."

I glare, and she cackles.

"Fine," I say. "You're still my nanny … for now. But once all this shit gets sorted, we're going to be making some changes ... starting with your last name."

She swallows thickly, but doesn't argue.

"Are you okay with going?"

"I am," she says. "As long as I have you to make sure no one is mean to my little girl."

"That's not happening," I promise. "Okay, I'll reply that we're going, but I'm telling him that I'm bringing along my girlfriend and her daughter, not my damn nanny."

Before she can argue, I stalk out of the room and up the stairs to wake up Addie. Before I go in, I text my brother rather than emailing.

> Hey, Addie and I will be there for the picnic. I'll book a room soon. FYI, I'm also bringing my girlfriend and her daughter.

I expect him to throw a fit or at the very least ask a million questions, so I'm shocked when he replies with:

> I'm glad you're dating again. I look forward to meeting them and seeing my niece.

Well, that went easier than I thought it would. Now, I just have to make sure I keep my promise and make sure nobody, especially my family, does a single thing to hurt my girls.

I'm about to pocket my phone when another text comes through. I expect it to be from my brother, but instead, it's from my dad.

HENRY

> I'm with Eric at a fundraiser. Why am I just finding out that you're dating a single mom and bringing them to the company picnic?

> Maybe because you have yet to even meet your granddaughter.

HENRY

> I would if you acted like you were part of this family instead of the Kingstons.

> I'm not having this argument again.

My dad hates that I chose to work for Kingston Limited rather than our family company. You'd think instead of making accusations, he'd look at himself in the mirror.

HENRY

> Fine. What's her name?

I groan at his question.

> You're not running a background check on her.

"Dada!" Addie yells, announcing she's awake.

> I gotta go. We'll see you for the picnic, and I expect you to be nice.

Of course, my dad doesn't reply, and I know this

won't be the end of it. He's probably already contacting his investigator to find out who Kira is. He only asked me what her name was, hoping I'd give it to him and make it easier for him to dig into her background.

After what went down with Nora, he gave me a huge lecture about knowing who I was involved with. After my mom had left him, he had become more bitter than he already had been and never married again. He thinks because one woman hurt him, all women are like that. But I refuse to have that same mindset. My mom ran because she couldn't handle the lifestyle. Nora ran because I hadn't involved myself in enough of the lifestyle.

But Kira is different. I can feel it in my gut and in my heart. And I know, unlike my mom and Nora, she's not going anywhere.

"Hey, Ryder," Kira says, snapping me from my thoughts. "I got you something."

I glance up and find her holding a pair of men's swim trunks, covered in pink flamingos and half-eaten doughnuts. The same design she bought for herself and the girls.

"Now, you can eat your own doughnuts." She smirks.

She might think she's funny—and, okay, she is—but the fact that she went out of her way to buy me shorts to match them just made my fucking day.

"Nah," I say, snatching the shorts out of her hand

and leaning in to kiss her sweet lips. "I appreciate the shorts, and I'm definitely going to wear them, but I'm still snacking on your doughnuts."

Twenty

KIRA

"Do you want to grab a coffee on the way?"

I glance over at Ryder and nod absentmindedly, too nervous to speak actual words. After an amazing weekend—between a date night with Ryder and spending the rest of the weekend with our girls in our own little bubble—it's Monday, and Ryder took the day off to go to the attorney's office with me to discuss my situation.

Ana offered to keep the girls while we went, so we dropped them off, and now, we're on our way into the city. I know I need to get a divorce—and believe me, I want one—but it's like messing with a hornet's nest. You know it's there because the hornets are visibly hanging out on it, but unless you mess with it, they'll leave you alone, so you do what any sane person would do—you leave it the hell alone.

Since I left Brian, my goal has been to stay under the radar—don't mess with the hornet's nest. But the moment I file, that's all going to change. Because once Brian's nest has been shaken, he's going to know exactly where to go to come after me.

Ryder swears he'll make sure we're protected, and I believe that he'll try, but he also doesn't understand what Brian is capable of because on Ryder's worst day, he could never be as horrible of a human as Brian is.

"Hey," Ryder says, taking my hand in his and entwining our fingers. "It's all going to be okay. We're not doing anything today. We're just going to talk to the attorney and see what our options are and how we go about it."

We ... our ...

It's when he uses words like that, I'm reminded that I'm not alone. With my mom, I always feel like a burden. She loves me—I know she does—but she can barely handle her own life on a good day. With Raymond, I was nothing more than a good time. Brian wanted to own me. But when Ryder talks to me, it's as if we're a team—in this together.

"Thank you," I tell him, lifting our hands and kissing the tops of his knuckles. "Regardless of what happens, thank you for being here for me."

"There's nowhere else I'd rather be."

After getting coffee and breakfast, we head to the

attorney's office. Her name is Debra Katzen, and she's younger than I expected. For a moment, I'm worried that she's too young and inexperienced to handle my case, but after I explain my situation—that I don't want anything but to be legally divorced—and she starts speaking, I know I was wrong.

"I have a PI on retainer," she says. "He's been investigating Mr. Williams since Ryder and I spoke, and I already have enough on him to have him disbarred. But we're not done digging, and we won't stop until we have enough to bury him."

"Do I even want to know what you have on him?" I ask.

I knew Brian was shady from the conversations I'd overheard, but I tuned it out—ignorance is bliss and all that.

"If you do, I'll tell you," she says with a shrug. "But if you don't, that's what you're paying me for. I'm going to make sure that when we file for divorce, he won't be able to contest it."

"Is that legal?" I whisper.

Debra glances at Ryder, who places his hand on mine and squeezes and then nods at her.

"Men like Brian don't play by the same rules," Debra says. "He's a high-powered attorney with a lot of connections. He's done enough shady shit that if it were to come out, it would end his career. In a perfect world, you should be able to file for divorce and get it, but Brian's in a different world, and in order to get what you want, you're going to have to play by his rules, which means getting our hands a little dirty."

I nod in understanding. "I don't need to know," I decide. "As long as nothing can be linked back to me, I don't care what needs to be done to get him to sign those papers. But what I am worried about is, once we file, he'll know where I live, and he'll come after us."

I glance at Ryder and say something I've been thinking about, but not wanting to voice. "Maybe Violet and I should move somewhere else."

"What?" he hisses. "Why?"

"It's one thing to put myself and Violet at risk. I did this. I married him, and I have to deal with the fallout. But I don't want to put Addie or you in the line of fire. If something happened to that sweet little girl or you …" I shake my head and sniffle back my emotions. "He's a monster, Ryder, and he will stop at nothing to come after me once he knows where I am."

"You're not going anywhere," Ryder says. "And that asshole isn't going to know where you are."

"How? Don't we have to put my address on the divorce papers?" I ask, confused.

"Ryder's purchased a post office box here in Houston," she explains. "And I've put my office address on file in case anything needs to be signed for. He'll know the state you're in, but that's it."

"And when is all this going to go down?" I ask,

already dreading the day Brian receives the divorce papers.

"The PI is still digging," Ryder answers. "But we're planning to serve him right before the Fourth of July."

"Won't we be ..."

And then it hits me. Ryder's thought of everything. Including making sure that we're out of town when the papers are served, just in case Brian somehow finds a way to figure out where I'm living.

"While he's being served, we'll be on the beach, hours away from Rosemary," I say out loud.

"Bingo," Ryder says, setting his hand on my thigh and squeezing. "I promised nothing would happen to you and Violet, and I'm going to do everything in my power to make sure that holds true."

"If you have any questions, you can call me anytime." Debra slides her business card across the desk.

I wonder how much Ryder is paying her for her to be available twenty-four/seven. It must be hundreds of dollars an hour.

"Hey," Ryder says, leaning in. "Whatever you're thinking, stop. We're in this together. It's you and me and our little girls against the world."

And just like that, I fall a little harder for the man who I wasn't expecting to turn my life upside down in the best way possible.

"Mommy!"

The moment Violet spots me, she jumps up from the couch, where she was watching a movie, and runs toward me, not stopping until she crashes into my legs.

I've only just wrapped my arms around her when a high-pitched voice yells, "Mama!"

I look up and find Addie toddling over. She mimics Violet by wrapping her tiny arms around my legs, and I stand there, frozen in place, shocked by her word choice.

"Mommy, I had so much fun," Violet says without missing a beat.

"Mama!" Addie repeats, lifting her arms so I'll pick her up.

Without thought, I do so, and the moment her face is near mine, she slobbers kisses on my cheek.

"Hey, Monkey," I say, giving her a kiss on the tip of her nose.

"Mommy!" Violet repeats, only for Addie to copy her again.

"Mama!"

"It seems somebody has become a parrot," I say with a laugh, trying to make light of it even though my heart is pounding behind my rib cage at the thought of this sweet little girl thinking I'm her mother.

I bend down slightly to give Violet my attention, and Addie clings to me like the monkey she is. "Yes, sweetie?"

"Can we go swimming when we get home? I haven't been in the pool in forever!"

"You were in the pool yesterday," I point out.

"That was so long ago," she whines.

"We'll see. Go clean up any mess you made so we can get going."

Violet runs off, and I turn to Ana, refusing to look at Ryder. "How were they?"

"Angels," Ana says. "Neither has had a nap though, so they'll probably pass out in the car. How did your appointment go?"

"It was informative," I answer, not wanting to get into the details in front of Violet.

"You'll have to tell me all about it this weekend." She glances at Ryder. "You're still good with watching the girls, right?"

"Of course," Ryder says, snaking an arm across my shoulders. "And it's not *watching* when I'm taking care of our kids. It's called parenting."

"Good answer." Ana smirks while my heart damn near leaps out of my chest. "Be here at six," she says to me. "We're ordering in food, so come hungry."

"Sounds good."

Violet comes back, declaring her mess is clean, and then we head out. The ride is quiet since the girls did just as Ana had predicted and passed out before we made it out of the driveway.

After the girls are lying down and I don't spot Ryder anywhere, I head downstairs to make myself a cup of coffee. While the espresso is dripping, my phone dings with a text, but before I can check it, strong arms wrap around me from behind. I drop my phone and turn around, looking up at Ryder.

"Hey," he murmurs, lifting me onto the counter and then leaning in and pressing a tender kiss to my lips.

"Hey." I wrap my arms around his neck and my legs around his waist. "About earlier …"

"I wish you were Addie's mom."

"What?"

"I was never in a rush to settle down, but like anyone, when I went on a date, I'd try to imagine what it would be like to be with the woman long-term. Could I see myself waking up next to her for the rest of my life? Coming home and discussing my day with her? Could I see her as the mother of my children?

"After the first date, I knew Nora wasn't someone I could see myself settling down with. She was self-centered from the beginning, and the only reason I continued to date her was because I was having a moment of loneliness and she pushed. And then she got pregnant."

Ryder sighs and drops his head to my chest, and I drag my fingers through his hair. He's still in need of a haircut, but I like the way his silky strands feel between my fingers.

"I couldn't see Nora as a mother, and the truth is, she wasn't meant to be one.

"But when Addie called you mama..." He looks up and locks eyes with me. "I could see it. The way you love and care for her. You're patient and nurturing and everything I've ever wanted for my daughter."

He palms my cheek, and I nuzzle his hand.

"But it's more than that," he continues. "I see us. Raising our kids together, having more babies, taking family trips, sneaking to get moments alone."

He waggles his brows, and I choke out a laugh through the lump in my throat.

"When I look at you, I see everything."

He uses his thumb to swipe away a fallen tear and then kisses the spot where it was. "Are those good or bad tears?"

"Good," I tell him. "I know part of the reason she said it is because that's what Violet calls me. But the second the word came from her lips, I felt like it was meant to be. I love her the way I love Violet, and I don't give a shit that she's not mine. If it were up to me, she would be."

"Fuck, I love you," Ryder says, pressing his forehead against mine. "I can't wait until you're divorced so I can make you and Violet mine."

"Violet?" I ask, confused.

Ryder lifts his head and looks at me. "The way you love Addie is the same way I love Violet. I don't just want you, Kira. I want you both. I want us to be a family, and when the time comes and if Violet and you are okay with it, I would love nothing more than to be her dad."

My heart swells at his words. All I've ever wanted was for Violet and me to be part of a real family.

I palm his cheeks and press my lips to his. "I want that too," I murmur against his mouth. "I want to be a family."

He kisses me back, and I get lost in our promises for the future until my phone vibrates against the counter, bringing us out of the moment. It's a reminder for the text I got earlier, but didn't check.

I tap the screen, and Marie's name appears, along with a text.

> Hey! Haven't heard from you in a while. Want to do coffee?

"You should go," Ryder says.

"Huh?" I glance up from my phone.

"Go have coffee with her."

"Oh." I didn't realize he had seen her text. "The girls aren't up yet ..."

"I mean, by yourself," he says with a chuckle. "I can handle them when they wake up. You deserve to have some alone time. You do so much for us."

"I'm going to have a girls' night this weekend," I point out.

"One has nothing to do with the other," he says. "Go meet your friend for coffee, tell her all about our night the way women do."

He smirks, and I roll my eyes.

"Maybe then she'll realize how serious we are about each other and she won't be so negative."

"You really don't mind?"

Brian hated me having girlfriends, and Raymond never got along with my friends in college.

"Would you care if I were going to meet Julian for lunch?"

"No."

"Exactly." He grips my hips and sets me on the floor, then tips my chin and kisses me.

"But you also don't work for me," I say. "I'm on the clock right now."

"I'm done with the fucking clock," he murmurs. "You're fired."

I gasp, and he chuckles.

"Let me ask you a question, and be honest."

"Okay."

"If you could do anything, money no object, what would you do?"

I think about that for a moment. I went to school to be a teacher, and when it was just Violet and me, that was what I wanted to do. And I still do, but now, with Addie in the picture ...

"I want to be your nanny. I love being with Addie and Violet. I know in August, Violet will start school, and I always thought I'd get a job teaching, but that would mean putting Addie in day care, and I want to be the one to take care of her, not someone else."

I shrug, and Ryder's face splits into a smile.

"Are you Violet's nanny?"

"What?" I laugh. "No. I'm her mom ..."

But the second I say the words, I know where he's going with this.

"Then, you're not Addie's nanny either." Ryder pulls me into his arms. "I don't want you to feel like I'm taking away your choices the way your ex did. I don't want you to feel like you're stuck or you can't leave. So, for now, I'm going to continue to pay you, but you're no longer Addie's nanny. You're mine, and I'm yours, and if at any time you no longer want to be home with the girls, you say the word, and we'll handle it *together*. If you want to go have coffee with your friend without the girls and I'm available, I want you to go. Understand?"

"Yes."

"Good." He gives me a quick kiss. "Now, go have coffee with your friend, and when you get home, we'll figure out dinner."

Twenty minutes later, I arrive at the coffee shop to meet Marie. She's not there yet, so I order us both a coffee and something to eat and have a seat. A few minutes into drinking my iced latte, I see her strolling in.

"Hey, I ordered you a coffee and a muffin." I point to her drink and food as she sits.

"Thanks." She glances around. "Where's Adeline?"

"Who?" I ask in confusion because nobody calls Addie by her real name.

"Addie," she clarifies. "Sorry. I know someone else with the same name. I just assumed that was her real name."

I nod in understanding. "She's with her father. Both girls are at home with him. They were napping when I left."

"Are you sure that's wise?" she asks, taking a sip of her coffee.

When I raise a questioning brow, she clarifies, "Leaving your daughter with a man she barely knows."

"She knows Ryder very well, and I trust him." I think back to the past few days, and I can't help but smile when I add, "He told me he loves me."

Marie's eyes go wide. "Already? That seems kind

of soon, doesn't it?"

"I know you're worried about me, and I appreciate it, especially since both of us have been through some tough times with men, but Ryder's different. He's even hired an attorney to help me divorce Brian."

Marie nods, but doesn't say anything for several minutes, and I wonder if she's lost in thought, thinking about what she's been through. I don't know the extent of what happened to her, and I don't want to push, but maybe talking to someone will help. And that's when an idea comes to me.

"My friend Ana is throwing a girls' night this weekend. You should come. Her friend Paige will be there. We're going to drink and eat and let loose."

"Oh, no, I can't ..."

She shakes her head, but I'm not accepting no for an answer. She needs other women in her life. Isolating yourself is never the answer.

"Yes," I insist. "It will be a great time, and if you don't want to spend the night, you don't have to. When's the last time you had a girls' night? C'mon. Say yes, please."

I playfully give her the same puppy-dog eyes Violet gives me when she wants something, and Marie gives in.

"Okay, okay, I'll go. Text me the address, and I'll meet you there."

"Yay! It's going to be so much fun!"

We spend the next few minutes chatting until

Marie checks her phone and says she forgot she has an appointment she needs to get to. With the promise of seeing each other this weekend, we say goodbye, and I head back home to my family.

When I walk in the door, the place is quiet, so I check the back and find Ryder throwing Violet into the pool and Addie cheering him on from the steps.

After quickly changing into my swimsuit, I head out back to join them.

The moment Addie catches sight of me, she yells, "Mama!" as she toddles out of the pool and over to me.

I scoop her into my arms and then bring her into the pool with me as Ryder throws Violet again and she comes up, giggling.

I snuggle into his side, and he kisses me tenderly.

"Did you have a good time?" he asks.

"Yeah, the break was great, but truthfully, I'd rather be here. I used to feel trapped within the walls of my home, but here, with you and our girls, it feels like it's where I'm meant to be."

Ryder grins and nods in understanding. "Yeah, I feel the same way."

Twenty-One

KIRA

"Oh my God, I am stuffed."

I throw myself back onto the couch and clutch my stomach, sure I've eaten my weight in sushi and junk food. Ana wasn't lying when she said she'd handle the food for our girls' night.

"Same," Paige says with a groan. "We should order from this place for our book club discussion."

"Oh, yes," I agree. "Ryder loves sushi."

"Did you ever hear back from your friend?" Ana asks.

I pull my phone out of my pocket and find a text from Marie.

> I'm so sorry! An emergency came up, and I can't make it. Rain check?

"She had an emergency come up."

I send her a text back, asking if everything's okay, and then repocket my phone.

"Oh, that's a bummer," Paige says. "Everything alright?"

"I think she's been through a lot." I shrug. "I get it. It's hard to let people in, especially strangers."

"Maybe next time," Ana says with a smile. "Because there will be a next time."

"Should we watch a movie?" Paige asks with a yawn.

We've spent the past several hours eating, drinking, and gossiping.

Paige and her boyfriend are having a bit of trouble because he's been told that when his contract is up in September, they have a job for him back in London, but Paige doesn't want to move again, and he promised this was the last move.

Ana and Julian have decided they're done having babies, and Ana is going to stay home until their daughter turns one, and then she'd like to go back to work full-time.

When I mentioned that even though I love being home with Violet and Addie, I feel like it's wrong for Ryder to pay me, Ana said she gets it because she's no longer working and doesn't feel like she's contributing to the household.

But then Julian overheard and said she and I were contributing more than any job we could have outside the home. We're taking care of the most important people in our lives, and that's worth more than any job we could have. I never thought about it like that, but I get it, and I can see where Ryder is coming from.

"A movie sounds good," Ana says, "but if I fall asleep halfway through it, it's not my fault."

Paige finds a cute old-school romantic comedy on the television and clicks play, and within thirty minutes, both women are passed out.

I should be as well, but I'm nervous about sleeping at someone else's house. I never know when my nightmares are going to strike, and the last thing I want is to wake up the entire house with my screams. So, instead of going to sleep, I continue to watch the movie despite how tired I am.

As if Ryder can sense my inner struggle, he sends me a text.

RYDER

Are you asleep yet?

I'm scared...

The phone rings immediately, so I get up and go to the guest room, closing the door behind me, and then call him back. Since it's a video call, his handsome face fills the screen.

"Hey," he says, his features etched with concern. "What are you scared about?"

Just seeing him and hearing his voice already has me feeling slightly better.

"Having a nightmare and waking everyone up."

"Ahh. Well, when you sleep with me, you don't seem to have any."

The past several nights, I've slept with Ryder in his bed. Ever since we spent the night together, he's insisted on me sleeping in his room, saying now that he knows what it's like for me to sleep with him, I can't take it away.

We always wake up before the girls, so it's not a big deal, but even if they did wake up first, we've made it clear we're dating and we love each other, and Violet is okay with it.

With Addie calling me Mommy, Ryder's mentioned wanting to give Violet the option to call him Dad since she brought it up before, but I think it's best to wait. Whereas Addie is young and doesn't really understand the term, aside from the fact that it's what she hears Violet calling me, my daughter fully understands, and I don't want to confuse her if things don't work out with Ryder and me. I know Ryder is serious about us, but my past has me needing to give him more time to make sure he doesn't change his mind because I'm not sure my heart—or Violet's—would be able to handle him walking away, especially if he told her he'd love to be her dad.

"Kira, are you okay?" Ryder asks, shaking me out

of my thoughts.

"Yeah, sorry. I just ... I think my nightmares have lessened because I feel safe with you."

I lie on the bed since I'm already in my pajamas and sigh in exhaustion. "I hate that even though Brian's nowhere near me, he still appears in my nightmares and affects my life. I feel so weak."

"You're the strongest woman I know," Ryder says, conviction laced in his words. "Having nightmares doesn't make you weak. It makes you human."

I nod even though I don't feel very strong right now. I'm a grown adult who should be able to sleep in someone's guest room, yet all I want is to be home.

"Baby," Ryder says after a few minutes, "you want to come home?"

My eyes fill with liquid, and I nod quickly. "Yes," I choke out. "I really do."

Twenty minutes later, I'm pulling up to our house, thanks to Ryder calling a private car service for me.

The second I get out, the front door opens, and Ryder appears. I run toward him, dropping my bag on the ground. My legs wrap around his torso, and I bury my face into his neck, inhaling his masculine scent.

He kicks the door closed and carries me through the

house as I brush kisses along his neck and collarbone. He's shirtless, so I move to his shoulder and then back up to his jawline, wanting to feel him everywhere I can. He smells like the perfect mix of comfort and home.

When we get to his room, I lean back slightly and then pull him toward me for a kiss. I was only at Ana's for less than six hours, yet I'm ravenous for this man. It feels like I haven't touched him in days rather than hours.

"I need you inside me," I murmur against his mouth, "now."

Within seconds, my cotton shorts and underwear have been pushed to the side, and Ryder's thrusting into me as my back hits the wall and his mouth devours mine.

He continues to slam into me from the bottom, hitting me in the perfect spot that all too quickly sends me over the edge, taking him with me.

"Fuck," he breathes into my mouth. "I need this—you and me forever. Tell me you're mine, Kira. Tell me you're mine forever."

"I'm yours," I tell him without thought. "Forever."

His mouth is on mine once again, kissing me like I'm his lifeline. He walks us to the bathroom and sets me on the counter. Once he's turned the shower water on, he pulls my shorts and underwear down my legs, drops them onto the floor, and then spreads my thighs. When his cum starts to drip out, I try to close them, but he shakes his head as he runs his fingertip along my seam and then thrusts a couple of digits into me. They make a squishing sound, and my cheeks and neck turn hot.

"Once you're divorced, will you get rid of your birth control?" He glances up at me, his face deadly serious.

"What?" I whisper, confused by his question because there's only one reason someone gets off birth control.

"I want to fill you with my baby."

His fingers start to move in and out of me while his thumb finds my sensitive clit, and I find myself moaning in pleasure.

"Would you want that?" he asks, his eyes not leaving mine as he finger-fucks me faster ... harder. "For me to fuck you over and over again until you're carrying my baby inside of you?"

His words shouldn't be such a turn-on, but, holy shit, they are.

"I want everything with you, Kira," he says, sounding the most vulnerable I've ever heard him. "I want the ups and downs, the highs, the lows. I want to raise our babies together and make more. Since you moved in, you've slowly morphed this house into a home, and I can't imagine going back to the way it was before you."

He brushes his lips against mine as he increases the pressure against my clit, and that's all it takes for pleasure to rush through me.

I moan into his mouth, and he kisses me harder, scooping his hands underneath me and carrying me into the shower. It's a good thing since my legs are trembling from the two orgasms that he's given me.

Setting me down, he quickly disposes of his clothes and then goes about washing my hair and then my body. I've never had a man take care of me after sex the way Ryder does, and it has me falling even harder for him.

Once we're both clean, he wraps a warm towel around me, and I pad through his room so I can get pajamas from my bedroom.

When I return, he's already lying in bed with the blanket folded over, waiting for me to join him. I climb into his bed and snuggle into his chest, and he runs his fingers up and down my back.

"I meant everything I said earlier," he murmurs. "I want everything with you ... starting with you moving your stuff into my room."

I snap my head up because that sounds a whole lot like ...

"Are you asking me to move in with you?"

"You already live here." He chuckles. "But I am asking you to move into my room. I love you, baby. I've been hooked on you since the moment we met, and I don't want you here as my nanny. I want you here as my girlfriend and, soon, my fiancée and then wife."

I swallow thickly, suddenly overwhelmed.

"Talk to me," he says, using this thumb and

forefinger to lift my chin.

"It's not that I don't want the same things as you. I do," I tell him. "But I guess a part of me always assumed that, eventually, Violet and I would move out. I never thought this would be our permanent home."

"It can be whatever you want it to be," he says softly. "I don't want to pressure you, so just think about it. There's no rush."

I nod in understanding and rest my head back on his chest. "Thank you, Ryder," I whisper as my eyelids start to become heavy. "I've never truly felt safe until now."

"You'll always be safe with me," he promises just before my eyes close, and I fall into a nightmare-free sleep.

Twenty-Two

RYDER

"Are you ready? When we go in there, you have to say *surprise*!"

"I can do that!" I hear Violet say.

"Can you say it?" Kira asks.

"Yeah!" Addie yells, making me chuckle.

When I woke up to Kira being gone and a note saying not to move, I remembered that today is not only Father's Day, but also my birthday. So, after taking a piss, I laid back down and spent the next half hour getting caught up on some work emails while I waited for the girls to show up.

The door opens, and Kira, Violet, and Addie walk in with balloons, presents, and a tray filled with my favorite breakfast—an iced latte from the coffee shop down the street and chocolate-glazed doughnuts. I'm a simple guy—what can I say? Since I work out, I don't eat a lot of junk food, but I once told Kira that my guilty pleasure was chocolate-glazed doughnuts.

"Surprise!" Violet exclaims.

"'Prise!" Addie copies as she climbs onto the bed and crawls over to me.

"Happy Father's Day and birthday," Kira says, leaning over and giving me a quick kiss.

It's been almost a month since she started sleeping in my bed full-time—although she hasn't moved her stuff in yet—and we started showing PDA in front of the kids, and I've never been happier. In two weeks, we're heading to the beach for the Fourth of July picnic, and Kira's asshole of an ex will be served divorce papers.

My hope is that he'll sign without issue, but if he tries to start shit, I have enough to end him. That piece of shit has his hand in all types of illegal pots, and if he doesn't want to lose his career, he'll sign.

"Thank you," I tell the girls.

"We made you gifts," Violet says, handing me the bag in her hand.

"Oh, yeah? Should we eat breakfast first or open presents?"

"Presents!" Violet answers.

"That's because I already fed the girls doughnuts." Kira laughs. "They were up very early, and once they saw the doughnuts, there was no way they were waiting for you to wake up."

"All right, presents first."

I hand the tray to Kira, who sets it on the dresser, and then take the bags from both girls.

I open Violet's first since she's practically champing at the bit and find the most adorable handprint card.

"Is this your hand?" I ask.

"Yep! Addie made one too!"

"Me! Me!" Addie giggles.

"*Ryder*," I say, reading Violet's card out loud, "*happy birthday. I hope you have fun. Love, Violet.*

"I love it. Thank you." I lean over and give her a kiss on her cheek, then open the card Addie got me. It has a smaller handprint, but unlike Violet's messy yet legible handwriting, there are scribbles everywhere with Kira's handwriting above. "*Happy birthday and happy Daddy's Day. I love you. Love, Addie.*

"Did you make this?" I ask my daughter, who nods happily. "Thank you, Chunk." I pull her into my arms and kiss her cheek.

"Addie got to make you a birthday and daddy card," Violet says. "But since you're not my daddy, I didn't." She shrugs like it's not a big deal, but her eyes are sad, and her tone matches.

One day, when Kira is ready, I'm going to make that little girl my daughter, and then she'll have a damn dad who will love her and protect her and take care of her for the rest of her life. But for now, because Kira isn't ready for me to make that kind of commitment yet, I say the only thing I can say ...

"I might not be your dad, but that doesn't mean I don't love you or my card. This is the best gift I've ever been given because it's from you."

Violet smiles softly. "I made it all by myself, and I helped Addie make hers, too, 'cause she's a baby and she couldn't use the paint alone."

"That was very nice of you. Thank you."

"We also made you a cake," Violet says.

"What?" I gasp. "Doughnuts and a cake? I think it needs to be my birthday every day."

"No way!" Violet giggles. "Then, you'll be too old."

"That's true," I agree. "Now, what else is in these bags?"

I pull the gift out of Violet's bag and find a brand-new blue tie.

"I picked it out! Do you like it?"

"I love it. And blue just happens to be my favorite color. Wanna know why?"

"Why?"

"Because blue is the color of your mommy's eyes."

"And mine!" Violet notes.

"And yours."

I glance at Kira and find her smiling, her eyes filled with a mixture of sadness and happiness.

I love you, I mouth to her.

I love you more, she mouths back.

Soon, I tell myself. Soon, I'm going to make Kira

and Violet mine, and then I'm going to spend the rest of my life spoiling the hell out of all my girls.

"Open your gift from Addie," Violet says, bringing me back to the present.

I do as she said, and inside, I find a jewelry box. When I pop the box open, nestled inside are the most adorable monkey cuff links.

"Addie couldn't exactly pick out a gift," Kira says with a laugh, "but when we were looking at the ties, I saw those and thought they were very fitting for Father's Day."

"They're perfect," I choke out.

This is the first gift anyone has ever bought me for Father's Day, and it's the first time in years that anyone has ever given a shit about my birthday. In previous years, if my dad was in town, we'd go to brunch, but in our family, you don't buy or make—as he would call it—"cheesy" gifts. And we sure as hell don't do sentimental.

"So, we were thinking," Kira says, handing me back my coffee and doughnuts, "since today is your day, we would do something you enjoy."

"Oh, yeah? We're going golfing?" I joke.

"Actually, we are!" Kira laughs. "Kind of." She smirks. "I don't think the golf course would be too thrilled with the girls trying to hit balls, so instead, we're going mini golfing!"

The girls cheer, and I throw my head back with a

laugh.

"Sorry," she says. "It's the best I could do with two kids."

I tug her toward me and wrap my arms around her waist. "Mini golf sounds perfect. Thank you." I pull her face toward mine and give her a kiss, needing a quick taste of her to hold me over.

Later, once the girls are asleep, I'll show her just how much all this means to me.

DAD

> I saw your call, but I'm in a meeting. We'll see you for the Fourth of July picnic, right? Your brother mentioned something about you dating your nanny? Please tell me you're not making another stupid decision regarding women. We'll talk when I see you.

I GROAN AT HIS TEXT AND REGRET CALLING TO WISH him a happy Father's Day. I should've known better.

> There's nothing to talk about. Kira is my girlfriend, and she and her daughter are coming with me to the picnic. If that's going to be a problem, let me know. We don't have to go.

DAD

> Stop being dramatic. I just want what's best for you. I'll see you then.

"Everything okay?" Kira asks, climbing into bed.

"Yeah, just dealing with some family shit," I say vaguely, not wanting to repeat what he said.

It's been the perfect day, thanks to her and our little girls, and I don't want to ruin it with my dad's bullshit. The man wouldn't know what was best for me if it smacked him in the face.

"I'm sorry," she says, lying on my chest, like she does every night. "My relationship with my mom isn't the best, but she really does care."

"You don't talk about her much," I mention, rolling to my side to look at her.

"I can't call her without risking Brian finding me. He knows how to track devices, so we agreed not to communicate until everything was handled with him. Mom has her issues, but I still miss her. She's the only family Violet and I have."

"That's not true," I say, rolling us over so I'm hovering above her. I went damn near two years without being sexually intimate with a woman, and now, I can't handle a couple of hours without touching Kira. "Addie and I are your family too." I lean over and kiss the tip of her nose. "Only two more weeks until the papers are served, and then you'll be able to talk to and see your mom again." I lean down and snag her bottom lip, sucking it into my mouth.

"There's a chance Brian is going to fight this, you know," she murmurs, wrapping her arms around my neck.

"There's nothing to fight. You're taking nothing from him. It even states in the paperwork that you'll repay him for the vehicle that was stolen if he can't get it handled with the insurance company."

"I know, but he's not the kind of man to let this go without giving me hell."

"And we'll be prepared for that," I promise. "Now, enough about him …" I run my fingers through her hair and tilt her head up. "The only thing I want to focus on is thanking you for today."

"Mmm," she moans. "Now, that I can get on board with."

She looks at me and, with a devious smile, says, "Remember when you mentioned wanting to take my ass?"

Jesus fucking Christ.

"Yeah?"

"Well, I was thinking …" She pushes me off her, lifts her shirt over her head, leaving her in only a tiny thong, then flips onto her hands and knees. "As my birthday present to you"—she glances back at me and wiggles her ass—"I could give you my ass."

Best fucking birthday ever.

Twenty-Three

KIRA

> I'm on my way. Let's meet at the coffee shop, and then we can walk to the library with the girls.

I SHOOT OFF A TEXT TO MARIE AND THEN GRAB THE diaper bag I prefilled with everything I'll need for today. I wasn't planning to go for coffee, but Marie texted, apologizing about bailing on the girls' night and offering to buy me a coffee. Since I'm a coffee addict, I can never say no to coffee.

"Girls, let's go," I call over my shoulder as my phone rings in my back pocket. When I pull it out and see that it's Ana, I hit Accept and stick it between my face and shoulder, so I can multitask.

"Hey! How's it going?"

"I'm bored."

"With two kids under two? I doubt it," I say with a laugh while I get Addie buckled in and then make sure Violet's seat belt is on.

"Okay, maybe not bored," she says. "But I'm restless. Don't get me wrong—I love being home with my babies, but I don't like being cooped up in the house. I'm used to being on the move."

"I get that. It's why I take the girls out a lot. I'm meeting Marie for coffee, and then we're going to the library. There's a story time happening this morning. Want to join?"

"Hell yes! We'll meet you there."

"Sounds good."

I hang up, double-check I have everything we need, and then click the gate. It's only a short drive to the coffee shop, and once we arrive, both girls get excited over getting their chocolate milks. Since I'm the first one here, I snag a table that will seat everyone and then wait for Marie and Ana to arrive.

Ana arrives first with both babies and Paige with her.

"Hey!" I stand and hug both women. "You don't have work?" I ask Paige.

"I do, but my boss is awesome." She winks at Ana. "I'm just having coffee with you guys, and then I'm heading into the office."

"Is your friend here yet?" Ana asks.

"No, she should've been here—" The sound of a text cuts me off, and when I glance at my phone, I find a message from Marie, saying she had a last-minute emergency and can't make it.

"Everything okay?" Paige asks.

"Yeah, Marie can't make it."

"She seems to cancel a lot," Ana mentions. "Should I take it personally?" she says with a small laugh.

"Honestly, I didn't tell her you were coming, so it's definitely not you. I think she's just a bit flaky." I shrug. "But she's nice, and she doesn't seem to have many friends—something I can relate to."

"Well, you have us," Ana says. "Can you watch them while I order my coffee?" She points to her son and daughter in the double stroller.

"Of course."

Paige and Ana grab their coffees and pastries and then have a seat.

"Have you guys started reading the book of the month?" Paige asks.

"Yes! It's so good."

Last week, we had our book club discussion, and it was so much fun. A few more women from their work joined, and they were so nice. Ana went live in the book group, and we talked about the book. The ladies loved that Ryder actually had read the book, and a few made some flirty comments, but Ana made it clear he was taken, which was unnecessary since it's online and we'll never meet any of these people.

"I love that Ryder reads to you," Paige says. "He's like the ultimate book boyfriend, only real."

"Speaking of boyfriends, how's it going with John?" I ask.

"I think John's going to take the promotion," Paige says with a frown. "He said he would be a fool not to."

"So, are you going to move back to London?" Ana asks.

"I don't think so," Paige says with a sigh. "I was moved around so much, growing up, and I told him that I wanted to make Houston our home after he was offered a position here. I love it here. I love my job, being near my friends. I love John, but I don't know if it's enough to move again. And I know that sounds horrible."

"No, it doesn't," I tell her. "I get it. I moved quite a few times because my mom could never get it together, and it sucks. Now that I know what a home feels like, I can't imagine leaving."

Ana grins. "I love that you and Ryder have found each other. You guys are perfect for each other."

"I don't think anyone is perfect," I say with a small laugh. "But I've fallen in love with him. He's such a good dad, and he's so protective. He loves with his heart on his sleeve and unconditionally. I can't wait for this crap with my ex to be done with so we can move forward with our lives."

"It will happen," Ana says, reaching out and squeezing my hand. "And as for you"—she glances at Paige—"I'll support whatever decision you make, but I'll miss the hell out of you if you leave."

"Ugh," Paige groans. "Why can't life be easy?"

"Mommy, can we go to the library now?" Violet asks, setting her empty cup on the table.

"Mama!" Addie mimics, filling my heart with love.

She lifts her arms, and I pick her up and set her in my lap.

"We'll go to the library in a few minutes," I tell both girls. "Just let us finish our coffee first."

I hand Violet my phone so she can watch a show on the Disney app since she doesn't have a device of her own, and Addie scrambles to watch as well.

"Ryder is lucky to have you," Ana says softly. "Julian and I were so worried about him after the crap *she* pulled. I knew it would take a special person to bring him out of his shell. Thank you."

"You don't have to thank me," I scoff, shaking my head. "I came to Rosemary, looking for a fresh start, and found love, and I owe it all to you. You gave a homeless single mom a chance, and I'll always be grateful to you."

Just as I'm taking a sip of my coffee, a text comes through from Ryder.

> Good morning, beautiful. Have a good day with our girls, and I'll see you when I get home. Don't cook. I'm bringing dinner home.

"Ryder?" Ana asks with a knowing smirk.

"He's everything I've ever wanted and never thought existed. He wants me to move in with him permanently—like, share a bedroom and make it our home. He refuses to call me his nanny." I lean in so Violet can't hear. "He wants to make Violet his," I whisper. "And if it were up to him, we'd be married as soon as my divorce was official."

"But ..." Paige prompts.

"I'm scared. Sometimes, I feel like what's happening between us is too good to be true. Like I'm waiting for the other shoe to drop. And in my world, it always does."

"I've learned the hard way that, in life, we have two choices," Ana says. "Live in fear of what could happen or simply live for today. For years, I lived in fear, but since I met Julian, I've finally started to live for today, enjoying every moment we spend together, every memory we create. Sure, bad things can happen. Life isn't always easy, and nothing in life is guaranteed. But the question is, what kind of life do you want to live?"

There's only one life that comes to mind. "I want a life with Ryder."

"Then, live your life," Ana says. "And don't let fear hold you back."

"It's okay," Paige adds when I don't say anything. "I get it. It's easier said than done."

Isn't that the damn truth?

"I feel like we forgot something."

Ryder chuckles softly and places his hand on my thigh. "That's the third time you've said that since we left. If we forgot something, it's not a big deal. There are tons of stores. Whatever we need, we can grab."

"Okay," I say, taking a deep breath.

It's July 3, and we're on our way to the beach, where we'll be spending the weekend with Ryder's family for their annual Du Ponte Enterprises Fourth of July picnic. My head should be here with Ryder and the girls, but instead, I'm worrying about Brian being served divorce papers.

Ryder told me everything is going to be okay, but until the papers are signed and the divorce has officially gone through, I won't believe it.

"Kira," Ryder says, shaking me from my thoughts, "I can practically feel you vibrating with stress. Breathe, baby."

"I'm trying," I choke out. "But I can't help it. I can feel it deep down—something is going to go wrong."

"And it might," he says, taking my hand in his and bringing it up to his lips for a tender kiss. "But I'll be right there by your side, and we'll face whatever is flung our way together. I've hired security for when we get back, and he'll be everywhere you are when you go out. He's trained to handle men like Brian. And Debra is going to keep us updated on Brian's next move."

He entwines our fingers together and kisses each of my knuckles, and I slowly start to calm down.

"We're staying at a beautiful hotel on the beach with the girls, and we're going to have a great time. Don't let this ruin our weekend. Whatever happens, we'll deal with it when we get back."

"Okay," I agree as Ryder pulls up to a luxurious resort.

As he drives around to where the valet is waiting, we pass a massive three-level stone fountain.

A gentleman opens my door, and I thank him, then proceed to grab the double stroller for the girls.

"Mommy, look!" Violet points to the wall of the hotel, where the address reads 5005. "Five, just like me!"

"Not yet." I ruffle her hair playfully. "I still have one more week of you being four."

Violet rolls her eyes like she's four going on fourteen, and I groan, making Ryder laugh.

"I can't believe my little girl is going to be five next week," I say as we head inside with the girls. "It feels like she was a baby just yesterday."

"Have you thought any more about where you want her to go to school?" Ryder asks, referring to the conversation we had the other night when I brought up needing to sign her up for kindergarten.

He's planning to send Addie to a local private school—even though she's years away from starting school—and suggested Violet go there as well. I looked it up, and it's ridiculously expensive, but it has the reputation of being one of the best. Apparently, there's a wait list to get in, but with Ryder's name, he assured me we'd have no problem getting her in on short notice.

"It's hard to let you pay for it," I admit. "I know if we're going to have a future together, I need to get used to the fact that you have money but ..." I wave around the extravagant hotel lobby we're standing in and sigh. "It's just a lot to get used to."

"Kira," Ryder says, glancing at me, "I don't just have money. I have billions of dollars that I'll never spend in our lifetime. Paying for Violet's education won't even make a small dent in my account. I want to take care of you both."

"Ugh," I groan, shaking my head. "Let's talk about this next week, after she's turned five and I've accepted that she's no longer my baby."

Ryder chuckles. "You got it."

We step into line to check in, and Ryder slides his arm across the back of my shoulders and leans in, planting a soft kiss to the curve of my neck.

"I love the way you smell, like sweet coconut," he murmurs. "I made sure to get us a room with a hot tub, and tonight, after the girls are asleep, I'm going to eat you and then fuck you in that hot tub."

"Mmm. Is it bedtime yet?" I whisper, making him chuckle.

Ryder gets us checked in, and then we head to the private elevator that will take us up to the penthouse. Along the way, he's stopped by several people he knows who work for his dad. They're all polite and give me hope that maybe this weekend will go better than Ryder predicted.

"We're staying on the same floor as my dad and brother," he mutters as the elevator dings and the doors open. "Hopefully, we won't run into either of them until the end of the weekend."

We walk straight to the first door and are about to walk into the room when his name is called from behind us.

"Dad," Ryder says, stopping and turning around.

"I'm glad you could finally make it." Mr. Du Ponte glances from his son to me. "I'm Henry Du Ponte." He extends his hand and smiles, showing off his perfectly straight white teeth.

He's older—in his late sixties, if I were to guess—but he's in shape. He has the same hazel eyes and mesmerizing smile as Ryder. I imagine he was handsome when he was younger—probably looked just like Ryder, and I'd bet Ryder will look similar when he's older—but with all the work Mr. Du Ponte's had done to evade aging, he almost looks fake.

"I'm Kira," I tell him. "It's nice to meet you, Mr. Du Ponte. And thank you for allowing us to attend your event."

"Of course," Mr. Du Ponte says. "And please, call me Henry. Eric and his wife brought along their nanny as well."

Just as he finishes his sentence, another door opens, and out walks a couple dressed like they're going to the country club and not to the beach.

"Eric, son!" his dad says. "Perfect timing. Your brother and his nanny just arrived."

"Dad," Ryder hisses, "Kira is not—"

"Ryder, I'm glad you could make it." His brother gives him a one-armed hug that forces Ryder to let go of me. He's the spitting image of Ryder, only a bit older, and his wife is gorgeous. "And you must be Kira, right? I'm Eric, and this is my wife, Patricia."

"Nice to meet you both," I say. "This is my daughter, Violet." I gesture toward my daughter, who's too focused on the video on my phone to notice anything or anyone else.

"I was just telling her that you brought your nanny as well," Henry says, glancing at his watch. "You should introduce them and let the cousins spend some time together while we go to lunch."

"Dad!" Ryder barks, making his dad stop talking. "Kira is not my nanny. She's my girlfriend. And if you keep this up, we're going to leave as quick as we came."

Henry rolls his eyes. "Stop being dramatic. I get it. You're lonely, son, but don't worry. Isabel Buchanan is here. Do you remember her? Her father is—"

"Seriously?" Ryder hisses. "Stop!"

He looks at Eric for help while I uncomfortably shift from foot to foot, having no idea what to do or say.

"Stop him, or I'm leaving," Ryder demands. "You asked me to come to this shit, and I'm here, but I'm not going to spend the weekend listening to this crap, and I'm not going to let him pull this shit right in front of my girlfriend. I love her, and if I have it my way, I'll be marrying her sooner rather than later."

My heart swells at Ryder's admission. I mean, I already knew how he felt, but I love that he's not ashamed to admit it to anyone. He loves with everything in him, and I feel so blessed to be loved by him.

"How?" Henry accuses. "She's still married, son. Or are you so blinded by a beautiful face that you didn't bother to look into her past?"

What the hell?

"Of course you had her investigated," Ryder growls.

"Well, one of us needs to think with the correct head. After what happened with that last woman."

"Enough!" Ryder barks in a tone I've never heard him use before.

Instinctively, I jump back and trip over the wheel of the stroller. Before I hit the ground though, Ryder catches me. His eyes meet mine, and they morph from angry to apologetic.

"I'm not doing this with you," he says to his dad, his voice low. "You asked me to come to the company picnic, and I'm here. Can you for once in your life act like a normal dad? You haven't even met your granddaughter yet."

"A *normal* dad?" Henry spits. "Do you hear yourself? This is why you—"

"Dad, stop," Eric finally says. "Ryder knows what he's doing, and he's not going to make the same mistakes he made with Nora." He looks at Ryder. "Dad is just trying to help. Let's start over. In case you guys forgot, I'm in the middle of a campaign, and we need to put on a united front in public, so you two can't be at each other's throat."

Oh my God. Did he just make this about him?

I hold back my groan, not wanting to draw attention to myself, and wish I hadn't convinced Ryder to come this weekend. Ryder warned me about his family, but I didn't fully grasp what he was saying until now.

"Okay," Henry says. "Why don't we go have lunch, and we can talk about this in private?"

"No," Ryder says. "There's nothing to talk about. I'm done."

The way he says it sends a chill up my spine because he's no longer angry—he's over it.

"Ryder," Eric warns, but Ryder ignores him.

"No," he repeats calmly. "I've had enough. We haven't even been here five damn minutes. This"—he jerks his chin toward his brother and dad—"isn't a family. It's a fucking business transaction, and it's not the way I want to live my life." He looks at his dad with an expression that backs up his words. "We haven't even made it to our room, and you've already alienated the woman I love. I can't do this anymore. Growing up, all I wanted was for you to love me, but you'll never see us as anything more than business, and while Eric is okay with that, I'm not.

"You got custody of us to stick it to your ex-wife because she wouldn't bow to your every whim. So, not only did I grow up without a mom, but I also grew up without a dad. Grandfather is the only person who's cared about spending time with me. And thankfully, despite the odds, I didn't end up like you."

"Your mother didn't give a shit about you," Henry hisses. "I got custody of you to save you from the ridiculous life she wanted to stick you in. She's spent the last several years living like a damn hippy in some shitty RV." He scoffs. "That expensive home you live in, the luxury cars you drive, the cushioned life you live are because of me!"

"No!" Ryder barks. "It's because of me. I haven't touched a dime of the money *Gramps* gave me. Everything I have—the house, the cars, the life—is because of me."

Addie whines, and Ryder reaches over and picks her up, holding her tight against his chest.

"I'm not going to expose my daughter to you or your world. I'm done trying to be a part of this family. I want my daughter to grow up feeling loved and wanted and cared for—things I never felt because you were too busy trying to be king of the castle."

"You've always had a thing for the dramatics," Henry says.

"Begging someone for attention isn't being dramatic," Ryder points out. "But now, you don't have to deal with my dramatics because as far as I'm concerned, I'm no longer part of this family."

He glances at his brother, looking like he wants to say something, but instead, he shakes his head.

"I'm done," are his final words before he takes my hand in the one that's not holding his daughter and walks us back to the elevator.

The ride back down to the lobby is filled with quiet tension, and I don't ask what we're doing, not wanting to upset Ryder further. I don't think he'd lash out at me, but he's upset, and I think he just needs a moment to calm down.

When we get downstairs, he requests our vehicle and bags and then buckles Addie into her car seat while I follow suit, making sure Violet is buckled in.

"Are we going to the beach?" Violet asks in confusion when she realizes we're back in the SUV.

"We are," Ryder says. "But I was silly and took us to the wrong hotel."

He sticks his tongue out at her, clearly trying to defuse the situation, and it works when she sticks hers out at him in response.

He drives a few minutes down the road and then pulls into another hotel.

"Wait here," he says, leaning in and giving me a quick kiss before he jumps out.

A few minutes later, he returns with a soft smile splayed across his face. "You guys ready to go to the beach?"

Violet cheers in excitement, and Addie copies, neither of them having any idea all that just occurred.

"I think that's a yes," I say through a laugh.

We get the girls out once again, and the valet says they'll bring our bags up for us.

I didn't think it was possible, but somehow, this resort is even more luxurious than the last one. Just like last time, we ride up to the top floor, only when we get off, there's only one door on the floor.

"Don't worry," Ryder murmurs as he swipes his card on the door to unlock it. "I made sure this suite has a hot tub too."

He shoots me a panty-dropping wink, and just like that, the tension fades away, leaving Ryder, the girls, and me in our own happy little bubble.

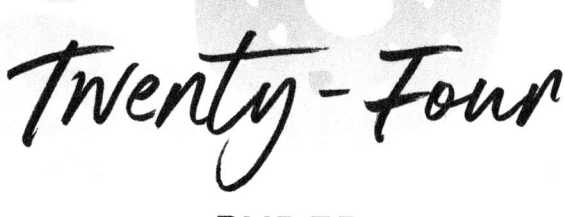

Twenty-Four

RYDER

ERIC

Please come back. Let's talk about this like adults.

ERIC

Are you really going to just cut off the entire family?

GRAMPS

I heard what happened. What hotel are you staying at?

I IGNORE THE MESSAGES FROM MY BROTHER AND TEXT my grandfather back the name of the hotel we ended up at. A moment later, he messages back that he'll see us soon.

I'd rather not get into this shit with him when all I want to do is enjoy my weekend with my girls, but my grandfather has always had my back, so I'm not going to push him away simply because his son is a dick.

"The girls are getting hungry," Kira says, plopping her wet behind next to me on the lounge chair we rented for the day by the pool. "I was thinking lunch and then a nap."

She shoots me a flirty wink, and I pull her into my arms while we watch the girls play at the splash pad. Since Addie isn't a strong swimmer yet—although she's learning—the splash pad is perfect for them to have fun and be safe.

"My grandfather is on his way over," I tell her. "He'll want to meet you, and he's only seen Addie a few times. Once he gets here, we can go eat."

"Daddy!" Addie yells, making me do a double take because did she just call me ...

"I think she picked it up from me," Kira says with a laugh. "I always refer to you as Daddy. She also called me Mommy earlier. Her vocabulary is increasing by the day."

"Jesus," I mutter, shaking my head. "As much as I like the idea of her growing up, I'm not sure I'm ready for this."

Addie calls me again, and Kira laughs.

"C'mon, *Daddy*. Better go play with your little girl

before she's too grown to want to play with you."

I glare her way, and she cackles, skipping over to the girls. We play in the water for another few minutes until I spot my grandfather standing in the corner, watching us. He's dressed casually in a collared shirt and khaki dress shorts with his Sperry leather boat shoes. He's aged since the last time I saw him, and I hate the thought of him getting old. Once he's gone, I'll literally have no family left in my life, aside from Addie.

"Gramps!" I say, extending my hand to shake his since I'm too wet to give him a hug. "You got here quick."

"Came right over when you texted me the name of the hotel," he says. "I'm sorry about your dad, son. We warned him to behave, but he just couldn't do it."

"I'm done," I tell him. "I've tried so many times, but this was the last straw. I'm almost forty years old, and I've spent my life wanting that man to accept me while knowing he never would unless I was following in his shadow. But I can't do it anymore. I've fallen in love, and she's been through hell, and I'm not going to expose her to people like my father."

My grandfather smiles and nods. "Love, huh?"

"So fucking in love," I admit with a laugh.

"Well, all right then, let's have lunch so I can meet her."

I call the girls over and introduce Kira to my grandfather, who insists she calls him Walter or Gramps.

After we dry off and get the girls dressed, we get a table at the resort restaurant and have a nice lunch. Gramps spends the meal getting to know Kira and Violet while bonding with Addie. The entire time, I wonder why the hell my dad couldn't be more like his father. All I ever wanted was a family to be a part of, and yet all he's ever wanted was to be successful. He cares more about the fact that I chose to work for Kingston rather than Du Ponte.

"Your grandmother would've been proud of you," Gramps says after lunch is over.

Kira insisted on taking the girls up to the room to lay them down for a nap while I walked my grandfather to the valet to say goodbye.

I wish we could've spent more time together, but he has to be at the Du Ponte Enterprises picnic since he still owns the company. He might've handed the reins over to my dad, but he's still extremely active in the company. He had planned to retire, but then my grandmother passed away, and he didn't know what to do with himself.

"I miss her," I admit. "I miss spending the weekends and summers with you both, and I hate that Addie doesn't have family in her life, like you and Gram."

"I can't replace your grandmother," Gramps says, "but I've decided to retire ... for real this time. I'm in my eighties, and I feel like all I've done in my life is work. I was thinking I could come visit. Rent a place near you and—"

"Absolutely not." I shake my head. "You're the only damn family we have. I have a house that's way too big with far too many rooms. You can stay with us."

Gramps smiles and squeezes my shoulder. "I'm proud of you, Ryder. Keep loving hard and living your life how you see fit. Your dad will never change, and your brother won't get his head out of your father's ass long enough to think for himself. You deserve to be happy. Marry that woman and start your own family."

Gramps pulls me into a hug and murmurs, "I'll see you soon, my boy," and then gets into his waiting vehicle.

As I walk back to the room, I see several more texts from my brother and dad and know I need to do as Gramps said, so I do something I should've done years ago. I send a text to my dad, letting him know that I'm done and to not contact me anymore. And then one to my brother, telling him that as much as I would love to have a relationship with him, I can't have our father in my life anymore. If he wants to get to know me, I'm here, but until then, I need to focus on my family while he focuses on his political future.

Dad sends back a text, telling me I'm being ridiculous, so I block him, and my brother texts that once the election is over, he'll reach out so we can talk. I roll my eyes and don't bother responding.

When I get up to our suite, Kira has changed into

dry clothes and is lounging on the couch, watching a show.

She glances up at me and smiles softly. "Your grandfather is a good man."

"Yeah, he is," I agree. "He said something today that made me think. He said I deserve to be happy. To marry you and start my own family."

I pull her into my lap, and she straddles my thighs as she wraps her arms around my neck.

"That's exactly what I plan to do, baby. And I know I should wait. Hell, you're still legally married to another man. But I can't."

I palm her backside and carry her into our room and set her on the edge of the bed. Then, I go to my suitcase and pull out the ring box I packed.

"I've been carrying this with me everywhere in case the perfect moment arose," I tell her. "But I've realized that there will never be a perfect moment, and I don't want to wait any longer."

I get down on one knee and look up into her soulful blue eyes. "I need you to know how much I love you and that I want to spend the rest of our lives together. I know you can't marry me until you're divorced, but this ring symbolizes so much more than just marriage."

I pop it open, and the diamond glitters in the light. "This ring symbolizes my commitment to you and your daughter. I love you both and want to spend my life taking care of you, the same way you take care of Addie and me. I want you to look at this ring on your finger and know that you're loved unconditionally. That you have a family. You're not alone anymore, and no matter what happens, you have me."

"Ryder," Kira breathes, swiping a tear from her cheek.

"I love you, and I want to make you mine in every way I can. Kira Miller, will you wear my ring and one day marry me?"

I barely finish before she's nodding and jumping into my arms. I tumble back onto the floor, and she straddles my hips, landing on top of me, giggling with happiness.

"Yes, Ryder," she says through her laughter. "Yes, I'll marry you."

I grab her left hand and push the ring onto her finger, taking a moment to admire it on her hand. "The sales associate said it's a pear cut," I tell her. "But when I saw it, all I could think of was that I wanted to put this ring on your finger and make you happy every day for the rest of your life. The ring reminded me of a teardrop, and I want this to be the only tear you wear." I chuckle, hearing myself. "I know that sounds cheesy but—"

"No," Kira says. "It doesn't sound cheesy at all. I love it, and I love what it represents. I spent many days trying to be tough for Violet, only to spend my nights crying ... until I met you. I never knew love could feel this good, and I hope five, ten, hell, twenty years from now, it still feels like this."

"It will," I promise, sitting up on my elbows so our faces are close. "It will because we'll work every day to make sure it does."

I wrap my fingers around the back of her neck and pull her face down to mine. Our mouths fuse, and our tongues unite. I kiss her hard and deep, hoping to convey every emotion I feel for this woman, knowing nothing I do or say will be enough. That's how much I love her.

Our clothes quickly come off, and then Kira is sinking onto my cock right here on the floor. We kiss while I massage her clit, and as she rides me with everything she has, I whisper against her lips how much I love her and can't wait to marry her. And as I come deep inside her warmth, I remind her that I'm going to give her the entire fucking world. And unlike the asshole who lured her in with false promises, I mean it—starting with making sure she gets that goddamn divorce as soon as possible so she can put that entire fucked-up situation behind her.

"Guess what today is." Violet skips into my office and grins.

"Um …" I put my finger on my chin and pretend

to think hard. "Wednesday?"

"No, silly!" She giggles. "Today is—"

"Your birthday!" I finish before she can. "How old are you now? Seventeen?"

"No!" She laughs again. "I'm five! And you know what that means? I get to go to school!"

"It does," I agree.

I was supposed to work at the office today, but I took off to spend the day with Violet for her birthday. We're planning a barbeque this weekend, but since today is her actual birthday, I wanted to be here to make it special.

"Mommy and Addie are still asleep." She shrugs. "Guess we gotta celebrate my birthday without them."

I chuckle and glance at the time. It's only six in the morning. She must've woken up early, excited for her birthday.

"I think your mom would be very sad if we celebrated your birthday without her, but since they're asleep, what do you say we go to the doughnut shop and pick out your favorites for your birthday? And while we're there, we can get some for them as well."

"Yes!" Violet cheers.

After leaving a note for Kira, in case she wakes up while we're gone, we take off to the doughnut shop in town. The entire way, Violet talks about how excited she is for school.

Since Kira gave me the green light to get her enrolled

in the private school nearby, I'm planning on contacting them this week. The wait list is over two years long, but it's nothing my last name, along with a generous donation, won't take care of.

I used to be ashamed to use my last name, thinking it meant I accepted the shit my father had pulled, but then Gramps reminded me that my last name was his before it was my father's and I deserved to use it just as much as my brother and father. I don't use it often, but for Violet to attend the best school in our area, you can bet your ass I will.

When we arrive downtown, I find a parking spot and then take Violet's hand in mine and walk us over to the doughnut shop. While we're walking and she's talking, something strange comes over me. I glance around, feeling like we're being watched, but when I don't see anyone, I chalk it up to paranoia.

It's been five days since Brian was given the divorce papers, and we haven't heard anything yet. He has thirty days to respond, and I wouldn't put it past him to wait until the last second to do so. I have an ace up my sleeve that will force his hand, but I'm holding on to it until it's needed.

We're standing in the long line that wraps around the corner when Violet moves closer to me and stops talking. I glance down at her, and she looks nervous. My paternal instincts kick in, and I move her to the other side of me.

"You okay?" I murmur so only she can hear me.

"I think I saw Brian," she whispers, her eyes wide with fear.

Normally, I'd assume she saw someone like him, but since Kira filed for divorce and he knows the major city we live near, I wouldn't put it past him to find out exactly where she lives. I was hoping it would be harder for him to find them, but when you have money, you can make shit happen. I know that firsthand. Which is exactly why I hired security for the girls. Because I'm not taking any chances.

"Come here."

I lift her into my arms, and she holds on to my neck like it's a lifeline while I glance around, trying to find him. I've only seen a few pictures of him, but I made it a point to memorize what he looked like to be on the safe side.

"Do you still see him?" I ask a few minutes later.

Violet lifts her head and looks around, then shakes it.

Hopefully, she was wrong, and it wasn't him that she saw, but I'm not taking a chance. So, until we're inside, I carry her, and only once we're in front of the counter do I put her down so she can pick out her doughnuts. We go with a dozen, plus chocolate milk for her and Addie, and once I've paid, we take our goodies home.

When we step inside, Kira is standing in the foyer with Addie on her hip and tons of balloons and presents waiting for Violet—and all thoughts of Brian are pushed aside.

"Are these all for me?" Violet shrieks.

"Yep," Kira says, smiling at her daughter and then at me.

Last night, I insisted on picking up balloons for today. We talked about putting them in her room for when she woke up, but she woke up too early.

"Can I open the presents?" Violet asks.

"How about we eat breakfast first?" I suggest, knowing Kira will need coffee. "Then presents."

"Okay! Addie, look what I got us." Violet shows Addie her chocolate milk, and she squeals in delight.

We eat our breakfast, and then Violet opens her presents. Kira bought her a new bike that she's been wanting as well as a cute vanity for her to put on her play makeup. She also got her some cute clothes and a couple of dolls.

When she gets to the last present, Kira eyes me in confusion since I didn't tell her that I was buying Violet anything. The present says it's from the both of us though because I don't want Violet to think her mom wasn't part of it.

"Oh my God!" Violet yells, tearing the paper. "It's an iPad!" Violet drops the box on the table and runs over to give her mom a hug. "Thank you, Mommy! This is the best present ever." Once she's hugged her, she comes my way and wraps her arms around me. "This is the best birthday ever."

I clean up Addie's sticky fingers while Kira helps Violet open the box. When she asks if it works like Kira's phone, I let them know that I've added it to my plan so it has data and can be used anywhere. It's an iPad mini, so it's the perfect size for her little hands.

Kira shoots me a look of awe and disbelief, and I simply shrug. I warned her that I planned to spoil them, and I meant it. Violet might not be my blood, but just like Kira, she's mine to take care of. And that's exactly what I'm going to do.

Twenty-Five

KIRA

"Violet, let's go!"

"Okay," Violet says, jumping up from the couch. "I need to grab my iPad!"

It's been two weeks since Ryder surprised us both with the device, and I have a feeling I'm going to have to set some limits on it. Luckily, she'll be starting school full-time soon, and she'll be busy. I wanted to chide Ryder for purchasing something so expensive, but the smile on my daughter's face stopped me. To him, it wasn't about the cost, but about making her birthday memorable and all about her.

We went to the park so she could ride her new bike, and when we got home, I made her favorite dinner. We had her favorite cake for dessert, and then we played her favorite games before bed. And even though Ryder insisted on paying for everything, it felt good to know that I had more than enough money in the bank to provide it all for her myself.

When the weekend came around, our friends came over to celebrate Violet's birthday again. We spent the day in the pool, and Ryder rented a bounce house. We grilled burgers, and afterward, we sang "Happy Birthday" to her again with everyone cheering. I took pictures, and then I did something I hadn't done since I ran away—I texted them to my mom.

I spoke to Ryder about it when he mentioned Violet had thought she saw Brian, and we decided that I was done hiding. My relationship with my mom was barely hanging on by a thread as it was. That night, I called her, and we spoke for a long time. I thanked her for everything she had done to help me escape and told her about my new life in Texas. She asked when she could see us, and I promised that once things settled down, I would get her a flight to come visit.

"Mommy!" Addie squeals, lifting her arms so I can pick her up.

We've been home the past week since I've been nervous about leaving, but the girls are getting a bit antsy, so when Marie asked to meet up again, I gave in. Jacob, my bodyguard, will be driving us and will stay close—but not so close that it's obvious—in case Brian shows up.

We meet at the coffee shop, and Marie hugs me,

saying it feels like we haven't seen each other in forever.

"I know! It's been crazy. Between serving my ex with divorce papers, going away for the Fourth of July, and—"

Before I can finish my sentence, Marie grabs the hand I was waving in the air and gasps, "Are you ... engaged?"

"I am," I gush.

"But you're still married."

The tone in her voice instantly puts me on the defense.

"I know, but that's only because of Brian. Once he signs the papers, I'll legally be divorced, and Ryder and I can get married."

"Mommy, can we go to the park?" Violet asks.

"Sure." I look at Marie. "Would you like to join us?"

"Of course. It's a beautiful day out."

I give the girls their chocolate milk, and we walk outside toward the park with Jacob following far enough behind us that I don't have to explain anything to Marie.

When we get to the kiddie play area, Violet jumps out of the stroller and runs straight for the slide while Addie says, "Out, *pease*!" so I can help her out.

I've only just picked her up, and I am about to place her on her feet when a masculine voice that still haunts my nightmares speaks my name, making me spin around.

"Brian," I gasp. "What are you doing here?"

"It's time to come home," he says, his voice calm, like he didn't beat the crap out of me and then throw me down a flight of stairs and leave me for dead. Like I didn't file a restraining order against him and run away the moment I found out he was going to get away with what he'd done.

"You've been playing games long enough," he continues, his eyes—the same color as Ryder's yet so different—locking on me. While Ryder's hazel eyes are warm and comforting, filled with love, Brian's are cold and devoid of any emotion.

He reaches out to grab my arm, saying, "Get your daughter, and let's go," and I stumble back with Addie in my arms.

I've come a long way from the woman I was when I was with him, and I won't allow him to touch me in any way. He lost that right the moment he hurt me, and that will never happen again.

Sensing my distress, Addie whimpers, "Mommy," and instinctually, I tighten my hold on her.

"Don't come any closer!" I demand just as Jacob steps between us.

"That's enough," he says to Brian, who looks shocked to see another man defending me.

He must've followed me here, but since Jacob kept his distance, Brian didn't realize I wasn't alone.

"Who the fuck are you?" Brian hisses. "Holy shit, Kira, you're really whoring yourself out, huh? First the accountant and now him."

Oh my God, he's been following us—or at the very least, he had me investigated. Which makes sense since he found me here.

"Mommy!" Violet screams, running to my side. "You get away from my mommy!" she yells.

"I'm going to tell you one more time," Jacob says. "Either leave or I'm calling the cops. You're already breaking your restraining order. You can leave without causing a scene, or we can do this with a scene. It's up to you."

"Mommy, Mommy!" Addie whines, trying to get my attention.

"Shh, it's okay, Monkey," I murmur, refusing to take my eyes off Brian. I don't trust that man not to do something stupid, and my only goal right now is to make sure Violet and Addie are safe.

Brian glares at me for several seconds, but he must realize this isn't going to end how he wants because he nods once and raises his hands. "Fine. But this isn't over."

With his threat lingering in the air, he turns and walks away, leaving me shaking like a leaf.

I sit on the bench with Addie in my lap and Violet by my side. "It's okay," I tell them both, needing to say the words out loud to calm myself down.

"Kira," Marie says, reminding me that she's still here since she hasn't said a word this entire time, "what is going on?"

"That was my ex," I choke out. "Brian."

"It sounds like he's very much still in love with you."

I whip my head around to look at her. "Excuse me? No, he's crazy and abusive." My hands and voice are shaky, but I'm doing everything I can to hold it together, not wanting to upset the girls.

"Or he's desperate," she volleys. "Love makes people do crazy things."

Remembering everything Marie has told me about her ex, I inhale a deep breath, realizing that maybe she's been through more than I know. Because there's no way anyone in their right mind would say that everything Brian has done to me was out of love.

"Do you think maybe things are going too quickly?" she asks. "You're still married, and yet you're engaged to another man, and his daughter is calling you Mom. I'm worried about you."

Marie places a hand on my elbow that's meant to be comforting, but mixed with her words, it's anything but. She's had a problem with Ryder from the first time we met, and now, even after knowing Brian was abusive, she's trying to convince me to … what? Go back to him?

"I think you should consider getting your own place," she continues. "What's your email? I can send you some listings. I have a friend who works in real estate."

She pulls out her phone, and all I want to do is get away from here—from her. But since I don't want more conflict, I rattle off my email and then stand so I can make my escape.

"I'm going to go," I tell her. "The girls and I are shaken up, and I think it's best if we go home."

"Okay," she says, standing as well. "If you need anything, I'm here. And I'll send you those listings tonight. I know you believe being with Ryder is the right thing for you, but I think you should consider your options. You don't want to move too fast and—"

"I get it!" I snap, having had enough of her. "Jacob, can we go now?"

"Wait," Marie says, eyeing the guy curiously. "Who is that?"

"The man Ryder hired to protect me. I need to go." Without waiting for her to respond, I set Addie into the stroller while Violet climbs in, and then we take off.

Thankfully, Jacob is driving because I don't think I'd be able to. When we get home, Ryder's car is in the driveway, and he's waiting for us by the front door.

Since I haven't told him what happened yet, I glance at Jacob, who says, "I texted him once your ex was gone."

"Thank you," I murmur. "And thank you for what you did."

"It's my job, ma'am. I'll also be filing a report, so you'll have to do so as well. That way, it's on record."

"Of course. Thank you."

I get out, and Ryder is already at my door, pulling me into his arms.

"Fuck, baby," he mutters. "When he texted me, my heart sank at the thought of that asshole being anywhere near you and our girls."

"You did the right thing, hiring Jacob. I was so scared, and if he wasn't there, I don't know what Brian would've done. But he was."

While Ryder grabs Addie, I get Violet. Since it's nap time, we lay the girls down, but instead of going downstairs, I lie with Violet for a little longer, thinking about everything that transpired today.

I knew Brian would come for me. It's not in his DNA to let this go. That would be the equivalent of him losing, and men like him don't like to lose.

One of the reasons why I left my mom behind was so that he would leave her alone. Now, instead of it only affecting me and Violet, I've dragged Ryder and his precious daughter into the mix.

"Hey, you okay?" Ryder whispers, sticking his head inside.

I glance at a sleeping Violet and nod, then carefully climb off her bed and meet Ryder outside the door.

"I thought maybe you fell asleep in there," he says, taking my hand and guiding us over to his room.

"I was just thinking," I tell him honestly.

He lies on the bed and pulls me into his arms.

"About what?"

"Us ... Brian."

Ryder quirks a brow and sits up slightly. "What about us?"

"He's not going to stop, and I don't want this to affect you and Addie."

He sits up all the way and pulls me into his lap, encircling his arms around my waist, and I swear I've never felt as safe as I do when I'm this close to Ryder.

"We're in this together," he says, tipping my chin so I'll look at him. "We'll handle it together. Don't go putting ridiculous thoughts into that beautiful head of yours. I'm here because I want to be, and I don't want to be anywhere else. Him breaking the restraining order only helps our case. You and Violet and Addie are safe, and you'll stay that way."

He flips us so I'm on my back, and his mouth meets mine, kissing me so hard that it takes my breath away. Quickly, our clothes are removed, and then Ryder's lips are back on mine, sucking, licking, nibbling.

He parts my thighs and pushes his fingers into me, his mouth never leaving mine as he fingers me hard and deep. Unlike when he makes love to me, he's ravenous, desperate, and I know that despite him promising to keep us safe, he's scared ... of something happening to us, of me leaving him. Of the entire situation being out of his control.

"Hey," I say, palming the sides of his face. "I'm not

going anywhere. I'm staying right here with you and Addie. We're in this together."

He sighs in relief and nods. "Together," he murmurs before kissing me again.

His thumb finds my clit, and he massages it with just enough pressure that, within seconds, I'm climaxing around his hand.

He waits for me to ride out my orgasm, and then he spreads my legs with one hand while gripping his hard shaft with the other. He strokes it a few times and then pushes it into me.

Instead of fucking me, he watches as his thick shaft slowly enters me, filling me deliciously, and then pulls out, taking my pleasure with it.

"Ryder," I breathe, lifting my hips, "I need you inside me now."

He drops down, his hands landing on either side of me, and then pushes into me, this time not stopping until he's all the way in. His mouth devours mine, tasting me, while his body moves against mine in a slow rhythm, coaxing another orgasm out of me.

This time, when my release hits, Ryder comes as well, his cum coating my insides.

"Soon," he whispers into my mouth. "Soon, you're going to take that fucking implant out so I can fill you with my babies."

When Brian used to talk about me getting pregnant—not knowing that I was on birth control—I'd get nervous, the thought of another man leaving me while I parented on my own in the forefront of my thoughts. But when Ryder says it, I can imagine it. Him spoiling me, being a hands-on dad and husband. Family trips and holidays. Watching our children grow up together.

"Soon," I agree, realizing that Ryder's so much more than just my fiancé—he's my best friend.

And I know when he said we were in this together, he meant it. And I have no doubt that when we take the next step, he'll be right by my side.

Twenty-Six

RYDER

"Did you see?" Kira says, appearing in my office out of nowhere. "Violet got in!" She runs over and jumps into my lap, wrapping her arms around my neck. "Thank you for taking care of that."

She peppers kisses all over my face, and my heart warms at how easy it is to make her happy.

"I need to fill out the forms and email them over to them. Can I use your laptop?"

She bats her pretty lashes, and I chuckle.

"Of course. You know, if you want one of your own—"

"My phone is fine," she says, shaking her head. "And since you don't mind me using yours…"

"Not at all." I lift her and then stand, setting her back down on my seat. "You fill out the paperwork while I start lunch."

Since I'm home today, we're grilling and spending the afternoon in the pool.

I lean over and give her what's supposed to be a chaste kiss, but it quickly turns heated.

"Later," I murmur. "I need to get the grill going."

"Fine." She pouts playfully. "Later."

With one more kiss, I head out of my office and down to the kitchen to get lunch started, noting to wake the girls up soon from their nap.

It's been a little over a week since Brian showed up and we filed a police report on him. Our attorney is going through the proper channels to have it investigated since it's our word versus his and he's got an alibi, saying he was in his home state—nowhere near Kira—when the report was filed. The asshole thinks he's smart, but I have the money and means to make sure he doesn't get away with this.

I'VE JUST FINISHED MAKING THE BURGER PATTIES, AND I'm firing up the grill when Kira and Violet come down the stairs.

"Hey," Kira says, leaning over the plate I'm holding and giving me a quick kiss. "Patties look good."

"Did you finish filling out the paperwork?" I ask.

"Almost. Violet woke up, so I figured I'd make the

side dishes and finish the paperwork after dinner." Kira glances at her daughter. "Want to help me make the mac 'n' cheese?"

"Yes!" Violet exclaims. "Can we make it double cheesy?"

"Of course." Kira taps Violet's nose, and the two of them disappear into the kitchen.

I turn the grill on and scrub the grates while it heats up. Once it's ready, I place the patties on the heat and close the lid.

I head back inside to check on the girls, but when I get into the kitchen, it's empty. My phone rings, and I pull it out of my pocket, seeing Kira's name and picture on my screen.

"Are you calling me from inside the house?" I laugh.

"No." She laughs back. "We were out of bacon for the mac 'n' cheese, so we ran to the store. I pulled into the parking lot and realized I didn't tell you. Sorry, my mind is all over the place."

"It's okay. But you shouldn't have left without me. You don't have Jacob with you."

Since I was working from home, I told him I'd call him when we needed him. There's no point in him hanging out outside the house.

"Oh shit," she hisses. "I'm sorry. I didn't even think. I'm already here. I'll just run in and out."

"Okay, but stay on the phone with me," I insist.

I hear Kira turn off the car and speak to Violet

about taking her hand so they can hurry. The sound of the wind from her walking through the parking lot fills the silence, followed by the opening and closing of the store doors.

Some would say I'm being paranoid and over the top, but when it comes to my girls, I'm not taking any chances.

"Oh, hey," I hear Kira say. "Yeah, just grabbing some bacon." There's shuffling and another voice, and then Kira says, "Hey, Ryder, I just ran into Marie. Let me call you right back."

Not wanting to sound like a crazy person, I agree and then stare at my phone, waiting for her to call me back.

I remember that the meat is still on the grill, so I run out and flip the patties.

Still no call back.

When the burgers are done, I plate them and turn off the grill, then head back inside.

But she still hasn't called me back.

Ten minutes later, Addie wakes up from her nap, so I grab her and change her diaper and then call Kira—because what the fuck?

Her phone doesn't ring, instead going straight to voice mail, so I call again and again. After the third time, I start to freak out, so I pull up the Find My app on my phone and click on Kira's name. It shows she's at a park, which makes no damn sense.

I try to call her again, but it continues to go to voice mail. So, I do the only thing I can think of and go in search of her.

After strapping Addie into her car seat, I take off down the road, following the tracker the best I can. Fifteen minutes later, we pull into the park, and the tracker takes me toward the back, where there's a lake.

My heart is pounding against my rib cage, telling me that something is wrong. Shit's not adding up. How the hell did she go from the store to the park? And why would she do that?

I click Refresh, but it still shows she's here. And then the status changes to Unknown, making my gut clench. This makes no sense.

I get out with Addie and walk toward the lake, and that's when I notice tire tracks in the dirt. I'm not an investigator, but I find it weird that a car would drive straight toward the lake, the tracks disappearing into the water.

I don't know what's going on, but something's wrong, and I'm not going to waste my time trying to figure it out on my own. Instead, I call the police and explain what happened.

An hour later, they're pulling my fiancée's SUV out of the water. Julian picked up Addie because she was hungry and cranky, and I was freaking out—still fucking am.

"Sir, there's no one in the vehicle," the officer says.

"And the inspection camera hasn't located any bodies in the lake."

"Then, where the hell are they?" I yell because it's not every day your fiancée's vehicle gets pulled out of the fucking lake.

Don't get me wrong—I'm thankful as fuck they're not in the vehicle, but we still have no idea where they are.

He shakes his head. "We're having a team search the area, but there's no sign of struggle from the vehicle. It looks like someone left the keys in and let it roll in."

"This doesn't make sense! Her phone showed they were here."

"And her phone has been recovered. It was in the vehicle. But they aren't here. Is there any reason she would want you to think she disappeared?"

I open my mouth to say that she would never do that, but then it hits me.

"Brian," I hiss. "Her ex. She has a restraining order on him because he assaulted her. She went into the grocery store and … Marie!"

The officer is looking at me like I've lost my mind, so I explain, "Kira and Violet went into the grocery store, and she ran into her friend Marie. She might know what happened to her." Except I don't know her last name or phone number.

"If you know her login information, you can log in to her phone from yours," the officer explains.

"Everything is saved on the cloud."

Oh shit. He's right.

"I need to file a missing persons report for Kira and her daughter."

"We can do that. Why don't you go home and see what you can find out about that friend of hers, and an officer will meet you at the house to file the report?"

"Thank you," I choke out, knowing deep down that something is wrong.

Kira would never leave without telling me, which means someone took her. And based on the scene in front of me, they were hoping to either make it look like suicide or steer me in the wrong direction long enough to get her out of town.

Fuck! I promised Kira that I would keep her and Violet safe, and I've fucking failed.

When I get home, I wake the computer up, hoping since Kira was working on it last, I can figure out what her login information is. I minimize the screen with the school forms, and another screen pops up—her email. I look at the most recent one that's opened and see an email from Marie but no last name. It has a list of available properties to rent in Houston.

What the actual fuck?

For a second, my heart stutters, and I think the worst—I was wrong. She left me. But then I remember who Kira is, and I know damn well she would never do that. If she didn't want to be with me, she would tell me. She wouldn't take off to go get fucking bacon and not come back, and she sure as hell wouldn't drive her car into the lake.

I don't know why she has an email full of properties for rent, but I have no doubt there's a reason, and once I get my fiancée and her daughter back home, we'll discuss it.

I do a search and find an email she sent to herself with usernames and passwords. I copy and paste them and send them to myself.

I'm trying to log out and log in when the doorbell rings out through the house. Assuming it's the officer, I run downstairs, but when I swing the door open, I find Nora standing on the other side. She's dressed differently than she used to—in a pair of jeans and a flowy top—and her hair is darker and one color, the highlights completely gone. Whereas she used to scream money, she now looks normal.

"What are you doing here?"

"I want my family back."

Jesus fucking Christ, this can't be happening right now.

"How the hell did you get through the gate?"

"You put it as our daughter's birth date." She rolls her eyes. "It wasn't difficult to figure out."

She steps through the door, and I lift my hand to stop her.

"*My* daughter, not yours," I point out.

"That's why I'm here," she says, stepping closer to

me. "I made a mistake, Ryder. I miss you."

She presses her hand to my chest, and I swipe it away, moving out of her touch.

"I can't do this right now. My fiancée and her daughter are missing, and I need to find them."

"No, what you need to do is focus on your family. Kira is obviously focusing on hers."

The fact that she knows my fiancée's name has me taking a step toward her.

"What the hell did you just say? And how do you know Kira's name?"

"I know a lot more than you think," she says with a shrug.

Her nonchalant response sends a chill straight up my spine. Something is off... a lot of fucking *somethings*, and I have a suspicion that, somehow, my psycho fucking ex is caught up in the middle of it all.

Stalking toward her, I reach out and slam my front door closed, and then I wrap my fingers around her neck, pushing her against the wall. "Tell me how the fuck you know my fiancée's name! She's missing, Nora!" I tighten my hold on her enough to make it clear my threat is real. "I swear to God, if you had something to do with that, I will make you pay."

"She's not missing," she chokes out. "She's back where she belongs. She left with her husband because they're a family."

"She wouldn't do that."

"Yes, she would!" she screeches, making me flinch. "She belongs with him, just like I belong with you. I messed up, but I can fix it. I can be a good wife, I promise. I can be a better mom than her! I was just struggling, but I've fixed everything."

My blood turns cold, and the worst feeling passes through me.

"Nora, what did you do?" I ask, trying to remain calm because killing her won't get me answers.

"Did you know she's still married?" she hisses, ignoring my question. "She was never yours. She's his, just like you're mine."

"Nora…" Fuck, all the pieces are clicking into place, and I'm not liking the picture they're creating at all. "Tell me you didn't do something you can't take back."

"Adeline was calling her mom!" she cries. "She's not her mom! I am. This house is mine! You're mine! The money is mine!"

And then it hits me…

"Are you Marie?"

She smirks. "That bitch is too trusting."

Fuck. Fuck. Fuck.

Now, it all makes sense.

"Where is she?" I ask, tightening my hold on her a little more, done with this bullshit.

My ex-wife is off her fucking rocker, and she's the reason Kira and Violet are missing.

"Where she belongs. With her husband!"

"He's abusive!" I yell, losing my cool and slamming my hand against the wall beside her head. "If you handed her over to him—"

A knock on the door cuts me off, and I rush over to it, swinging it open and praying it's Kira even though she would never knock.

It's not her though. It's two police officers in uniform.

"Ryder Du Ponte," one of them says. "My name is Officer Glen, and this is Officer Remington. We're here to file a missing persons report on a"—he glances down at his phone—"Kira and Violet Miller."

"Her last name is Williams!" Nora says, further confirming that she knows who my fiancée is and is most likely responsible for her being taken. "She's married and with her husband."

The officer glances from her to me in confusion.

"Kira has a restraining order on him," I explain. "His name is Brian Williams. If she's with him, it's against her will and even more imperative that we find them as soon as possible. I have reason to believe that my ex-wife has something to do with it."

"Stop worrying about her!" Nora screams. "She's not yours. She's his! I'm yours. Focus on me."

"Let me tell you something," I say, grabbing her arm and pulling her toward me. "If I find out that you had anything to do with Kira's disappearance, I'm going to make sure you rot in prison."

I shove her toward Officer Remington. "She's trespassing. We have a legal agreement stating that she's not allowed to come within five hundred feet of my residence. I want her arrested. And if you don't believe me, I can show you proof."

I pull up the restraining order on my phone, and as I do so, Nora tries to run. Before she can make it to the door though, I slam it shut, refusing to let her get away.

The officer approaches her, letting her know that he's going to take her to the station, and when she smacks him in the face, he pulls her hands behind her back and says she's under arrest for assaulting an officer.

Once she's gone, Officer Glen says, "Do you have any idea where your fiancée could be?"

"No." I shake my head. "Her phone and car ended up at the bottom of the fucking lake."

"Maybe she has another device," he suggests. "An Apple Watch or—"

"The iPad!" *Fuck! Why didn't I think of that sooner?* "Violet never goes anywhere without her iPad mini, and it's trackable."

I pull out my phone and scroll down. And sure enough, her iPad mini is on my list since it's on my account.

"It's showing she's about thirty minutes north of here." I turn my phone around so the officer can see it. "I need to get to them. With her car in the lake, someone had to have taken them there, and I have no idea if they're okay."

"We can get a team together," the officer says. "If her ex is armed, you don't want to just barge in there."

"Okay," I say, snatching up my keys. "Then, let's do this."

On the way, I contact Kira's attorney to let her know what happened. She lets me know that if Brian took her, he's fucked. The charges that she'll throw at him will send him to prison for years. Then, I call Julian to check on Addie and update him.

"Nora is Marie?" Ana gasps.

"She all but confirmed it," I tell them. "Marie is her middle fucking name. It didn't even click into my head. I feel so fucking stupid."

"Fuck that," Julian says. "Nobody would have thought like that unless they were as crazy as she is."

"It makes sense," Ana says. "She bailed every time I was there. She knew I'd recognize her in a heartbeat."

"She changed her hair color and dresses less high-class, but, yeah, if you saw her, you'd recognize her. Only Kira's never seen her because I have no pictures of her in the house. Fuck!" I slam my fist against the steering wheel. "If something's happened to either of them …"

"They're going to be okay," Ana says. "Just stay positive."

"I was supposed to keep them safe," I murmur. "I failed."

"Nobody could've expected any of this to happen," Julian says. "The important thing is that you know where they are, and you'll get to them before anything goes down."

We hang up, and I focus on following the tracking information for the iPad. The police officers took down the location as well, but I can't stop watching it in case they move. It's my only shot at getting to them.

The tracking app takes us down a dirt road off the beaten path, and we end up in front of an older house. Officer Glen has me park down the road, not wanting to alert anyone that we're here. He wants me to hang back, but I refuse. If something's wrong with my girls, I need to be there. This is all my damn fault. I took them into my home and promised I would keep them safe. And I've failed.

I wait by the bushes, so as not to give them away, while they quietly surround the perimeter. I don't know what's happening, but after several minutes, one of the officers knocks the door in, and several guys rush in.

A few minutes later, an officer comes over and says, "We found the suspect in the kitchen. He's been injured, and we've called for an ambulance. We did a full sweep of the house, and it's empty."

"What? That doesn't make sense." I run toward the house and inside, not giving a shit about anything but finding Kira and Violet.

The second I see Brian lying on the ground, blood

oozing out of his head, I push past the officers and grab him by his shirt.

"Where the hell are they?" I demand.

"That bitch damn near killed me," he slurs. "I need help. She drugged me."

"Where are they?"

"Hopefully dead in the fucking woods."

I throw him back onto the floor and go in search of Kira and Violet. When I spot Violet's mini backpack, it confirms they've been here, and for her not to take it with them means Kira probably acted quickly, and then they ran out.

"Don't touch it," an officer says behind me. "It's evidence."

"I'm going to look for them," I say. "They have to be somewhere."

And who the hell knows if they're okay? It's late, and it's pitch-black outside. They must be terrified.

Twenty-Seven

KIRA
EARLIER TODAY

"Oh shoot. We don't have any bacon."

"We can't have mac 'n' cheese without bacon," Violet says.

"C'mon. We'll run to the store."

While I grab my keys off the hook, Violet grabs her mini backpack she brings everywhere she goes, and we take off toward the store.

I'm just pulling into the parking lot when I remember I left without telling Ryder.

"Are you calling me from inside the house?" he says with a laugh when he answers.

"No." I laugh back. "We were out of bacon for the mac 'n' cheese, so we ran to the store. I pulled into the parking lot and realized I didn't tell you. Sorry, my mind is all over the place."

Between Violet getting signed up for school, filing for divorce, and Brian showing up, my head feels like it's going to explode.

"It's okay," Ryder says. "But you shouldn't have left without me. You don't have Jacob with you."

"Oh shit," I breathe, having completely forgotten that I'm not supposed to go anywhere without someone to protect us. "I'm sorry. I didn't even think. I'm already here. I'll just run in and out."

We're already at the store, so it would be dumb to go all the way back, just to have Ryder come back out to get it.

"Okay, but stay on the phone with me," Ryder insists, reminding me why I love this man.

Growing up, I thought it was normal for men to be selfish. They would take and take from my mom, and I assumed that was just how it was. Especially since both Raymond and Brian were the same way.

But Ryder is different. He puts those he loves before himself. And I want to get to the point where I can do that as well. I feel like he does so much for us, and I want to do that for him as well. He always says that me loving him is enough, but it doesn't feel like it is.

Violet and I get out of the car, and I take her hand in mine so she stays close to me. The phone is to my ear, but I'm not talking to Ryder, wanting to be aware of my surroundings.

"Look, Mommy! It's Marie."

"It is," I say as Marie walks over. "Grocery shopping?" I ask to be polite.

"Yeah," she says. "You?"

"Just grabbing some bacon."

"Did you look at the listings I sent you?"

Not wanting Ryder to hear this conversation, I let him know I've run into Marie and that I'll call him right back.

I pocket my phone and sigh. "Marie, I appreciate everything you're trying to do, but I'm not looking to move out. I love Ryder, and he loves me. We're engaged, and once I'm divorced, we'll be getting married."

Marie's jaw clenches. "I really wish you had listened," she says. "Don't say I didn't warn you."

Without waiting for me to respond, she stalks down the aisle, leaving me wondering what the hell is going on.

Taking Violet's hand in mine once again, I quickly find the bacon and check out, wanting to get back home.

We're almost to the car when Marie pulls up and gets out.

"Hey, Kira," she says. "About earlier."

I stop to hear her out, but that's a mistake because I'm not paying attention to my surroundings, and before I know what's happening, a pair of strong hands grabs me from behind. I try to scream, but a cloth is shoved into my mouth to muffle the sound.

I'm thrown into the back seat, along with my daughter, whose hands are restrained. She screams at the top of her lungs, and Marie leans in and stuffs her mouth with a cloth.

"Shut up, you fucking brat!" she hisses.

I can't speak because my mouth is stuffed, but I look at her in utter shock, confused as to why she's doing this.

"They're good to go," Marie says to …

Oh my God. The man who restrained me gets into the front seat, and his hazel eyes meet mine.

Brian.

Marie is working with Brian. But why?

"Next time you want to steal another woman's husband, make sure you know whose husband you're trying to steal."

With a glacial glare, Marie slams the door, and Brian takes off while I'm left even more confused. Whose husband was I trying to steal? Ryder? He's not married … right? There's no way he would be creating a life with us if he were still married. He told me he was divorced. That Addie's mom wanted nothing to do with them. Late at night, when we were whispering our truths in bed, he told me he paid her millions of dollars, and she walked away, signing away her rights to that precious little girl.

Could she be Nora, Ryder's ex and Addie's bio mom?

I think back to all the times we met for coffee. The

way she was pushing for me to take things slow. And the first time she said Addie's name ... oh my God! She called her Adeline.

There's no way the woman I befriended is none other than Ryder's ex-wife and egg donor. That would be too much of a coincidence—unless it wasn't.

Oh God. I suddenly feel sick. All the times I confided in her about Brian, thinking she was my friend. She was gaining information to use against me. She was never my friend. She just wanted me out of the way so she could get her family back.

Bile rises in my throat, but I swallow it back down, not wanting to throw up with a cloth in my mouth. I glance up at Brian, but he's not saying a word, focusing on driving.

Since I can't speak to Violet to comfort her, I make eye contact with her and then nod for her to scoot closer. She edges as close to me as she can and then rests her head on my shoulder. I use my chin and the side of my face to try to soothe her the best I can while I watch the road, trying to figure out where Brian is taking us.

It would be a long drive all the way back to his house, and would he really be dumb enough to bring us there? He must know that Ryder is going to come looking for us. When I don't call him back or show up at the house, he's going to go in search of us.

I try to reach into my back pocket for my phone since my hands are restrained behind my back but instantly realize I don't have it. Either Brian or Marie must've taken it from me. Hopefully, Brian has it so Ryder can track us, but I doubt they didn't consider this. If Marie and Brian have been working together from the beginning, that means they've been planning this for months so they had time to think about everything.

The drive ends sooner than I expected at an old wood cabin in the middle the woods. I tried to follow the signs and turns, but at some point, the asphalt road turned into dirt, and the signs disappeared.

"Don't even think about running," Brian says, glaring at me in the rearview mirror. "There's nothing but woods surrounding us. You'll get lost and eaten by an animal before you're ever found."

I don't know if he's just saying that to scare us or if it's true, but it's something I'll consider when Violet and I escape. Because we will escape. My hope is that Ryder will find us, but if he can't, I'm going to get Violet and me out of here. I would rather risk the wildlife than be held captive by Brian.

"Let's go," he says, opening the door and pulling on my elbow.

Since I can't speak, I glare and throw my elbow so he can't touch me.

"Listen here," he says, yanking me toward him. He grips my cheeks with one hand and squeezes so hard that it hurts. "That crazy chick was going to kill you, so be a little fucking grateful that I insisted on handling you myself and don't act like a bitch."

His eyes are devoid of all emotion, and I know nothing I say will convince him to let us go, so instead, I nod once in agreement. If I want to get Violet and me out alive, I need to play nice. Messing with the hornet's nest will only get you stung.

Brian stares at me for several seconds and then nods back. He removes his fingers from my face and then leans into the car to pull Violet out. She fights him, and when he finally gets her out, her eyes are filled with tears.

I lock my eyes with hers, silently begging her to be good so he won't hurt her, and as if she understands, she calms down and goes straight to me.

"You've always babied her," Brian mutters. "Let's go."

He pushes us toward the house and then unlocks it, using a code that he doesn't hide from us. I repeat the six numbers over and over in my head in case I need them later.

When we get inside, the place is furnished, but it's not Brian's taste, telling me this isn't his house.

"It's been a long day," Brian says, closing the door, "so you're going to make us dinner, and we'll head out tomorrow morning."

I refrain from rolling my eyes. Only Brian would kidnap us and then demand I cook for him, like we're picking up right where we left off before he nearly killed me and I ran away.

"I'm going to take this out," he says, "but if you scream, it's going back in. And before you think it's because someone can hear, they can't because there's no one around to hear. I just don't want to listen to you scream when I already have a headache."

He pulls the cloth out of my mouth, and I keep my mouth shut. Then, he pulls it out of Violet's mouth, and she follows my lead. She's hiccupping from crying, but she tries so hard not to make any noise.

"Turn around," Brian says.

He unties my hands, then does the same thing for Violet.

"I missed you," he says to me. "We were supposed to be creating a life together, and you disappeared. It hurt, and I was mad, but I know you were upset as well. I lost my cool and hurt you, and I'm sorry. It'll never happen again, but you have to understand that I thought you were cheating on me, and look what happened when you left. You spread your legs for another man, like a whore."

He tenses his jaw, and I stay quiet, not wanting to say the wrong thing. Finally, he sighs and shakes his head.

"Violet, go watch TV while your mom makes dinner."

"Can I ... can I go to the bathroom?" she whispers, breaking my heart.

It's my job to keep her safe, and I've failed. Ryder told me not to go anywhere without him or security, and I messed up. Now, we're both in danger.

"Go ahead," he says. "Just keep in mind, if you do anything stupid, I'm going to have to hurt your mom. And I really don't want to do that."

Violet whimpers but nods in understanding.

Once she's in the bathroom, Brian looks at me. "You fucked up, Kira. And it's going to take some time to make things right. But hopefully, things will go back to normal soon."

This man has seriously lost his ever-loving mind if he thinks I have any intention of letting anything between us *go back to normal.*

"You can start by showing me you can still be a good wife," he continues. "There's food in the fridge. Go start dinner."

Violet comes out of the bathroom, and I smile softly at her, wanting to scoop her into my arms, but refraining because I don't want Brian to get mad and do anything stupid.

She sits on the couch, and Brian hands her the controller so she can watch TV. He sits on the couch next to her and opens his laptop. Since she seems to be relatively safe, I start on dinner while I try to think of a way out of here.

I make a simple grilled chicken dinner with steamed broccoli and rice. While we sit at the table and eat,

Brian talks about what's going on with the law firm he's a partner at, like it's a normal day. I respond when he asks me questions, not wanting to upset him, and quietly encourage Violet to eat because I know she must be starved.

After dinner, I do the dishes and then give Violet a bath. Brian is out in the living room, working on his laptop, so while I wash her, I whisper so only she can hear.

"You're doing so good, sweet girl. I don't know how, but I'm going to get us out of here, I promise. You just keep being good. Okay?"

She nods and then wraps her arms around me. She's wet, but I don't care. I hold her tight and whisper, "I love you more than all the stars in the sky," while she silently cries in my arms.

"I love you more than all the stars and the moon," she whispers back, "and I really miss Ryder and Addie."

"I know. I do, too, but we'll see them soon."

After her bath, I help her change into pajamas that Brian brought with him because he thought of everything, proving that this has been planned, and then I tuck her into bed. I hate that she's sleeping alone in the room, but that's what Brian said needs to happen.

"Is she sleeping?" he asks, not even bothering to look up.

Before we met Ryder, I thought it was normal for a guy to not help with bedtime or kiss his child good night. I thought it was because Violet wasn't Brian's, but now, I see that not all men are like this. Ryder says good night to Violet every night. He helps tuck her in, and he kisses her on her forehead, telling her that he loves her and to have sweet dreams.

"Yeah," I tell him, thankful that he's nothing like Ryder, which means he'll stay away from Violet because he doesn't care enough to pay her any attention.

Brian nods, then looks up at me. "Go take a shower. Wash that other man off you. Then, we can go to bed, and you can start trying to prove to me that you're not a whore."

I swallow anxiously at the thought of Brian touching me but nod in understanding, not wanting to piss him off.

"Do you have clothes for me?" I choke out.

"In the master bedroom, on the dresser."

I keep my shower quick so Violet isn't left alone for too long and then get dressed in the bedroom, thankful that Brian hasn't attempted to come in. While I'm in here, I see his luggage, and after checking to make sure he's still busy on his laptop, I search it for anything that can help me. I'm about to give up when I notice his bottle of sleeping pills in his toiletry bag. He takes them to help him sleep. Without them, he'll toss and turn all night and then have trouble focusing the next day.

Quietly, I open the bottle and pour three into my hand. He normally takes one, so three should make him pass out. Before I close the lid, I add a few more because, fuck it, if it kills him, so be it.

Since he brought my hair dryer, I use it for the noise while I crush up the pills and then push the powder into a tissue that I fold up tightly and then stick into my pocket.

When I come out, he's still working. I glance around and notice the bottle of scotch on the counter. He drinks every night while he works.

"Would you like a drink?" I ask softly, trying not to sound suspicious.

He glances up at me and smiles, and I'm reminded of why it was so easy to fall for him. Because he's a master at hiding his darkness under his disarming smiles and charming words.

"That would be great. Thanks."

I grab his glass and, without him seeing, pull the tissue out and drop the crushed pills into the bottom, then pour him three fingers, just like he likes. I mix it the best I can and pray he doesn't notice.

"Here you go," I say, handing him the drink.

He takes it from me, then pats the seat next to him. "Sit with me," he says, and I do, hoping to distract him while he drinks.

"When we get home, things are going to be different," he promises, taking a sip of his drink. "I know you ran because I'd hurt you, but next time, I need you to make better choices."

I nod robotically, wondering how someone who looks so normal can be so fucked up.

"I'm sorry," I murmur.

"I know you are," he says, patting my thigh and then running his hand up my flesh, not stopping until he's too close to the apex of my thighs.

He squeezes my leg, and I glance down at his hand, wanting to demand he take his fucking hand off me, but instead, I swallow it down and smile sweetly, praying that Violet and I make it out alive.

Brian takes another sip of his drink and types some more on his laptop while I sit obediently, watching as his drink slowly disappears.

Usually, when he takes a single pill, he passes out within thirty minutes, so I'm hoping since there are several pills, he'll pass out quicker and go into a deep sleep.

"Hey, Brian," I say, hoping to distract him and wanting some answers. "How did you meet Marie?"

"You mean Nora?" he scoffs. "Crazy bitch found me. Said she knew where you were and offered to help me bring you home." He glances over at me, his eyes glossy, telling me that the pills are working. "You really should work on who you let into your life."

Don't I fucking know it?

"I thought she was my friend," I admit.

"That's because you're far too trusting. You've seen the criminals I defend and the shit they pull. You've got to be smarter than that." He shakes his head, but it's slow because he's fading fast. "Just be glad I insisted on taking you back," he slurs. "If I hadn't, she would've taken you out."

"Well then, thank you for saving us," I bite out, trying to remain pleasant.

He opens his mouth to respond, but his eyes flutter shut and then open, as if he's struggling to stay awake. "Fuck, my head is all—"

His words stop. He looks at his drink and then to me, and my heart sinks because he knows.

"You fucking bitch!" he slurs. "What did you give me?"

He reaches for me, but I'm quicker. I jump up from the couch and run to the kitchen. I consider grabbing a knife, but instead go with the frying pan I used to make dinner. I think hitting him with it will create more of an impact than stabbing him. I've never stabbed anyone before, and if I don't take him out, he's going to come after me, and I won't win.

"Fuck!" he roars. "What did you give me?"

He comes around the corner, and without giving myself a chance to think, I swing the pan at his head, hoping it will knock him out, just like in the movies.

The first swing knocks him off-balance, but he doesn't pass out, so I do it again and again.

Brian tries to fight me, but the pills are too strong, and he's too dazed and weak to take me down. I hit him once more, and it knocks him to the floor. The side of his head is gushing out blood, and he's struggling to get up.

I'm not sure if he's going to pass out or come after me, so I throw the pan down and run to the room Violet's in. I pick her up and make a run for it out of the house.

Brian is still on the floor, trying to get up, so I run as fast as I can while holding my five-year-old, and I keep running until we're lost somewhere in the woods.

Then, I stop and look around and wonder what the hell I was thinking because we might be out, but I have no phone and no idea where we are.

Maybe choosing the woods over Brian wasn't the best idea after all.

Twenty-Eight

KIRA

"Mommy, I'm so tired," Violet whines, "and my feet hurt."

She was too heavy, so I had to put her down. But since I didn't think any of this through, we're both walking through the woods barefoot.

It's late and dark, and every time I hear a noise, I'm not sure if it's Brian or an animal—and I'm not sure which one I'd prefer it to be.

"I know, sweet girl. But we need to find a road."

She sighs, but doesn't argue, and we continue to walk.

I have no idea if we're walking toward a road or farther into the woods, and I'm scared shitless, but I'm trying to stay brave for my little girl.

I'm also worried that if the pills don't kill Brian—

which I doubt they will—and we don't get help soon, he's going to wake up and be the one to find us.

We walk for several more minutes, and then I see a flash of light come through the trees, lighting up the area.

"Mommy!" Violet gasps, having seen it as well.

"That must be where the road is," I tell her.

And if the lights were able to hit us, it must not be that far.

I guide us in the direction of where the light was with a newfound hope that we'll find the road and hopefully someone to help us while praying it's not Brian looking for us.

And then I hear a voice—the one I've been thinking about since we were taken—call out our names, and I pick Violet up and run toward it.

"Kira! Violet!"

"Ryder!" Violet and I call out at the same time.

"Ryder! We're here!" I yell.

"Ryder!" Violet screams.

"Kira! Violet!" we hear again. "Where are you?"

"Keep yelling, Ryder!" I shout. "We can hear you."

We keep calling each other's names like a horrible game of Marco Polo. And then we see him. Standing at the edge of the woods.

The second he spots us, he takes off after us and doesn't slow down until we're in his arms.

"Oh, thank God," he cries. "It's really you."

He peppers kisses all over my face while Violet stays squished between us, crying and thanking Ryder for finding us.

When he's done kissing me, he takes Violet into his arms and hugs her tightly, kissing her forehead.

"I've been looking for you guys for hours," he says, his eyes filled with tears.

"Brian took us and ..." I let my words linger, not wanting to tell him in front of Violet that I drugged Brian.

"I know. The police found him, and he's on his way to the hospital."

My heart sinks. A huge part of me hoped he would be found dead so this would all be over.

"C'mon. Let's get you girls home, where you belong."

"Wait!" Violet says. "My backpack. I left it in that house."

"I know," Ryder tells her. "It's how we were able to find you. The iPad's location was on. But we can't get it because the police need it. But I promise, tomorrow, we'll go buy you a new backpack."

"And a new iPad?" she asks.

"Whatever you want." He kisses her cheek. "I'm just so glad you're both okay. Now, let's go let the police know I found you. They have several men looking for you as well."

After we're both checked out and we answer the police's questions—and Ryder insists we answer the rest tomorrow after we've gotten some sleep—we head home.

When we walk through the door, the house feels different ... empty.

"Where's Addie?"

"She's sleeping at Julian and Ana's. I needed to focus on searching for you guys."

I nod in understanding.

We put Violet to bed, letting her know that if she's scared or she can't sleep, she can come to our room, but she's exhausted, and she falls asleep before we make it out of her room.

"I saw the properties," Ryder says when we get to our room.

Despite having already showered, I feel like I need another one.

"I never would've—"

"I know," he says, not letting me finish. "The idea that you were planning to leave me flashed through my mind for a second, but then once I thought about everything we've been through, the way you love me and know that I love you, I knew you wouldn't leave me."

Ryder grips the curve of my hip and pulls me toward him. "That woman, Marie, who you thought was your friend ..."

"I know," I choke out. "She's Nora." I shake my head, feeling so stupid.

"She showed up here shortly after you disappeared, begging for me to take her back. She's how I knew you were with Brian. She ran her mouth, and I was able to piece it all together." He leans over and brushes his lips against mine. "She's been arrested, and with all the laws they broke, they're both going to prison for a long time."

"Good. They deserve it."

Ryder glides his hand around to my butt, but I shake my head.

"I need a shower. I feel dirty."

His hands still. "Fuck, Kira. I'm sorry."

Wait, what?

"Why are you sorry?"

"I'm over here, trying to touch you, and I didn't even consider ... fuck! Do you need to go to the hospital? You said you were okay, but I didn't think about ..."

"What are you talking about?" I ask in confusion.

"Did he ... rape you?" he chokes out.

Oh!

"No!" I shake my head. "No. He didn't touch me. Well, he touched my leg, but it was after I drugged him, so he was too out of it to do anything more."

"Oh, thank God," Ryder breathes. "I mean, if he had, I wouldn't have judged you. It wouldn't have been your fault."

"I know," I tell him, framing his face. "Thankfully, he didn't. But being there with him, I still feel kind of dirty. I'd like a shower and for you to make me forget about today. Preferably at the same time."

I smirk, and Ryder grins.

"Your wish is my command."

He lifts me into his arms and walks us to the shower. After setting me on the counter, he turns the water on, and while it heats up, he removes his clothes and then mine.

Once we're in the shower, he goes about soaping me up and scrubbing every inch of me. He runs the loofah along my shoulders and down my arms and then gives my breasts his full attention. When they perk up at his touch, he leans in and draws one nipple into his mouth. He nibbles on it playfully and then runs his tongue along it, teasing me.

When he backs away to continue cleaning me, I pout, but he only smiles as he drags the loofah down one leg and up another. I part my legs to give him easy access, and he grants me the sexiest boyish grin.

He makes a show of cleaning my most intimate area, making it a point to rub his knuckles across my clit. Electricity courses through me, and my body craves his touch.

"More," I breathe, pushing my pelvis into his hand.

Ryder's eyes lock with mine as his fingers dance across my pussy and then stop at my hole between my legs. He parts my lips and then thrusts his fingers into me.

"Yes," I hiss. "Harder, please."

With his hazel eyes never leaving mine, Ryder works me over expertly until I'm screaming out his name and coming all over his hand.

"Good?" he murmurs, slowly pulling his fingers out and lifting them to his mouth. He makes a show of licking my juices off them and then moans like the taste of me is all he needs to survive.

"So good," I tell him, reaching down to stroke his cock so he can fuck me.

"Not yet," he says, gently removing my hand.

When I pout, he chuckles softly before his expression turns serious.

"I was terrified I was going to lose you today. I'm going to take my time worshipping you, memorizing every inch of your body. Making you come over and over so that I can ingrain the sounds you make into my brain."

"You don't have to memorize anything," I tell him, pressing my hand to his chest, right above his heart. "You have me. Every day for the rest of our lives."

He swallows audibly and nods. "I was so fucking scared, baby."

"I was too," I admit. "But we're home safe, and we're okay."

"I love when you say that." He palms the side of my face. "*Home.* This is your home. Tell me you're not going anywhere. And as soon as those goddamn divorce papers are filed, you're going to marry me and let me adopt Violet and make this *our* home."

I'm nodding along as he speaks until he says something that has me stepping back. "You want to legally adopt Violet?"

"Are you serious?" He gives me an incredulous look. "Of course I do. I've been holding off until I knew you were okay with it. Trying to take shit slow. But I love her, Kira, the same way I love Addie, and I would like nothing more than to be her dad."

Tears prick my eyes, and I'm thankful the water hides them, but still, Ryder notices—because he notices everything.

He leans in and kisses the tops of my cheeks. "I love you and that little girl more than every goddamn star in the sky. And you're both mine."

I encircle my arms around his neck and pull his face down to mine. "I love you. More than the moon and every star."

Our mouths crash against each other, and our tongues unite. The kiss isn't gentle. It's rough, filled with desperation to show each other how deeply we feel.

Ryder lifts me against the cold tiled wall, and my

legs wrap around his waist. And then, without wasting another second, he fills me with his long, thick cock.

Unlike our ravenous kissing, he makes love to me slow and deep, as if he wants to stay in me forever. Like he can never get enough. And I feel the same way.

Ryder doesn't stop until we've both found our orgasm, and even then, he stays inside me, raining kisses all over my face, my breasts. And even though I know why he's doing it—because he wants to memorize every inch of me—I let him. Because there's nowhere I'd rather be than in Ryder's arms, with him inside me, worshipping me.

RYDER

"Mommy!" Addie runs into the house and goes straight for Kira, sounding like she hasn't seen her in a week when it's only been eighteen hours.

"Chunk!" Kira picks her up and twirls her in a circle, raining kisses all over my daughter's face. "I missed you."

"Miss you!" Addie giggles.

She wiggles down and runs over to Violet, who hugs her tightly.

"I missed you, Addie."

"Miss you!" Addie repeats.

"Damn, looks like I've been replaced," I joke when

Addie doesn't even bother to come over to me. "You going to give your dad a hug?"

I bend down, and Addie runs into my arms.

"I love you, Monkey."

"I lub you," she says, making my heart swell.

"We're so glad you guys are okay," Ana says, giving Kira a one-armed hug since she has her daughter in her other arm. "I can't believe that woman was *her*."

"I know." Kira sighs. "But our attorney said with everything they're being charged with, they'll both be serving several years."

"Good," Julian says, holding Kingston in his arms. "I hope they rot."

"Hey, Violet, what are you doing?" Ana asks, going over to where Violet has gone back to drawing at the table.

"I'm drawing a picture of my family," Violet says. "Mommy said we get to live here forever."

This morning, when Violet woke up, she asked if they could stay here, saying she never wanted to go back to Brian's house again. Of course, Kira and I explained that what Brian and Nora had done was wrong—although we called her Marie since that's how Violet knows her and trying to explain it would confuse her—and that she and her mom never have to leave again. This is their home, and we're a family.

"Ryder," Violet says, glancing up from drawing, "how do you spell your name?"

I walk over and kneel in front of her. "D-A-D."

She writes the letters, then looks back up at me. "That's not how you spell your name! That's Dad." And then her eyes go wide.

"I know," I tell her softly. "But I was thinking that maybe you'd want to call me Dad because I'd love it if you were my daughter, just like Addie."

"You want to be my dad?" she asks, her eyes filled with emotion.

"I would love to be your dad, if you want me to—"

My words are cut off by two tiny arms strangling my neck.

"Yes!" she cries. "I do. I want you to be my dad."

She looks back at her mom. "Can he, Mommy? Can he be my dad?"

"Yes, sweet girl," Kira says. "He can be your daddy."

"Did you hear that, Addie?" Violet says, looking at my daughter, who's in the process of breaking a crayon while attempting to draw like Violet. "Ryder's my daddy! That means you're my sister."

"*Sistah*! Daddy!" Addie parrots.

"Yeah!" Violet says, hugging her. "We're a family."

Kira's glassy eyes lock with mine, and she mouths, *Thank you.*

"You never have to thank me," I tell her, wrapping my arm around her back and pulling her into my side. "You guys are giving me the greatest gift I could ask for ... a family."

Epilogue

RYDER
EIGHT MONTHS LATER

"Is it everything you pictured, Mrs. Du Ponte?"

My beautiful wife nods with a smile that hasn't left her face since the moment I saw her walking down the aisle with our daughters on either side of her while they threw rose petals all over the floor.

When we discussed her walking down the aisle, my grandfather offered to walk her, and while she appreciated the offer, she turned to me and said, "It's not just us getting married. Our little girls are just as much a part of this as we are, and I want to walk down the aisle with them."

She didn't give a shit that she'd be sharing the spotlight with two adorable little girls. She didn't care that the photos wouldn't only be of her. All she cared about was how it would make our daughters feel as they walked down the aisle with their mom so we could officially become a family.

"It's perfect," she murmurs, reaching up and kissing the corner of my mouth. "Truly magical."

"Good," I tell her. "Because I want to give you the fairy tale. Only, in our version, there's no happily ever after because this is only the beginning."

I kiss her deeply, and she sighs into my arms. It's been a crazy eight months between Violet starting school and our exes being prosecuted, found guilty, and sentenced to several years in prison, Kira finally getting her divorce, Addie turning two, and us planning the wedding—well, mostly me because she still hadn't gotten used to the fact that I had money and she suggested we do something cheap, like get married in our backyard. And I wasn't having it, so I told her I'd handle it.

"Mommy!" Addie yells, champing at the bit to join us. "I go to you!"

"Come here, Monkey," Kira says, kneeling for Addie.

"You too," I say to Violet, who wastes no time, running over to join us on the dance floor.

The song transitions from our first song to the one I requested the DJ play next, knowing it would be the dance with our daughters.

While Kira twirls Addie around in her arms, Violet stands on my toes so I can sway us to the beat.

"Are you having a good time?" I ask.

"The best," she gushes. "And Mommy said when we get back, I get to make my name the same as yours and Mommy's."

My heart swells as my daughter looks up at me with happiness. Growing up, all I wanted was a family who loved me, and now, I'm surrounded by three girls who love me more than I could have ever hoped for.

"You do," I tell her, lifting her into my arms. "And I can't wait for you to have my last name. But you know you're already mine, right? It doesn't matter what your last name says."

"I know. Because love is what makes a family," she says, repeating the words I spoke earlier while we were reciting our vows.

"That's right. And I love you more than all the stars in the sky."

Violet grins and then counters with, "I love you more than the entire universe."

We finish our dance, and then the DJ announces that everyone can join us on the dance floor.

Addie and Violet take off to dance with the other kids while I dance again with my wife.

We spend the rest of the night dancing, eating, and celebrating with everyone.

When it's time for the garter and bouquet toss, I take advantage of my wife sitting in the chair, letting me feel her up with my mouth.

"Ryder," she hisses through her laughter when I take it a bit too far and lick at her center.

What? It's not like anyone can see what I'm doing under that puffy dress.

Plus, it's been a long ass time since I've been inside her. First, she was on her period, and then she insisted we wait until our wedding night.

When I come out from under her dress with her garter between my teeth, everyone cheers, and Kira laughs.

The single men are prompted to step forward, and then I fling it behind me. When the crowd erupts in laughter, I turn around and find my grandfather standing there with the garter in his hand and a shocked expression on his face.

"Get it, Gramps!" I say with a fist bump.

"Okay, single ladies, it's your turn," the DJ announces.

Several women step forward while Kira stands and turns around so her back is to them. With a quick countdown, she throws it so far that it passes all the women and lands on …

"Oh shit," I hiss as Kira spins back around.

"No! No way!" Paige yells, standing and stomping toward Kira with the bouquet in her hand. "Take it back. I don't want this." She thrusts it at Kira. "We all know I'm never getting married. So, take it back and do it over again. It would be wasted on me."

"I don't think it counts if I do it again," Kira says nervously.

"Fine," Paige huffs, snatching the bouquet back. "I'll just burn it!"

"Paige, honey," Ana says, coming over, "I know you're in a dark place right now, and you have every right to be, but burning Kira's bouquet is not the answer."

Paige nods and sniffles as Ana guides her off the dance floor.

"I feel so bad for her," Kira mutters, shaking her head. "What John did ..."

"He's an asshole, and she deserves better," I say.

"Now, it's time for the cake," the DJ announces.

"Mmm." Kira grins. "I can't wait to try it." Then, she mock glares. "And if you stick it in my face like the videos you showed me, I'll withhold sex tonight."

I bark out a laugh. "I wouldn't dare, *wifey*."

"Wifey." She giggles. "I like the sound of that, *hubby*."

After we cut the cake—and I don't stuff it in her face because I'm sure as hell not risking upsetting my wife on our wedding night—we say good night to the girls since they're going back to our house with Kira's mom, Denise, for the night.

After much discussion, we helped her mom move to Rosemary. I got her set up in a cute condo close by, and Ana hired her as a secretary for Kingston. Kira and her mom have spent the past several months working on their relationship while Denise has gotten to enjoy being a mom and grandma. She loves spending time with the girls, and even Addie calls her Grandma now.

Tonight, I've booked us a suite at the hotel where the reception was held, and tomorrow, we're taking off on a Disney cruise with the girls and Kira's mom. We wanted this to be a family trip, and in a few months, we're planning a trip for just the two of us.

When we get up to the presidential suite, Kira fawns over it for a few minutes before she ushers me into the bedroom, has me unzip her dress, and then tells me to wait here for her.

While I wait, I get undressed since the tux isn't exactly comfortable and throw on a pair of basketball shorts and a T-shirt.

I'm starting to get worried about Kira taking so long when I look up and find her standing in the doorway, wearing the sexiest lingerie that I've ever laid eyes on. It's white lace and see-through, leaving damn near nothing to the imagination. And all I want is to rip it off her and bury myself deep inside her.

"What do you think?" she asks, stepping into the room.

Her hair, which was up, is now down in waves, and her makeup is long gone. She looked exquisite today, like a fairy-tale princess, but right here, she's a whole different type of beautiful.

She's real.

She's mine.

"I think I'm the luckiest guy in the world to be able to spend my life with you."

Her eyes turn glassy as she shakes her head.

"It's not luck, Ryder," she says, sauntering over to me. "It's because you're a good man."

I part my legs, and she stands between them.

I glide my hands over her hips and around to her luscious, bare ass, thanks to the thong she's wearing, giving it a squeeze.

"You're sweet and selfless, and you respect women," she murmurs, reaching around and unclipping her bra. It slides down her arms, and she lets it fall to the floor. "And you love our daughters and me with every part of you."

I nod, choked up with emotion.

"I'm not with you out of luck," she continues, hooking the thong in her fingers and pushing it to the ground. "I'm with you because you're so damn easy to love."

She kicks the material away, leaving her completely naked in front of me. "From the moment I met you, I was hooked. And a year later, I can't imagine not loving you ... not being loved by you."

Her mouth descends on mine, and I pull her into my lap, needing to feel her warmth. My hands twist in her hair as I deepen the kiss. Her lips are soft, and her tongue moves in perfect sync with mine. We continue to kiss until kissing isn't enough. And I need to be inside her.

I shift slightly, releasing my cock from its confines, and then Kira rubs her pussy up and down my shaft, her juices coating me while she finds her pleasure.

Within seconds, she's coming all over my cock, and I'm damn near shooting my load before I've even had the pleasure of being inside her.

"God, I love everything about you," she moans against my lips.

"I need to be inside you now," I murmur, lifting her up so I can place her on my cock.

But before it can happen, she says, "Wait! Stop," and I freeze in place.

"What's wrong?" I ask, needing to be inside her like I need my next breath.

"I forgot to tell you. It was supposed to be a surprise, but you need to know in case anything's changed."

"What?" I breathe, wondering what the hell is so important that it can't wait until after I've fucked my wife into tomorrow.

"I took out the implant," she says.

It takes a second for me to wrap my head around what she said. "Your implant?"

"My birth control," she clarifies. "I had it taken out."

Wait ... does that mean ...

"You're not on any birth control right now?"

"Nope." She shakes her head.

"So, if I come in you …"

"I can get pregnant."

Holy fucking shit.

"And you're okay with getting pregnant?" I ask, just to make sure.

"Yep, hence me taking it out. Are you?"

The thought of me filling her with my cum and creating a baby with her has me lifting her over my cock and slamming her onto it.

"I take that as a yes," she groans, her eyes rolling back in pleasure.

It's been a while since we've had sex, and the way her pussy chokes my cock like a vise has me damn near coming.

"It's a fuck yes," I murmur, gripping the curves of her hips and using them to guide her up and down on my cock.

I trail fiery kisses down her neck, licking and sucking on her heated flesh. I take a pert nipple into my mouth and suck on it, and her walls clench around my cock.

"Fuck, you feel so perfect," I murmur, kissing along her collarbone and up her throat. "Like you were made just for me."

Her delicate hands cup my jaw as her sexy lips reclaim mine once again. "Fuck me harder," she whispers against my mouth. "Make me yours."

And because I would give this woman anything she wants, I flip her onto her back, place her legs in the curve of my arms, and then fuck her with everything in me. Until she's screaming out my name as she comes all over my cock. And then I let myself go, spilling my seed into her, not stopping until I'm sure I've fucked her so deep that my cum will be leaking out of her for days.

"You know," she says once I've stopped and I'm lying over her, careful not to crush her, "I'm ovulating right now."

I glance at her and find her smiling. And fuck if that doesn't do something to me. I'm so hooked on this woman that it's not even funny.

"Good. I can't wait to see you pregnant with my baby," I say, fully aware I sound like a caveman. "But if you don't get pregnant, that's okay too." I lean down and kiss her soft, plump lips, so thankful that I get to call this woman my wife. "We have our entire lives ahead of us, baby. And I look forward to spending it with you."

About the Author

Nikki Ash is a USA Today Bestselling author of contemporary romance, focusing on single parent, secret baby, and surprise pregnancy romances. She spends her days and nights getting lost in words. When she's not writing, she's reading. From the Boxcar Children, to Wuthering Heights, to the latest single parent romance, she has lived and breathed every type of book.

Nikki resides in South Florida with her husband, two children, and dog that she considers to be one of her kids. When she's not reading or writing, she's traveling the world with her family—in search of inspiration.

Printed in Great Britain
by Amazon

Hooked On You

◆ A LOVE & WHISKEY NOVEL ◆

USA TODAY BESTSELLING AUTHOR
NIKKI ASH